Readers Love

'A wonderful holiday read'

'Tugs at the heart strings'

'Full of romance, joy and heartbreak'

'I laughed, I cried, and thoroughly enjoyed this book!'

LUCY KNOTT is a former professional wrestler with a passion for storytelling. Now, instead of telling her stories in the ring, she's putting pen to paper, fulfilling another lifelong dream in becoming an Author. Inspired by her Italian Grandparents, when she is not writing you will most likely find her cooking, baking and devouring Italian food, in addition to learning Italian and daydreaming of trips to Italy. Along with her twin sister, Kelly, Lucy runs TheBlossomTwins.com, where she enthusiastically shares her love for books, baking and Italy, with daily posts, reviews and recipes. You can find Lucy on Twitter @TheBlossomTwins or @LucyCKnott

Also by Lucy Knott

How to Bake a New Beginning
The Ingredients for Happiness

Wishes Under a Starlit Sky

LUCY KNOTT

ONE PLACE. MANY STORIES

HQ
An imprint of HarperCollins*Publishers* Ltd
1 London Bridge Street
London SE1 9GF

First published by HQ Digital 2019

This edition published in Great Britain by
HQ, an imprint of HarperCollins*Publishers* Ltd 2020

ISBN: 9780008348731

MIX
Paper from
responsible sources
FSC® C007454

Printed and bound by CPI Group (UK) Ltd, Croydon, CR0 4YY

For those who believe in fairy tales and the power of love; in all it's beautiful forms.

Prologue

The deep and smooth voice of Dean Martin croons through my mind, forcing me to relax. A smile curves up at the edges of my lips. The lyrics of his hit song 'That's Amore' dance in my mind. The moon is certainly lighting up the sky tonight in all its pizza-pie elegance. It is full, a sparkling pearly white and casting its beautiful glow on the tourists that are lost in Venice's romantic charm. The Christmas season is in full force and it's evident everywhere I look. The streetlamps twinkle as glittering silver tinsel weaves its way around the otherwise dark poles. I can understand the magic and the romance this city is famous for.

I look to the moon and think of my parents and how this will be another Christmas without them. They moved to Colorado five years ago and with my workload and my husband's busy schedule I've only been out to visit them the once. It's unlike me and I don't know how I've managed this long without them. But back in London I have my job, my best friend Madi and my husband – I know my parents understand.

I shake away my wandering thoughts and embrace the charm of Venice around me. I soak up the joyful feeling of love and Christmas as I snuggle into my husband's side. It has been a while since we've done anything remotely romantic. With Scott being so busy at work and me being locked away in my office working on my next script for the past couple of months, we simply haven't found the time. Not that I haven't been trying. I've been shutting my laptop off early most nights for the past couple of weeks, throwing on my laciest pyjamas, waiting for Scott to come home. But it's all been to no avail. Late nights on set and in the office meant he usually fell asleep on the couch, too exhausted to even make it upstairs by the time he came drifting into the house. I'd wake to find him either passed out, or worse yet, gone, back to the studio to start the routine all over again.

So, this . . . this is nice. I cuddle up closer to Scott's warm side, and sneak my hand around his waist, under his suit jacket. Feeling his toned torso beneath the thin white cotton of his shirt still sends desire flooding through me, even after six years of marriage. He turns to me, a broad smile on his handsome face. Maybe my efforts haven't been going unnoticed after all. Maybe the lacy pyjamas caught his attention, and this is just what he needed, a break from the movie sets and back to reality to refocus, to remember that I am still very much here.

The moon makes his blue eyes glisten, taking me back to our wedding night and staring into them as we danced our first dance. That whole day was magic; that and nearly every day for the past six years too. My smile widens as the lyrics dance in my mind – the world is certainly shining tonight and I may have had a little wine. He kisses my lips softly. My hands fly straight to his sandy blonde hair, gently tugging at its shagginess. I am drunk on love and suddenly feel like a teenager again. At thirty years of age, that is a welcome feeling.

The gondola pulls up to the short pier where another loved-up couple are gazing longingly into each other's eyes, eagerly awaiting their turn on the love boat. By this point I am too wrapped up in Scott to pay attention to the gorgeous night-time scenes that Venice has to offer. We stumble down the cobbled streets, grabbing at each other, only pausing when kissing and walking becomes too difficult a task. We make it back to our hotel before the whole of Venice gets to see Scott in all his naked glory. I am getting impatient, which is not like me; his suit jacket and tie have already come off. I'm not opposed to public displays of affection – in fact, I adore seeing people in love – but I am usually more subtle in my approach. I don't know what has taken over me; the need to be wanted by Scott, maybe?

The concierge smiles and hands us the keys before I need to embarrass myself with attempting to ask for them in my terrible Italian. No doubt the man witnesses more impassioned men and women on the daily than he knows what to do with. The hopeless romantic in me thinks what a beautiful thing to observe each day at work. Then it remembers that really, I get to do the same, even if the scenes are mostly made up in my head and then played out by actors – it still counts as real love, doesn't it? Maybe the concierge should start writing down what he sees and turn it into a script too.

My mind is brought back to the present when Scott throws me on to the stunning four-poster princess-like bed and kisses me fervently. I do my best to keep up. It's not that hard. I have loved this man since I was twenty-three years old. Heat courses through me, my hips arch forward with wanting and I savour the touch of his lips all over my skin, as I melt into the quilt. My cream shift dress floats up over my thighs as I kick my ballet flats off my feet onto the floor. I try to ignore the occasional painful tug of my hair as Scott kneels on it – it's my fault, it's too long, he would say – and instead I focus on the desire in my veins.

I guess not all my romantic ideas are made up in my head. My latest Pegasus Entertainment rewrite may have been inspired just a little by the man currently covering my stomach with kisses. Come to think of it, so was the one before that and the one before that. I should really thank my husband for being such a brilliant muse for a romance writer, I think to myself, then get distracted as he lowers the weight of his body on top of mine. I think I can wait and tell him later.

*

We arrive back from Venice and I feel as though I'm walking on a fluffy, bouncy cloud. Scott and I have been together for eight years, married for six, but I smile with the magic that is still there in my heart after so long. I take our suitcases up to our bedroom. It's six in the evening and I'm ready for a hot shower; to get rid of the icky plane feeling I get whenever I travel. I feel Scott and I deserve an evening of red wine, maybe even a cheeky takeaway, curled up by the Christmas tree in front of the TV before the mad rush of the fortnight before Christmas descends on us.

I leave Scott to whatever is keeping him busy downstairs and turn on the shower; he might join me when he hears the running water. My body is still tingling with the feel of him from our passionate weekend. Do Italians add something to their water? I giggle as the water soaks my hair and drips off my eyelashes. I feel a sudden surge of emotion and a burst of sentimentality strikes me as my mind plays snippets of our magical trip to Italy. It had felt beautiful to have some time away; everything had felt right.

In the pit of my stomach I feel a tingle of excitement that this will be the year we take the leap and start trying for kids. Scott and I have talked about it and this weekend gave me a glimpse into the future; how perfect our lives have been thus far and how incredible the next step in our journey together will be.

Scott must be thinking what I'm thinking and ordering that takeaway, I muse to myself when he doesn't come up to the bathroom. I stop dawdling in the shower, keen to get downstairs and join him on the couch. I hastily towel dry, throw on my Christmas pyjamas – it's December after all – wrap my hair in a towel and head downstairs.

I'm walking into the living room when I see Scott in my peripheral vision sitting at the dining room table. He is smiling at his phone, the smile that after all these years still gives me butterflies. But when he sees me, I notice his cheeks flush and a forlorn gaze appears in his eyes. I wander over to him, wrapping my arms around him and squeezing him tight. I can sense his brain has already switched back into work mode and he's worrying about emails and the crazy schedule that December brings with it as he feels cool and tense to the touch, making my gut wriggle uncomfortably for some reason.

'How about I order us a takeaway and we make a start on the Christmas movies, so we can actually fit them all in this year?' I say, kissing his cheek, hoping to relax the knots in his neck and keep work thoughts at bay for at least a few more hours. Scott is rigid, and I feel a discomfort in the pit of my stomach that I can't place. Usually he can't keep his hands off me at this proximity. I understand it has been a tiring travel day, but something doesn't sit right.

'I think we should take a break,' Scott says. I sigh and a titter escapes my lips – all this tension over Christmas movies.

'OK, how about we watch a movie of your choosing tonight and then start up on the Christmas movies Christmas Eve Eve? We still have so many to get through and it's really not Christmas without a few romantic fairy tales,' I suggest, tucking my hair behind my ear, the wet strands having started to stick to my cheeks. I make to step into the hall when Scott repeats himself causing me to back-pedal.

'Not the bloody Christmas movies, Harper, though yes, a break from all that crap would be good.' His voice sounds hard. I'm confused as to what has suddenly made him so moody. I've never heard him call my favourite kind of movie *crap* before. We often watch them and gush over our own real-life fairy tale.

'Oh OK, I'm sorry,' I stutter through a nervous laugh. 'Would you like me to cook something, honey? If you want a break from

5

the takeaways, I can see what we've got in, whip something up?' I step out of the hall and back into the dining room now, eager to get Scott out of the chilly space and his 'just got back from vacation funk', and into the warmth of the living room and under the pile of blankets awaiting us on the couch. He's not making any effort to move on his own and remains still in the chair.

'You make it sound like those are my only two options. I want a break,' he says, his tone dull and deadpan.

My brain is going over his words before I speak. I feel as though every time I open my mouth, I say something wrong. 'Options,' I repeat slowly. 'Erm, no we can cook together, we can go out, we don't have to watch movies.' I tug on the hem of my pyjama top, not knowing what to do or say next.

'I want a break from us,' Scott says with a heavy sigh.

It's the tiny word at the end of his sentence that takes me completely by surprise and causes a sharp stabbing pain in my throat. I take a step back and try to digest the words Scott has just said, my brain muddled with talk of takeaways and movies.

'What do you mean "a break"?' I ask quietly, tripping up over each word. My brain is rattling in my head with all kinds of uncertainty and fear. Is Scott joking? Is this some kind of prank? What have I missed? Scott isn't moving, just sitting in the same position he has been in during this entire conversation, but he's looking at me and I hate that I don't recognize the look in his eyes.

'A break, like we take some time apart, give each other some space,' he says. His features are relaxed, and I hate that he looks more relieved than pained. I feel like a child flying over the handlebars of my bike, landing in a heap on the ground with a sudden whack. I can't find my breath.

'Why?' is all I can manage. I'm hunched over a little with my hand on my stomach. I've paced a few steps, so I can look at Scott. He flicks his hands up at my question, almost like a shrug, like he doesn't have an answer. But you don't suggest something as big as taking a break from your marriage without having an answer, surely?

'We want different things; I don't think it's working.' He runs a hand through his blonde hair. There's a buzzing sound in my brain, a rattle, a hum, making it difficult for me to understand what is going on. When was it not working? It was working fine the last time I checked.

'I want you.' The words slip out before I can catch them. Doesn't he know how much I love him? How can he be saying we want different things? Where has this come from? Never have we discussed wanting different things. What does he even mean by wanting different things? We got married because we wanted each other. We gazed out in the same direction with similar goals and dreams in mind.

'I want you too, but I think we need this break. Have some time to figure out if this is what we really want,' Scott says. I feel like my mind is playing a trick on me. If he wants me then what is there to figure out? He's talking to me with the same look he gives the Chinese menu when deciding what he wants; I want fried rice, but I want won ton soup too. But this is our marriage, it isn't flavour of the week.

'If you want me, Scott, then what is the problem? What is it that you need to take a break from?' I ask. My brows are drawn and my lips are trembling at the weight of the questions. This is a conversation I never thought I would be having and it's all happening too quickly for my body to know how to react.

'You want kids. What happens if I don't want kids?' he says. He is flipping his phone around in his hands. He's agitated, I can tell. He's looking out of the window now and my instinct is telling me that he's ready for this conversation to be over. Scott isn't a huge talker and we've never had an argument that warranted a discussion lasting more than five minutes, mostly because it would just be me talking and Scott would get fed up. I would have to reduce myself to a few words, get them in quickly before Scott kissed me, then it would be make-up sex and we'd be good.

'Do you not want kids, Scott?' I ask, perplexed by his question.

7

I'd never given thought to him not wanting kids because not once had he mentioned anything of the sort. Not once, not even one little hint had been given to me that would make me think my husband did not want kids someday. He joined in with conversations about what it would be like when we had our own children in the future. Heck, he had started conversations about when we would have them, what names he liked, what books he would read and games he would play with them.

I'm holding on to the back of a dining room chair to keep me upright. I want to sit down but there is a strange adrenaline keeping me standing. I want to fix this. Scott stays quiet, leaving my question lingering, like he doesn't have an answer. My dad is a fixer, a manly man with a molten core. I can be emotional, but I know I can fix this; I can be strong.

'Scott, if you're worried about kids, we can talk about it. If you don't want kids right this second, it's OK. We can talk about having them when we're both ready. If you never want them, then I'm not sure what to tell you, but you're right: maybe you need to take some time to figure out whether it's a never or just not right now situation,' I say. My words come out surprisingly calm, in contrast to the fast and shooting pains I keep getting in my chest. But Scott does this to me. I want to please him, I know that much. I can compromise. I just need to assure him that I am here for him, whatever he is going through, I'll stand by his side.

I look at my husband, at the man I love, and I know we can get through anything. I will be here for him, he will be here for me, it's what we do, what we've always done.

Scott stands up, still looking out of the window and not at me. I keep my grip on the dining chair, afraid that if I let go, I might fall.

'Why don't we go and relax for the evening and watch some TV, or if you'd like we can make a pros and cons list for babies. We can even look over the baby name list we wrote, and you can cross off any you don't like,' I say, my lips quirking up into a small smile, trying to lighten the mood and think of a solution to the dilemma we're facing. I don't necessarily think it warrants a break in our marriage. I think something like this needs to be figured out together; having kids is a huge deal. I understand Scott is scared. I had been talking about it a lot more recently, but to say he doesn't want them is a huge statement to make after six years of marriage. What has changed his mind? I'm struggling to stem my panic but am doing my best not to get hysterical and scare him even more.

'I'm sorry if I've scared you with all the baby talk recently. I see you with your nieces and nephews and I guess I can't help getting carried away. You're really great with them, you know. And you always come up with the cutest baby names. But if you want me to lay off on the baby talk, I will do,' I add, with a more confident smile. I release my hand from its death grip on the chair, wanting to go over to Scott and soothe him with a hug, but he isn't looking at me and I want to give him the space he needs. My heart rate feels like it's steadying. I can pocket the baby talk for a little while, if it's what Scott wants. Besides Christmas is just around the corner, we both have work to do and I can distract myself with Christmas cheer and our office Christmas party.

'I'm going to go and stay with Matt tonight, OK? It'll be OK; I'll figure it out,' Scott says as he turns towards me. My heart rate picks up once more, faster than the speed of light. I gulp hard, reaching out for the chair before my knees buckle.

'I don't understand,' I mumble, genuinely baffled by his response. I don't want him to go. Don't we need to talk about this together? A marriage is two people, having a baby requires two people; don't I need to know what he's thinking, where I stand in all this? The room feels cold and I can feel a drop of water from my wet hair trickle down my back, making me shiver.

'Scott, do you not want to talk about this together? You don't have to stay with Matt. If you don't want to talk about babies anymore tonight, that's fine too. Anything you want to do, that's

9

fine. I promise I can let it go, but you can still stay here.' My voice sounds needy. I'm confused. I'm not supposed to be needy – society would scoff at me right now – but this is my husband. We have slept by each other's side for the past eight years. My body trembles with fear. I don't want him to go.

Scott walks past me towards the hall, stopping to give me a kiss on the forehead before he reaches the door. 'No, it's OK, babe. I'll figure it out. I just need some time and we'll be OK. I think this will be good for us and I've told Matt I'm coming now,' Scott says, his voice somehow lighter. 'I'll see you soon.'

And he's gone. The door closes behind him and I immediately drop into the chair. The tears that I have been holding in since I heard Scott utter the words 'break from us', come spilling out in heaves, splattering on to the red robin placemat my mum made for me a few Christmases ago, from a picture she took in her backyard in Colorado. The robin looks magical perched on the snowy branch of a pine tree. In the eight years Scott and I have been together he has never made me feel uncertain, unsure and unwanted, and right now I feel all those things.

Where was his fight? Why were we not having a discussion like a married couple should when a problem arises? How could he just walk out so easily? I have so many questions that remain unanswered, all while my mind is trying to comprehend how our romantic trip to Venice led to Scott wanting a break and not even being able to sleep in the same house as me. My blood runs cold at the thought; I feel disgusting.

Out in the hallway I can see the twinkling lights from the Christmas tree reflecting in the mirror. I can hear the slight murmur of the TV, which Scott must have switched on, announcing tonight's Christmas movie on the Pegasus channel; reminding me of the fairy tales I helped write and how Christmas was one of the most romantic times of the year.

Chapter 1

It looks like a Christmas bomb exploded in the hotel and I love it. Madi has gone to get us another drink and I'm stood by the eight-foot Christmas tree that is covered in so much tinsel and fake snow, I'm surprised it's still standing. Everywhere I look there are trees and baubles and stars dangling from the chandeliers. It's what Christmas grotto dreams are made of. I try and focus on all my favourite things and keep my mind from wandering to the shambles my current home life is in. Scott came home the other night after three days and it was like nothing had changed between us. The banter was lovely, the sex was passionate and hot until the minute it stopped, and I turned to ice when Scott insisted the break was working and it was what we needed. I haven't heard from him in two days.

I'm swaying gently to the music – Michael Bublé's 'Let It Snow', of course. It's not really Christmas without Michael Bublé, is it? I soak up the words, trying to drown out my thoughts. The hotel is packed with people. I merrily smile and wave and chat to my co-workers. Suddenly I stop swaying and stand motionless in between the hustle and bustle. Through a gap in the clearing I can make out the back of his head. He is sitting at the bar chatting casually to a bunch of men in suits, colleagues I recognize from work events I had attended with him in the past. With Scott being in production, he attended events that didn't always include writers like me, but mainly the directors and producers and all the behind-the-scenes staff from the movie sets.

That's when it happens. I watch as a tall blonde approaches him. His face lights up, greeting the blonde with a smile. He places a hand on her hip and a delicate kiss on her lips. My stomach hits the floor with a vengeance making me wobble in my boots. I put my hand out to steady myself against the wall, feeling like a goldfish out of water. I can't breathe. The air is not reaching my lungs.

I can't let him see me like this, so weak, so pathetic. I try not to stare as I try to walk away, my legs not quite remembering how to do so as they shake with each step. Yet I can't seem to pry my eyes away from the scene. She's wearing a long gold sequined dress, half her luscious blonde hair pulled back with a few strands dangling around her beautiful face and her arms are resting on his shoulders, as she throws her head back and laughs at something he says.

I have to avert my eyes, but they won't budge. All I can do is stare as I stagger for air, a space to breathe. Maybe if I stare long enough it will go away. Maybe the longer I stare the more used to it my brain will become. What's that thing they say about spiders? The more you look at them and face them, the less scared you will become? Shoot, if it didn't work for me with spiders, I sure as hell don't think it is going to work now, because it seems the more I look, the more pain I feel.

I find a quiet corner, hidden by a gorgeous purple and silver Christmas tree, but I can still see him. I can still see her. My heart feels like it is about to burst through my rib cage, and I can't calm my short gasping breaths. I feel stupid. For a moment I think I might be sick. What am I doing? I need to get out of here. Just then Madi finds me and panic fills her pretty blue eyes when she sees me. In that moment I see them out of the corner of my eye. They kiss, full-on kiss, and I am eternally grateful that my best friend chose now to find me. I feel like I'm about to pass out from the uncomfortable pain I feel in my heart.

I torture myself taking one last look at them before Madi grabs my wrist and pulls me out of there; away from the Christmas party that I look forward to every year.

*

I jolt as a piercing pain stabs my chest and I shoot upright. I'm in bed. My pillow is soaked, and my body drenched in sweat. I pat myself down, pinching myself, telling myself it was all a nightmare, when I turn to see Madi lying in my bed next to me.

'Madi, what's going on?' I shout, the fear in my voice making tears fall fast and heavy down my face.

Madi stirs and blinks a few times, wiping her eyes before registering that I am awake and shouting at her. Her eyes suddenly dart open and she becomes alert, pulling me in for a hug.

'It's OK, sweetheart, it's OK,' she says softly, trying to soothe me. I don't find any words, just more tears.

'When is this going to stop, Madi?' I whimper. It's a week and a half until Christmas and it's not the first time I have had this nightmare, which isn't just a nightmare but my brain dredging up the events that took place last Christmas. My mind has re-enacted this scene over and over for the past twelve months, but since the countdown for the twenty-fifth of December began on the first of December, it has become the gift that keeps on giving every single night – hence Madi's presence. I feel drained and completely spent, lying on my bed having exerted no physical energy whatsoever. I try to rake my hand through my locks, but I'm sat on most of my hair which makes it difficult. Instead, I wipe at my tired eyes, causing the delicate skin around them to sting as I do so.

Madi retrieves a brush from the bedside table and slowly and tenderly starts brushing my hair. 'Harper, I'm your best friend and you know how much I love you. I value your feelings and respect every emotion you have gone through and you know I'd never rush you, but baby, enough is enough now. You can't do this to yourself any longer. I can't allow it.' She pushes my arm gently so she can tug my hair from under me and brush out the knots. I glance around my bedroom, Scott's and my bedroom, spot the overturned pictures and the occasional item of Scott's, and I feel ashamed. Not much has changed, and Scott hasn't lived here for a year.

'You've barely left the house, you've been neglecting your parents, your work is suffering, Harp. If your recent lines hadn't been such bloody brilliant pieces of writing and transformed those horror scripts, Lara would probably have fired you by now – but you're a romance writer, Harp. We're romance writers and I miss bouncing ideas back and forth. Come on, you need to get out of this house and file for divorce so you can move on with your life,' Madi says boldly. She's right. I know she is and I'm not mad at her honesty. I've never appreciated it more.

'Why don't you go and have a hot shower and I'll make us some breakfast,' Madi says, holding my face and looking me in the eyes. Her own are filled with tears and concern. I nod, but when she leaves the room the softness and safety of my blanket has me sinking back under the covers. My eyes are heavy and I no longer have the will to keep them open.

*

I take a breath in, torn and terrified. My finger hovers above the enter key on the laptop that is open on the desk in front of me. This isn't me. I don't do things like this. I don't snoop on my husband or invade his personal space. I've never had any reason to before, but that all changed last night after seeing him at the Christmas party. He's given me reason.

'Are you sure?' Madi whispers from behind me. My office is cold, reflecting how I feel inside. My hands tremble. No, I'm not sure, I'm not sure at all, but that doesn't change what I feel I have to do.

14

'Madi, it's been a little over a week since Scott walked away so casually out of my life, with nothing but a vague explanation and a promise that he would be back, that we would be OK, that he just needed some space. He chooses to speak to me when it suits him, popped in for sex when he fancied, all while not caring how much that affects me mentally. He texts me like I'm some old friend. Yet he cannot seem to find the time to give me answers as to what all this is about. He has watched me cry, he has listened to me fight for him all while shrugging his shoulders in response. And to top it all off, he doesn't think twice about kissing another woman at the Christmas party.' I pause. I don't quite know who I am talking about now. It all feels so absurd.

'Christmas Day is only a few days away, I need answers, Madi. I need to know if he's coming home for good. I need to know who she is. And if he doesn't think I'm worthy of any, I must find them myself,' I say softly. I am already spent and I haven't even logged in yet. I don't think I have ever been more nervous in my life.

'OK,' Madi says gently, putting a hand on my shoulder. 'Please know I love you and that I am here for you.' Then she goes and sits on the black leather couch, her fingers twisting around her hoop earrings anxiously.

Before I can chicken out and allow my brain to manifest more evil thoughts, I press enter on my husband's email account. At least I will know for sure what's been going on and I won't have to torture myself with guessing.

Nothing jumps out at me straight away, no woman's name I don't recognize. Then I see it. An email to his friend Matt, with the subject line: What am I going to do?

I gulp and, with a shaky hand, click on the email and watch the conversation fill the page. Words and sentences begin slapping me in the face, hard. 'We talk every night and every morning.' 'We're practically girlfriend and boyfriend.' 'Harper is stressing about kids.' 'No kids.' 'I get jealous when other guys go near her.' 'I love her.' And that last sentence just about does me in. I fly out of my chair, *sick rising in my throat. It takes all I have not to throw my laptop across the room and smash it to pieces. I can't look anymore. I feel like there is a monster inside of me; it terrifies me. I can't control it. I don't want this anger inside me and I'm mad at myself for allowing it in. But all my mother's words of wisdom, her soothing mantras, are not speaking to me right now.*

My soul mate, my world, it all sounds so childlike now – my person . . . there can be no such thing. I almost laugh despite the hot tears burning my cheeks. My husband is in love with someone else and has been for months and I had no idea. I can't make out from the messages how long he has been seeing her, how long he has been sleeping with her, but it was long before he brought up taking a break. The email dated back months before Venice.

Our marriage is over for him, and he forgot to tell me. Instead, he's led me to believe he's just having some breathing room, getting out of the house for a bit, staying with the boys a while before we got serious about kids, all like it was no big deal, like he'll be back. He even texted only a few days ago that I was being silly when I asked him if he wanted a divorce, like it wasn't that serious. He laughed it off like I was the mad one, like everything he was doing was normal. He didn't want a divorce, he wasn't seeing other people, we would be OK, he loved me; all just lies he was spinning.

*

My head is throbbing, I am dripping with cold sweat and someone is rubbing my forehead. There's a distinct smell of crispy bacon in the air. I force my eyes open, but it takes a few attempts before I can blink anything into a clear view.

Madi places the breakfast tray on the floor and scoots up next to me on the bed.

'Harp, we're not spending this Christmas here, OK? We're going home,' she says, assertively moving tendrils of hair out of my face. I am aware of the state I am in, what I must look like shrivelled up under the covers again. I have lost all sense of who I am. All I know is that I am a mess and very much on my way to repeating the events of last Christmas – cocooned in my bed, shutting out the world while Madi tries with all her might to spread some Christmas cheer with gifts and mince pies, with mild success. The whole world knows Scott had an affair. It's been twelve whole months. It's done, it's in the past. I need to move on.

'But this is home,' I mutter, wrapping my arm around her waist for comfort.

'Yes, it is, but I mean home, home; to your mum and dad's house. It might not be in London, but wherever your mum and dad are, that's home. We're going to Colorado.'

Chapter 2

Madi's living room smells like cinnamon and pine. Candles flicker from every surface. With the help of Madi's famous hot chocolate and bacon butty combo, I'm starting to get into the Christmas spirit. It's been a few days since the nightmares have haunted my brain and for that I'm grateful. I'm not sure whether to thank the amount of Baileys Madi sneaks into my hot chocolate or the back-to-back episodes of *Chuck* that she's been playing late into the evening every night before bed this past week. It's difficult to have nightmares when my mind is otherwise preoccupied by when Chuck and Sarah will get together and if I could one day write a script anywhere near as incredible as this show. Still, Chuck and Sarah's love is not enough to get me in the mood for the work Christmas party this year; instead, Madi and I have booked our flights for Colorado. We leave in the early hours of tomorrow morning.

I haven't been to visit my parents in Breckenridge in two years. If I'm honest I didn't take the news of my parents moving away very well at all. Spending time with them has always been one of my favourite things, so I was mad at them for moving and I don't think I have fully let go of my grudge. Though Scott got on well with his family he was much more independent and encouraged me to be the same. His family live in Greece and he had adjusted to that just fine. I felt I had to be a grown-up and be more like him. But I miss my parents every single day; I just never admitted that to Scott.

Madi on the other hand could see right through me. Trying to keep up the bravado this past year has been difficult to say the least. My parents had talked about coming over to London to be with me, but I pushed them away, telling them I was fine. In my darkest moments I didn't feel I deserved the sympathy. Madi was right the other night. Scott having an affair has taken over my life for a year – I can't go on like this. I need to get my life back on track. I look at the clock on the wall and realize I should hurry. I feel a pang of longing and a nervous anticipation that I will get to see Mum and Dad soon, but I must nip back to my house to pack first.

As I walk past the twinkling lights that wrap around Madi's stairs, I feel a small thrill of excitement thinking about my parents' house. If you thought Madi and I loved Christmas, well, my mum is a force unto herself. You can't move an inch in her house without tripping over a nutcracker. I can't imagine what their house in Colorado will look like with the backdrop of snowy mountain tops and log cabins. A big grin takes over my features and I welcome the burst of joy I feel in the pit of my stomach.

Back at my house I'm going through my wardrobe grabbing every knit and woolly jumper I own to throw in my suitcase. I'm doing my best to stop my eyes from lingering too long on Scott's belongings. The only time I have heard from him this past year is when he has texted wanting to pick up some clothes or items. I would then make sure I was at Madi's so I wouldn't have to speak to him while he collected his things. There's still a fair bit here though and I have no idea what to do with it all.

That day I found the emails, I'd called him up on the phone, my whole body tense, straining to keep up with the speed my heart was racing. Scott had told me that his relationship was none of my business, that I was being too emotional and that it wasn't all his fault. There was no apology, remorse or answers. When I had cried and pushed for more, he'd angrily, and with an irritated inflection in his tone, told me that he had been seeing his apparent girlfriend since February, before hanging up. He had been having an affair for eleven months and I hadn't even realized. What could I possibly say to him?

Twelve months on and I still feel raw. The house does nothing to curb my state of emptiness; it simply exaggerates it. Even averting my eyes from the framed photos of us as a happy couple doesn't stop me from feeling the pain. Being in the house without Scott, I can feel it – that loss, that numbness in my bones. I shiver, pleading with the voice in my head to let me get on with packing without torturing me with what the house once was. I don't want to think about the lazy Sunday mornings we spent curled up in that bed, me watching 'This Is Us', Scott playing games on his phone next to me, in no rush to be anywhere, content in each other's company. He'd been the only person I wanted to be snuggled up under the blankets with.

I hastily grab my glittery red Christmas jumper and stuff it in my suitcase. My eyes are getting a little cloudy. I'm blinking frantically to stop the inevitable, as I snap shut my suitcase and march out of the bedroom. Between the noise in my head and my banging the suitcase against every rail on my way down the stairs I don't hear the voices that are outside the front door until it's too late to hide.

All I see are feet – two pairs of feet – as they step into the house. I really, really, don't want to look up.

'Harper, I just came to grab a few things.' I hear his voice, but I can't bring myself to look at him. He usually texts first. He can't just turn up like this, unexpected.

'And you thought it would be a good idea to bring her with you, to see our home, our happy home, the one you and she destroyed?' I want to scream those words to him, but my mouth

20

is dry, and nothing leaves my lips. Has she been in our house before? The thought hasn't crossed my mind.

I can feel his eyes burning into the top of my head. It sends a chill down my spine and it feels so alien. I have known this man for nine years, but in this moment, he feels like a complete stranger, like I've never met him before in my life.

'You brought her here?' I finally mumble, hating that my words come out so small. I look up. She is standing in the hallway looking around at our belongings. I don't know her, I can't say she is a bad person, but I don't see empathy in her eyes. Her features are harsh, her lips pressed into a slight pout. She looks at me with a face that reads she is bored of the predicament she has found herself in and if I would just get out of the way that would be grand.

I hold on to the banister with my suitcase-free hand to avoid humiliating myself should my knees give way and I go crashing down the stairs. I grip the banister tighter – not going to let that happen, I feel stupid enough as it is. Scott looks well and their relationship is clearly flourishing; I can't show him how far I have fallen.

Scott sighs and turns to hand her the keys to our front door. 'Look, I'm not doing this now, Harper. It's not about her. She's none of your business. I just want to get my stuff. Speaking of which, we need to sell the house. Please don't play innocent in all this; it has both our names on it. I'm paying for a house I'm not living in.'

Any trepidation I had before about going to Colorado and being so far away from Scott if he needed anything, if he needed to talk, is gone. I pause as I place my hand on the doorknob. I'm not sure why; maybe I feel for a brief moment that he is going to call my name, to apologize for the hurt that he has caused me, to maybe tell me that this is just a quarter-life crisis but we can work through it – just something that would make me feel like the eight years of my life spent loving him have not been a total waste of time, or worse still that in all that time he never truly loved me. I twist the knob. He doesn't call my name, he doesn't stop me, but before I close the door behind me, I look back at the man I once loved and take a huge breath in. 'I would like a divorce,' I say with all the confidence I can muster, then step into the freezing London afternoon, closing the door behind me as though I'm closing a book at the end of a chapter.

With the ice in the air, the tears are falling down my face, stinging my skin as the frosty nip meets them. Then the tears truly come pouring out. The fight in me has gone, yet my body does not feel deflated or weak. There's adrenaline coursing through my veins, something that I haven't felt in a long time. It takes me a minute to register that the tears that are falling are not the same tears as before. I gasp, touching the water on my face. They are happy tears.

The exhausting, draining fight for Scott that I have been clinging on to has been replaced by a new fight. With those five little words 'I would like a divorce', I feel the weight that has been dragging me down over the last twelve months has lifted. I'm not fighting for Scott anymore. I'm fighting for me.

Chapter 3

'Switch it off,' Madi says in a stern voice. I'm trying as quick as I can to read the email from Lara, my boss, while Madi is breathing down my neck and mumbling about how mobile phones and Wi-Fi connections can affect take-off.

'You were telling me the other day about how I've let my work suffer. This is work. I need to read this,' I say, shifting in my seat anxiously as I glance at an air stewardess looking my way. I make out the words 'original script', 'deadline', 'sorry to do this to you before the holidays' and 'last shot for the romance department' before I hear a polite clearing of the throat from a shadow looming over me. I look up and smile innocently. It's not like we've moved on to the runway yet. I'm not exactly one for breaking rules; I will turn it off.

'It's Christmas, babe, didn't you get all your work done before the break?' Madi asks, offering me a chocolate button as the plane rumbles to life.

I squint, looking past Madi and out of the tiny aeroplane window, thinking over my to-do list. Though I can't promise any of it was my best work due to my silly funk, I got all my edits and rewrites sent back in time for the Christmas break. I'm sure of it. Madi pops another chocolate button into her mouth as the

23

plane starts moving towards the runway and I try not to panic over how badly I have let my life fall apart. I am normally more organized than this and remember work I have and have not done.

I absent-mindedly draw another button out of the bag, watching as Gatwick airport recedes into the background. I chew on the delicious chocolate morsel, preparing to keep my ears from popping painfully when it hits me.

I avert my eyes back to the top of the email, as my stomach begins to dance with nerves of excitement as the words start to make sense. I focus on reading in complete sentences, so I don't get muddled up or mistaken.

'Harper, I'm sticking out my neck here and putting your script forward. Out of all the submissions I received there are elements of yours I want to explore and keep going back to. You can't let me down with this one, Harper. I need your best work. I need it submitted no later than Christmas Eve before it gets looked over by the Pegasus production team. Best, Lara.'

There is a small cough to the left of me and when I look up, I receive another pointed glare from the air stewardess. Nodding my understanding, I switch my phone off and stow it away in my backpack under my chair, a flush of red in my cheeks when I hear Madi's teasing tut as I do so.

'My script, Mads. It's my original script.' I gasp, ignoring her mock scolding. 'Remember when, gosh it was ages ago now, when they had open submissions for original scripts and Lara let me enter one of mine?' Madi sits up straighter in her aeroplane seat, munching on the chocolate buttons as though they are popcorn, her perfectly winged eyeliner making her beautiful blue eyes wide, but they are further accentuated by the excitement behind them as I speak.

'She's chosen my script to be sent for production, but she needs it edited and tweaked no later than Christmas Eve.' I gulp, my words fading as I reach the end of my announcement. I lean back in my seat. I can't remember the last time I looked at that script. It will take me weeks to connect with the characters, go over the

24

plot and the actions and oh gosh, all that smushy romance stuff; how on earth am I supposed to edit it in six days and stomach all that fluff? Editing other people's scripts over the past year has been hard enough; actually editing my own romantic thoughts, well, I'm not sure I've got it in me, especially at this time of year.

'This is amazing, Harp. I'm so proud of you. She obviously believes it's going to be picked up for production and sees its potential if she's asking you for a finer cut. You've got this,' Madi notes, stuffing a chocolate button between my pursed lips. I let the chocolate melt on my tongue as I try and steady my breathing. My confidence upped and left me right around the time that Scott did and just like my husband, it hadn't returned. Twelve months of doubting myself as a wife, a lover, a friend and – worse still – a writer, has sabotaged one of the things I adore more than anything: my job.

I love smushy fluff. I was born to write smushy fluff. Love is my thing. So what if last Christmas my husband ran away with another women and left me without looking back? It doesn't matter that I'm currently on the cusp of a divorce and have spent the last year in a gloomy dark hole writing scenes that better fit a horror movie. My job is on the line and therefore I can totally remember what love feels like and write the best, mushiest, gushiest, romance movie the world has ever seen, or something like that, can't I?

Fighting the aeroplane's pull to have me sitting up straight in my chair as it lifts into the air, soaring at a steep angle, I lean forward against the force and ruffle through my backpack. It's rare I go anywhere without my backpack and my collection of notebooks and scrap pieces of paper. Without a shadow of doubt, I know my original script will be tucked into the back of one of my folders or pads. I like to print everything I'm working on so I can edit it away from my computer screen. Picking up a pen can bring on a whole new perspective and often sends waves of inspiration through me. I'm praying in this case it will do just that.

My fingers graze over a thick stack of paper bound together with a paperclip. I pull it from my bag as the plane levels out.

'Got it,' I whisper, pulling down the tray table and getting myself situated. Madi is watching me with a smile tugging at her plump red lips.

'What?' I say softly, a smile curving up on my own.

'She's still in there,' answers Madi, scrunching up the chocolate button packet. How many of those had I had? Returning my attention to my pencil case, I beam at Madi's words. She's right. I have dreamt of this day since I was a little girl: the chance to write scripts and have them made into real-life movies. Working for Pegasus is certainly the right place to live out my dream and I have been a part of so many wonderful projects, but this is the first time in five years that my own original script is being considered for a starring role. There's a flutter of the old me stirring inside me, a burst of childlike glee showing through the smile that has replaced my initial fear. I can do this. I can't screw this up.

*

I am wrapped up in my olive-green and grey wool cardigan, with thermals underneath my black leggings, long cream fluffy socks peeking over the top of my brown Ugg like boots, two layers of cotton vests and an oversized jumper, and I'm still not prepared for the frosty nip that slices through my bones the minute we leave the airport.

I'm not the only one taken off guard by the deep freeze of Breckenridge, Colorado in the middle of winter. Madi – in her long red pencil skirt with thermal tights and giant brown teddy coat – is shivering; I can practically hear her teeth chattering. Although the temperature is below freezing, I am sweating through my wool and my stomach feels like it's full of hyperactive jumping beans, as I search the line of cars pulled up in arrivals for my parents' faces. I can't wait to see them.

I force my frozen eyelids to blink in an attempt to see through the icy wind, when I see my mum frantically waving her arms like she is performing the YMCA, five cars away. She's wearing a smile that could give the Northern Lights a run for their money and it's like the pain of the last twelve months slowly dissolves. I can't help the tug of comfort that pulls at my heartstrings at the sight of her. I remind myself that it will not fare me well to cry if I ever want to open my eyes again, but oh how I've missed her.

Madi notices my mum too and is rushing over before I can pick up my suitcase. Her skirt swishes past me and I watch her embrace both my parents. My shoulders release some of the tension they have been carrying over the past few weeks as I watch the scene play out.

I'm being careful not to slip on any black ice as I navigate the snowy path to greet Mum and Dad, who I haven't seen in two years. The minute I am at arm's length my mother is grabbing me and kissing my cheeks.

'My darling, look at you,' she exclaims with her hands around my face, looking over my features, and then she is kissing me some more. My dad is hanging back. I manage to glance his way and he offers me a lazy wink and shrugs his shoulders. This is typical of my dad, never rushing my mum, standing back and admiring her while she does her thing. In my brain there is a catalogue of adoring looks that my dad has sent my mum's way throughout my life, some when my mum was returning his gaze and others where he would simply pause for a moment just to drink her in. It's no wonder I became a romantic screenplay writer.

My mum finally releases me and starts fussing over getting Madi in the car. Madi is smiling, her teeth still chattering away. I don't even mind the cold and I love snow, but today it is a complete shock to the system. I'd take a little London drizzle over my lips turning blue any day.

'Hi, Dad,' I say, wrapping my arms around his neck and standing on my tiptoes to do so. He is far more accustomed to the Colorado weather having lived here for the past six years. He and my mum decided they wanted to get away from the fast-paced London lifestyle; they wanted somewhere more peaceful, where they could get back to their roots and enjoy the outdoors. I was never indoors as a kid. We were often out in the wilderness or enjoying the parks as a family and I loved every minute of it. Sometime during University it became less of a priority.

My dad's greying hair is longer these days. He is sporting a five o'clock shadow and the softest red and black flannel parka I have ever felt. He instantly warms me with his hug. 'Hi, kid, it's good to see you,' he says, and I can't tell if it's the cold that's causing his eyes to water or he has real tears in his eyes. Whatever it is, I hug him tighter, feeling that pent-up stress in my shoulders relax once more. I don't have time to open up and tell him I've missed him as Madi is pulling at my jacket and tugging me into the car.

'Hot chocolate and a cosy fireplace are calling my name,' she says from inside the car.

I sigh and pull away from my dad's bear hug. 'I love you, Dad,' I manage and hope that in those four words he knows that I have missed him and thought about him every day in my two-year absence.

'I love you too, kiddo. Now come on, let's get you home.' He kisses my forehead and makes his way around the car to the driver's seat as I dive into the back seat next to Madi. I shiver as the warmth of the car hits me.

I hadn't realized how much I needed my parents, how much their presence comforts me. Or more honestly, I did realize it but have been pushing my needs and wants to the wayside, worried that needing parents was not what adults did. Scott has been coping without his; I wanted to be able to handle it too. But with all the madness of the past year, the anxiety over trying to be an adult is the least of my worries. My eyelids grow heavy as an overwhelming feeling of exhaustion washes over me, mixed with the feeling of being completely content and safe in the company of those in the car. I place my head back against the headrest and stare out the window as the car begins to move.

The last time I was here, sometime late February two years ago, Scott had been with me, watching movies by the fireplace and enjoying candlelit dinners under the stars like something right out of a rom-com. It had, in fact, ended up in one of my rom-coms. The snowy setting, the cuddling to keep each other warm – it had all been perfect.

I can hear his laughter in my head, thinking back to that day when I was jumping up and down on the spot pleading for his help to unzip my snowsuit, so I could use the bathroom. I had been sledding all morning with my parents and by the time we got down the slopes and back to our cabin I was desperate. He had found it hilarious, my face a panic-stricken picture, but he said I looked cute in my frazzled state, teasing me for what had felt like forever before he kissed me softly on the lips and helped me get out of my suit. When I got back from the bathroom feeling relieved and a lot less moody, he had made us hot chocolate and got the fire going in our room.

What am I doing veering down memory lane? I scold myself as I wipe the sniffles from my nose with my woolly sleeve. That person is gone now. I'm here with Madi and my parents and I want to enjoy every minute of this Christmas to make up for the last one; the one that he left in tatters. I've been a mere shell of myself for twelve whole months.

Outside of the car the pine trees whizz by in a blur. The sky is a beautiful clear piercing blue and I am momentarily mesmerized by its calmness. I can't miss this. I won't let life simply pass me by or have Scott take up any more of my brain.

I feel Madi grab my hand and squeeze it tight. We always spend Christmas together. Even after Scott and I got married, Madi was always a fixture on Christmas Day along with the mince pies with brandy sauce and the pantomime on the telly. I haven't had a Christmas without Madi since we were ten. It suited her parents for us to have her; it saved them the hassle of an excitable child harping on about Santa Claus.

Madi's parents attempted the parent thing but I don't believe they quite got what they were after. If they could have flicked through a child catalogue, they would have gone for something simple: quiet, elegant, girly, a yes-girl who did whatever they asked and never ever put a foot out of line and never had her neat tied-up-with-a-bow hair out of place. What they got was a bold, adventurous, colourful, cheeky and curious child they had no clue what to do with.

'It's so good to be here,' Madi pipes up. 'Harper and I have more than enough time on our hands to enjoy all the Christmas festivities, after Harper finishes her script that is,' she adds, giving me an encouraging glare. 'We haven't missed the Santa race, have we?' Madi asks about my mum's favourite holiday tradition: the Breckenridge Race of the Santas. You would think my mum has lived in Breckenridge all her life with how much she dotes on the place. She and my dad fit in seemingly as soon as they moved here, and I've never seen them happier. The whole town comes together to raise money for a charity each year and it is quite the spectacle to witness thousands of Santas running, jogging and walking down the main street of Breckenridge. Mum was quick to lend a helping hand and runs her own tea and cookie station for the Santas as they pass. She gets a thrill out of it and starts baking cookies in the middle of November to prepare.

'Oh, honey, I'm afraid you missed it. You'll have to come a little earlier next year if you want to be a part of it. Let me know and I can register you for the race or you can help me at the station,' my mum says chirpily, already getting ahead of herself and planning next year. My stomach does a triple backflip at the thought of next year, next Christmas. What will I be doing then?

There is a gentle snow flurry falling outside now and in between the giant pine trees are little cabins that look like gingerbread houses. Honest to goodness, my eyes dart around in search of

Hansel and Gretel. The multi-coloured lights that twinkle from the rooftops look like jelly tots. The dustings of snow settled on the window ledges could be icing sugar and the blow-up Santas and gingerbread men look like, well, Santa and gingerbread men, but they could almost be edible, made from cookie dough as they sparkle in the distance. I like where my mum and dad live. I had enjoyed my previous visit and understood why they wanted to move to a town that was home to less than five thousand people and had all the outdoor activities that two hippies would ever need, but this was something else.

I feel like I'm in another world as we pull up to my mum and dad's log cabin that they call home. I almost don't recognize it, it is covered in so many Christmas lights. There's even a giant Santa outside wearing sunglasses and a tie-dyed T-shirt. I'm pretty sure my dad had something to do with that one.

The place could be a backdrop for a holiday movie and my mind is starting to whirl with ideas that make my newly appointed task of editing my own original script seem less daunting – which I need considering my inspiration on the plane lasted all of two pages before I resorted to watching comedy movies with Madi. The mush got too much and the only person my brain thought to derive inspiration from was Scott. Needless to say, he didn't scream joy to the world or happily ever after. I'm hoping my mum and dad's place will. Madi jumps out of the car behind me as I am staring open-mouthed at my parents' Christmas grotto. She hugs me from behind.

'I can see it now,' she says. 'Next Christmas on the Pegasus channel, prepare for a *Very Hippie Holiday*.' Madi chuckles. She's gesturing with her arms as though the words are in front of her. 'I love it.,' she adds.

'Me too,' I say a little breathlessly. And I really do. I admit that I've been terrified to spend Christmas with my parents. Normally, their off-the-beaten-path natures and positive energy is contagious and leaves me feeling beyond blessed to call them my parents, but with everything I have been going through with Scott and work, I hadn't quite felt up to entering the land of the free spirit and 'love is all you need'. However, standing here in front of my parents' house, that love – their love – is suddenly making me feel a whole lot stronger and more myself than I have felt in a long time.

'Come on, honeybee, let's get you something warm,' my mum shouts from the wraparound deck. Suddenly, the nerves I felt about next Christmas and looking into the future at the Christmases after that don't seem so prominent or scary. In fact, the idea that I have no idea of what the future holds tickles me with excitement over the possibilities. I smile up at Mum and nod at the Santa Claus that's flashing up a peace sign as I walk towards the house. I need to find some of that peace within myself and trust what the universe is offering me. I think I've come to just the right place.

Chapter 4

I can hear the low hum of The Grateful Dead playing through the house as I stretch out my legs in my bed, enjoying the soft caress of the blue velvety blanket between my toes. I feel like I've gone back in time to when I was sixteen years old, to when it was the norm to wake up to the voices of Jim Morrison and Bob Dylan. I smile at the memories of relaxing with my dad on a Sunday, listening to his music and learning about the bands he grew up with. I miss the days where arguing with him over which Grateful Dead song was their hidden gem was my only care in the world. Ahh the voice of Jerry Garcia could soothe anyone's soul.

Except I'm not in my teenage bedroom. I'm in a large room with wooden beams and flower garlands draped around a stunning log fireplace. There are potted tall green plants either side of the double king-size bed and black and white photographs of mountains and trees hung up on the log walls. It's gorgeous. Through the sheer navy and gold star print curtains I can see that it is snowing and my heart flutters back to my sixteen-year-old self once more. Why Scott had insisted we stay in a hotel when we visited my parents escapes me; this room is a dream.

Maybe I could go back in time for the day, before I became an adult, before I met Scott, to when it was just me, my parents and Madi. The Grateful Dead was already playing. I could search out my dad and finish where we left off fifteen years ago in our Grateful Dead debate and spend the rest of the day frolicking in the snow. I am just about to make good on my plan when Madi bursts into my room carrying a tray of something that smells incredible, and my laptop bag. My stomach simultaneously growls in excitement and drops with dread.

'Right, this should be enough French toast and coffee to keep you fuelled and strong. You will not leave this bedroom until that manuscript is polished and sent and then the festivities can get underway,' Madi announces, placing the tray and my laptop bag on my bed.

I slowly start to sit up and tuck my wavy brown hair behind my ears. I feel like the princess from *The Princess and the Pea* in this giant bed. I want to protest but Madi moves closer. I am now sitting upright, and I see the giant stack of French toast with what can only be my mum's diary-free whipped cream, fresh berries and agave syrup. I don't want to say anything that will jeopardize Madi putting it in front of me.

'Thank you,' I say with a small smile as Madi sets the tray on the bed in front of me, trying to make sure nothing spills.

'I know you have a lot going on, but once this script is sent, we can see what Breckenridge has to offer in terms of festive fun and make our own traditions,' Madi says, moving away from the tray, satisfied that it isn't going to topple over and spill its contents. I begin to pour myself a cup of coffee from the cafetière when Madi kisses me on the head. 'Harper Hayes, work your magic and get it done,' she adds, dropping another kiss on my forehead and turning to leave. Though I'm not technically divorced yet, Madi has recently reverted to calling me by my maiden name and it makes me feel a little more like I'm taking charge and in control.

I take a sip of coffee and smile as the smooth flavour hits my taste buds. Guilt washes over me when I take in Madi's excitement for being here and her desire to take in as much holiday fun as we can. She didn't exactly have a Holly Jolly Holiday last year, what with being cooped up with me and trying to mend the pieces of my broken heart. She'd never hold that against me, but I can't put her through the same thing this year. 'Thank you, Mads, and thank you for being here,' I manage. Madi stops walking and turns to face me.

'I wouldn't want to be anywhere else,' she says before sauntering out the door in her pink and white polka dot dress that she has layered with a long-sleeved grey top. Talking about going back in time, Madi wouldn't be out of place in the Fifties. She embodies the word pin-up. She is sexy mixed with elegance and modesty and absolute perfection in my eyes.

We draw quite the eye whenever we venture out of our writing caves and brave the real world, together. Madi in her bright colours, bleach blonde hair, kitten heels and tattoos occasionally on show and me with my Rapunzel locks and a hippie dress sense that I never grew out of. I had flowers in my eyes as a kid and wanted to wear everything my mum wore. The long skirts, wool cardigans and lace everything. I adore lace. Just like when I was a kid, everything is either oversized or cropped and the more lace the better.

I prop up some pillows behind me and polish off two slices of French toast dripping with agave syrup, before I switch on my laptop.

I can do this, I say to myself. I can polish up and edit this script. The characters are in love; I know what it's like to be in love. I sigh and take another huge bite of French toast, making sure to cover it in whipped cream.

Jerry Garcia croons through my dad's old stereo. The lyrics from 'Sugar Magnolia' reach my eardrums. I smile. That would also be the name of my mum and dad's shop. They sell organic and natural, homemade, well, everything really, straight from their workshop. Soaps, candles, teas and baked goods; all beautiful and delicious. I can't wait to test out their new products while I'm here. That was my most favourite job growing up.

I close my eyes, savouring the sweet flavours lingering on my

35

tongue. I push any negative thoughts away and allow the happy memories to take over my brain, trying to envision Jerry Garcia singing the soulful melody to his love. Despite my not quite feeling the love myself, the music does make me feel more in tune with my creative self. I start typing.

It can't be more than an hour later and I'm lying on the side of the bed, my hair dangling over the edge and I'm swishing it side to side, a part of me hoping that my mum dusted the floor before my arrival. I have been hit with a sudden surge of writer's block.

My leading man is in a room with his ex. They are just talking when the ex makes her move, planting a kiss on his lips just as his fiancée walks in. I need the leading lady to believe it's not what it seems, but I'm stuck. Why should she trust her fiancé?

I sit up, the blood rushing to my head not helping matters. Come on, back to work. I try to rally myself. Viewers want to be whisked away in this beautiful fairy tale. Who says fairy tales aren't true? You must open your heart to love. Love is everywhere, and my job is to fill everyone's heart with love. I choke on the sweet taste of syrup that is lingering on my tongue. I didn't fill Scott's heart with love. Now that is someone else's job.

I push the laptop away at the unpleasant thought and climb out of the bed, tiptoeing to save my feet from the chilly wooden floorboards. I pick up a few logs from the wicker basket at the side of the fireplace and place them in the grate. With the matches I find on the mantel, I light the fire and sit cross-legged on the deep purple rug in front of it.

I can't keep doing this to myself. I don't want to think about Scott and his girlfriend. I want the nightmares of seeing them kiss to go away. But why can't my brain let go of him? I really need to finish this script. Lara has shown interest in my first original screenplay and has given me one more chance to prove myself as a romance writer; I can't mess this up.

I take a deep breath in and watch as each log in the fireplace ignites. I get lost in the rising flames and fiddle with the fluff of the purple rug. Affairs aren't exactly unheard of. It's just that I never in a million years saw Scott as someone who could do that. I would have done anything to make him happy, to work on the problem, if he would have just let me in on it.

I brush my thumb over the tiny heart tattoo on my left wrist. I had gotten it shortly after Scott and I got back from our honeymoon, seven years ago now. I had been in a state of newlywed bliss and on the spur of the moment, while I was with Madi when she was getting the rose on her shoulder, I decided to get one to symbolize my love for Scott and to remind myself that when things got tough to never forget the love we had for each other. Now he has simply moved on with his life. I know I must do this too, but I can't seem to find the switch inside me to flick it to 'stop thinking about Scott'.

I return to my spot on the bed and nibble on a now cold, but still delicious, slice of French toast and pour myself a lukewarm coffee and get back to the task at hand.

*

By 7 p.m., I've resigned myself to the fact that my screenplay is not going to be finished today. I make my way into the living room where I am greeted with a glow from the orange and yellow flames that sway in the fireplace, the light glaring from the TV and the multi-coloured lights that flicker from the tree in a corner of the room.

My mum's tree has always been beautiful, but out here against the rustic décor, the wooden ceiling beams and stone fireplace the lights, the flower ornaments and homemade wooden Santas and sleighs are something else.

Madi is curled up under a turquoise throw on one side of the L-shaped couch and my parents are snuggled up together on the other side. I make myself known and sit down near Madi, so I can pinch some of her blanket.

'What are we watching?' I ask, as my mum gets up and walks into the open kitchen that's part of the spacious living room area. Madi looks over at me.

'Oh, just a Pegasus Christmas classic that had a bunch of input from an incredible writer I know,' Madi answers, giving me a wink and pulling her long legs towards her so that I can get more of the blanket.

'It's one of yours then?' I say, genuinely smiling and returning Madi a wink of my own.

'So, did you get it finished?' Madi asks, sitting up straighter. My dad looks over.

I stretch my arms above my head, loosening the knots in my neck, as my brain stumbles over the word 'no.' With all eyes on me a wave of panic swoops in, catching me off guard. Reluctant to disappoint Madi and wanting to get the festive fun underway, I have no control over the words that spill from my mouth next.

'Yes, I did, I sent it all off too.' Inside, I'm cringing. I've just lied to Madi, but I can't bring myself to be the reason she doesn't get to celebrate Christmas for the second year in a row.

'Atta girl,' Madi says, offering me a high five. I grin and clap my hand against hers. Madi's eyes linger on mine a touch longer than needed and I quickly turn my attention to the TV, not wanting her to see the truth in my eyes.

'That's fantastic, sweetheart,' Mum says, coming up behind us with her own concoction of mulled wine. It's a blend of herbal teas, no alcohol needed, and I haven't had it since my parents moved out here. The cinnamon hits my nostrils and I immediately sink back into the soft couch, momentarily allowing my worries to melt away with each warm sip. But with the Pegasus Entertainment adverts buzzing in the background, my moment of bliss is short-lived. Not only do I have to put my past aside to write the best screenplay of my career, I now have to figure out how to do it in three days without my best friend knowing.

Chapter 5

The next day I make my way down to the kitchen with the hope that Madi might have decided to treat herself to a lie-in, so that I can grab some coffee and sneak in an hour or two of editing before she wakes. But the minute I enter the kitchen I'm greeted by my one and only, who informs me that my parents are out and that the day is ours for the taking. She's wearing her signature turquoise headscarf and her blonde hair is pinned up in a bun, with mint Converse and a white tee under a thin strap denim playsuit. She looks perky and bright making me yearn for a dose of what I would really prefer right now: a day with my favourite person. All thoughts of writing dissipate.

In comparison to Madi, I haven't parted with my oversized olive cardigan since we got off the plane, my hair is a tangled and knotted mess, and the black leggings I'm sporting could do with a wash. I have yet to put any make-up on my face. I stare at Madi's bold pink lips and envy them a touch. I catch her looking me up and down and I can see her brain ticking. My ensemble represents my frazzled state. I can't actually remember the last time I felt one hundred per cent myself, but looking at Madi I feel motivated to channel my usual vigour when it comes to choosing outfits every day.

I look up from my comforting mug of liquid gold in time to see Madi curiously give me a once-over, and then she smiles. I smile back, an idea coming to my mind.

'Mads, will you do my make-up today?' I ask, feeling a spark of happiness ignite in my stomach. I love it when Madi does my make-up. If she wasn't so brilliant at writing screenplays and if I didn't love working with her so much, I'd suggest she become a make-up artist. Madi responds by shooting up off her chair, grabbing her mug of coffee and hooking my elbow.

'Absolutely, Harp. It would be my pleasure. Then I thought we could go to the Handmade Holiday Market. Everywhere is within walking distance around here and Jerry was telling me whichever way we walk we will find something to do or see,' she says, marching in the direction of my room, taking me with her.

The spark in my belly is now a full-on flame; warmth takes over my body. The Handmade Holiday Market sounds perfectly idyllic and wonderful. Madi knows me so well. Plus, looking through the glass double doors and the large windows that surround my parents' house, I can't hide the patter of excitement that awakens in my stomach when I see the high mounds of snow and forest that they look out on to. I can see why my parents love it here. The trees are magnificent, towering over the house with their thick trunks and spindly branches with deep green thistles and a coating of icing-sugar snow. You could get lost pointing out every intricate detail that made each one so unique despite their shared name. In fact, I am getting lost in them and momentarily forget that Madi is waiting for my response.

'That sounds lovely, Mads; maybe I can pick up something for Mum and Dad,' I say. It's been ages since I got my parents anything truly thoughtful and the guilt hits my gut as I remember yet another gift card that I sent them in the post last year. Living so far away, it became the most practical option. It wasn't like it was entirely thoughtless. I love gift cards and think they're the perfect gift for people to treat themselves to something they ordinarily might not allow themselves to. I often used to get so busy at this time of year, what with Scott's family living long-distance too and him having a brother and sister and nieces and nephews to accommodate, gift cards were the easiest options all round, even though I hate to admit it.

'Ooh and we can find a cute brunch spot while we're out too. I wonder if the markets are like back home.' Madi cocks an eyebrow at me. We love finding local family-run cafés whenever we visit a new place. Even back in London we like to make it a fortnightly affair to visit a place we haven't eaten at before and go for a coffee or have a change of scenery while we're writing. And at Christmas, Nutella crepes from London's Winter Wonderland are a must. The guilt is stacking up this morning as I think of all the things I have neglected and brushed to the wayside over the past year.

'Brunch out sounds perfect,' I say as we enter my room. I rummage through my suitcase and pull out knits, leggings and floaty dresses while Madi sees to collecting my make-up. In the bathroom I throw some water on my face and with one look at my hair, decide that I'll let Madi see to it; she's been brushing my hair since we were three and always manages to detangle it without causing me too much pain. I go to hang up my dressing gown on the back of the bathroom door when I hear the sound of Elton John's 'I'm Still Standing'.

For a moment I don't know what to do. I haven't listened to break-up songs, because it feels like I don't deserve them. My fear over not being stronger since Scott left and the fact that I've allowed my situation to get me down, made me feel like a fraud. And forget about the sad ones – knowing I wasn't the only one in Scott's life, that I wasn't enough? Well, those sad songs rendered me crushed and humiliated.

I pause at the bathroom door at the sound of Elton's voice, mixed with the softer melodies of Madi's voice, and catch her wielding a hairbrush, twirling around the room singing along.

Without warning, laughter bursts out of me as I watch her swinging hips. The beat of the song reverberates off the walls. She spots me and throws me the can of hairspray. The chorus kicks in at the same time as my adrenaline takes over. Memories of dancing with my parents when I was a kid at all the festivals come flooding back, loosening my limbs. Gripping on to my make-believe microphone I join in Madi's impromptu karaoke and let Elton's words revive my spirit.

*

My dad was right. We've walked a stone's throw from the house and are currently contemplating which direction to take. One way looks to be nothing but forest, the most glorious trees that made visions of Snow White dance in my brain; the animals that we might come across, the trees that told stories in their bark. To the left stands gingerbread house after gingerbread house. If we go that way, I feel we will be gone for days exploring every minute detail of each garland and decoration that adorned each house. The path straight ahead bears no immediate destination, just a road that gleams with slippery snow and ice. In the distance, through the misty fog, there is a faint outline of mountains.

The cold air hits my face and I wave my arms out to the sides of my puffer coat. I feel like I am the leading lady in one of my holiday rom-coms, the world in front of me for the taking. A choice awaits me. For a moment I feel a shot of adrenaline course through me. There is beauty everywhere I look, and I want to run in all the directions, but I don't quite feel courageous enough and fear takes over the adrenaline abruptly. I look over to Madi, whose blue eyes are gazing somewhere far away. We tend to share the same dazed look when stories and plots are zipping through our minds. She's grinning broadly with her hands on her hips. I try to dispel my fear to appreciate this moment with her and take it all in.

'Which way?' I shout. My lips are buried behind my woolly purple scarf.

'I have no idea,' Madi shouts back, then she takes my hand and laughs. 'How about we take the path that looks to lead to the unknown? It seems like the more adventurous and dangerous option.' She wiggles her eyebrows at me, then hooks her arm through mine as we begin to walk up the treacherous path straight ahead.

'You forgot to add terrifying?' I say, raising my eyebrows at her, catching the double meaning behind her choice of words: the unknown path and the adventure. I know that, good or bad, what lies before me is going to be an adventure. I grew up with parents who believed the universe had plans for us and that we just had to trust it. I just hadn't accounted for those plans to include divorce and my heart feeling like it was in a million pieces.

Quite frankly, I am petrified of what is lurking in the unknown. But the less I think about that now, the better. I put one foot in front of the other and focus on the golden sun reflecting off the snow, causing rainbows to dance in the trodden-down snow that has turned to ice. If I don't quite trust the universe yet, one thing I know is that I trust Madi. I follow her lead and we walk in a calm and comfortable silence for what I feel is coming up to a mile.

I'm taking in as much of the surroundings as I can, but my head is down much of the time as I shield my face from the frosty breeze and do my best not to fall.

When I do look up, I feel as though I have walked through a portal that has transported us to The North Pole. Then I remember how my mother described Main Street at this time of year. It is like London's Winter Wonderland but the decorations, the atmosphere and the aromatic smells are multiplied by a thousand. The old-town-USA-style shops resemble nothing short of Santa's grotto. Each one bears unique tinsel, ornaments and magical window displays. The streetlamps are wearing candy cane stripes and the further we walk into the square, the more stalls we see selling everything from homemade fudge and chocolates, to homemade soaps and jewellery. Off to one side they have a Santa station and right before my eyes . . .

'Are those real reindeer?' Madi gasps. Her mouth opens wide.

'I'm going to say yes,' I reply, unable to take my eyes off Santa's pack animals. They are beautiful; their fur is shining as they make soft grunting sounds as the children put their palms out to feed them.

'This place is amazing,' Madi gushes as we begin to move again. I can sense Madi is walking towards the smell of whatever is floating up in the air that is making me drool. I can smell fried potatoes and tomatoes and hear sizzling coming from a giant pan. Then cinnamon hits me in a wave of sweet pleasure. I will be happy if the only decision I must make today is savoury or sweet or, more realistically, which to eat first.

The stalls are catching my gaze, but my stomach is following Madi, letting my brain know that food will be sourced and eaten first and then it can divulge in its creative need.

We find a stall that is serving pancakes and I can see Madi's eyes bulge as she stops before it, her eyes wandering over the menu. I know full well that she wants to order everything. I surprise myself having already made my decision that I want the pancakes with fried peaches. They smell heavenly. I watch Madi and then turn my attention to the man behind the counter. I give him a small smile to apologize for the hold-up, but he seems happy to study Madi and give her all the time she needs. He has a kind face when he nods at me to acknowledge my smile. His hair is blonde, his eyes are hazel, and his features are warm. He returns to preparing food.

Madi's thorough read of the menu is something I'm used to so patience isn't a problem as I am enjoying observing the scenes around me. I am fascinated by people-watching and have been from a young age. My parents always had the most interesting people round to our house when I was growing up from doctors, to gardeners, to struggling artists and teachers. I loved watching them interact with one another. My parents welcome everyone. It's not surprising really that I started writing stories and scripts in my head, imagining the exotic lives that these people led. But it was the love and passion that burned in the eyes of my parents and all those who visited that captivated me most, be it the love they had for each other or the love they had for their work and the world around them. It's no wonder I became a fan of Pegasus Entertainment.

The man finishes serving a lady in front of us and then leans casually against the wooden wall frame. He catches me watching him and gives me a confident nod. Madi looks over at me and follows my line of vision to the man and chuckles.

'I am so so sorry,' she says, waving her hands around. 'Sorry for holding you up, everything just sounds so good. Right, I know what I'm having,' she says, standing tall and pushing her shoulders back. Her cheeks are flushed red from our cold walk and her red lips are glistening with the morning dew. She looks beautiful. I step forward and wrap my arms around her shoulders. I love Madi and I love her confidence.

'No need for apologies, what can I get you . . .?' The man sticks out his hand and raises his eyebrows, searching for our names. His cheeks are flushed pink and my heart tugs a little at his kindness.

'I'm Madi and this is Harper,' Madi says, reaching out to shake his hand.

'I'm Colt, it's nice to meet you both.'

'It's nice to meet you too Colt,' Madi says. His eyes linger on the both of us for a few minutes and I wonder what's going through his head. Our accents give away that we are tourists, but maybe he knows my parents? My mum and I sometimes get mistaken for sisters. The thought makes me smile.

Madi reaches up to grab my hands that are dangling from around her shoulders.

'Please can we get pancakes and peaches for me and, Mads, what are you having?'

Madi orders her peach-stuffed waffles and Colt gets to work informing us that we can take a seat and he will bring out his creations once they are ready. Madi and I fall in step to find a table. I release my arms from around her neck but tuck an arm into hers as we walk.

We take a seat at a wooden table with little log benches; a heat lamp is standing tall to the side of us and I must admit that between Madi's and my impromptu dance party earlier this morning, the Colorado air, Colt's kindness and the smell of cinnamon peaches toasting, my fragile heart feels full. Currently my biggest concern is if Madi will let me try some of her waffles.

'Colt is sweet,' Madi expresses, rubbing her hands together. 'Everything on the menu looks so good, we might have to come back later,' she adds, excitement in her tone.

'This place is magical,' I say, looking around. I breathe in a lungful of the crisp air just as Colt appears and places two plates of incredible-looking – and smelling – dishes in front of us.

I thank him through a smile and give Madi a wide-eyed grin. It's hard not to smile genuinely when you're looking at a plate of bright orange peaches that are covered in sweet cinnamon syrup, alongside a stack of golden-brown pancakes drizzled in dark chocolate and a heavy helping of vanilla whipped cream. I think I love Colt.

The flavours hit my taste buds and I relax into each bite as it warms my body. My shoulders uncurl from around my neck where they were trying to keep the icy bite at bay, and I have to admit it's monumentality difficult to be unhappy with a mouthful of all the combinations that make up my pancake dish.

There's a long silence while Madi and I consume half of the contents on our plates, then without saying a word we each pick up our plate and hand it to the other, swapping dishes and digging in once more. We barely stop for breath. Not to be outdone by the pancakes, the waffles are out-of-this-world delicious.

Without warning on my last bite of waffle, my chewing starts to slow, my hands begin to tremble, and my eyes have gone misty.

I feel an overwhelming sense of happiness to be here in this setting with my best friend, but the love is suddenly mixing with a cocktail of unwelcome feelings inside of me. I don't deserve this happiness. I don't deserve this delicious food. I don't deserve for Colt to smile at me – he doesn't know me, he doesn't know the person I am.

'Am I a nice person?' The question comes out of my mouth before I have time to stop it. I can't quite figure out the inner workings of my brain. One minute it's happy, the next I feel like my soul is suffocating. When will the intensity of emotions that came with learning of Scott's affair and him walking away in such an unpleasant fashion leave me alone?

I didn't have the slightest clue that I wasn't satisfying him. Images of me wrapping my arms around him when he came home after work, smothering him with kisses and giddily talking about our future together are playing in black and white. How could I have been so selfish? What kind of wife was I?

I swallow down my waffle. My salty tears mix with the sweet syrup on my lips. My whole body has stiffened except for my hands that are trembling.

I must look like a right sight to the shoppers milling about the square.

Madi puts down her knife and fork and leans over to me, grapping my wrists. I'm chewing and sobbing simultaneously.

'Oh, no, no no, sweetheart,' Madi says, dabbing at my face with a napkin. 'Sweetheart, you have been my best friend since we were three. You know I tell you how it is. Harper, you are the nicest person. Do you drive me mad sometimes? Yes. Does your ability to talk for hours on end about a script you're working on sometimes make me crazy? Hell yes. Do I like pulling hairballs out of my drain every time you stay over? Heck no. Do I enjoy when you get hangry or when you are stubborn and won't let me choose the movie on a Friday night? Not really. But all those things do not make you a bad person. Scott choosing to lie to

47

you and cheat and disrespect your marriage does not make you a bad person. We all have things to work on, either together in a relationship or on our own. We can always better ourselves and our relationships; no one is perfect, including you, Harp. But that doesn't mean what he did was anything short of selfish, cowardly and cruel. This is on him, Harper, not you.'

Madi is leaning over the table, propped up on her elbows, looking me straight in the eyes and catching my tears with her tissue.

'Why does it hurt so bad, Mads?' I stutter. Madi brushes the hair from my eyes and wipes some more tears away.

'Because you loved him with all you had, and you shared a part of you with him that no one else got to see. Besides yours truly being your number-one best friend forever, he was your best friend. It's OK to miss him. It's natural to miss him. But don't ever let his actions make you feel guilty. What goes on in a marriage is discussed within a marriage by the two people in it. He should have respected you enough to communicate with you, to give you the chance to figure it out together and to look after each other the way you always have, and he didn't. I don't care if you made him listen to that Beach Boys song you love and he hates, on repeat every day, he should have talked to you about it and that's on him.'

I take a shuddery breath, grateful for the heat lamp that is keeping me warm despite my insides feeling frozen. I feel a mixture of pathetic and thankful, wondering what on earth I would do without Madi. She has been on this crazy roller-coaster ride with for the past year and has yet to try and jump off. I appreciate her for allowing me to voice my pain, as the minute I get my thoughts out in the open I feel freed.

'Thank you,' I whisper, picking up a tissue and seeing to my own probably very smudged make-up face, and dabbing the tears away. Allowing Madi to sit back on the bench, being propped up on her elbows couldn't have been the comfiest.

Just then Colt comes over and puts what looks to be a milkshake with two straws in front of us. He smiles, his warm and awkward smile. 'It's a Rocky Mountain hot chocolate. It makes all your troubles go away. I say that, but I can't guarantee it as you two are my guinea pigs – it's a new concoction. I was feeling inspired.' He glances sweetly at us both.

Colt nods and walks away after we thank him, and I notice Madi's lips already on her straw. As I see the creamy chocolate slowly shrinking further down the glass thanks to Madi devouring its contents, I quickly take a sip. I don't want to miss out. Not only does it look incredible, but it tastes it too.

With one sip I am transported to toasted marshmallow and creamy chocolate heaven. It's like a campfire in my mouth, in a good way. We devour the shake, which I'm certain had medicinal properties – maybe it's the cacao they use – before we walk past the hut to inform Colt that he must add his inspired concoction to the menu. Then we thank him for a scrumptious brunch before we go on our merry way for a mooch around the stalls.

I have enough sugar in my system giving me a high that I hope will keep me afloat for the rest of the day.

The Handmade market is everything I thought it would be and more. The stall owners are friendly and eager to talk to us about their crafts. I feel inspired to pick up my pen and write about it all. I manage to pick up something special for my mum and dad and my heart is warm with the anticipation of being able to give them their Christmas present in person this year.

I don't think about Scott for the entire afternoon as I take in every stall. Colt's milkshake worked wonders. Unfortunately, it worked too well as by the time we venture back to the house, my good intentions of turning on my laptop and looking over my edits have disappeared faster than our plate of pancakes and waffles, and I feel like I could fall asleep standing up the minute I lay eyes on my bed.

Chapter 6

It's five in the morning and two days before Christmas Eve and I can't contain my curiosity about the forest any longer. I put on my brown snow boots, throw my hair in a loose braid and scarf, and tell my laptop that I will be back in no more than an hour to see to finally finishing off my script. Then I wrap myself up in my wool cardigan and olive-green puffer jacket with my well-worn leggings and sneak out of the sleeping house.

The fresh-fallen snow crunches as I step onto the deck; the air is cool but pleasant. I can hear an owl hooting in between the trees. I take that as my guide and follow his calls. The moon and the stars are enough to light my way and, somehow, I don't feel scared being out here alone. My parents' house lies in darkness. I believe the Christmas lights are on a timer to conserve energy. I walk past the hippie Santa and towards the towering pines. As I walk closer, the grandeur of the trees hits me and I'm immediately enchanted.

I trace my hands over the bark. Shavings of snow have settled in the ridges and cracks giving it a frosty tint. If I look closely enough, I can see the fuzzy outline of each snowflake that is hugging the trunk. I peel my eyes away from the first pine and follow a straight path past the other, not wanting to weave in and out of the trees too much in case I get lost. I'm not as familiar with the forest as I'd like to be. Scott wasn't much of an outdoors man. The one time we ventured out here to visit my parents, he'd opt to stay indoors or visit the local bars and restaurants over getting up close and personal with nature.

As a kid I was always outside. Even in London, my parents walked everywhere, and I can count on one hand the weekends that weren't spent at a park. Family holidays were spent hiking in Cornwall, visiting farms in the Cotswolds, or backpacking around Yosemite in California. It wasn't until I got with Scott and moved into the middle of London away from my parents that I stopped paying attention to the great outdoors. And when my writing took over and I started working for Pegasus Entertainment I fell easily into a routine with Madi; curling up behind my desk, wrapping myself up in blankets on the couch, tapping away at my laptop. When we did acknowledge the outside world, it was for a walk straight to a coffee shop, parking our butts inside and commenting on the rustic, outdoorsy feel of the indoors; the irony wasn't lost on me.

Up ahead I find a clearing where a couple of trees have been cut down making short stumps perfect for sitting on. I sit down and pull out the notebook that I had stuffed in my coat pocket. I look up from my spot on the stump and where the trees have been cut back leads to an opening in the canopy where the sky peeks through. It takes my breath away. The stars are golden and twinkling against the lightening sky, there's a slight touch of pink mixing with the wispy grey and blue as the sun is beginning to rise and I can hear the faint twit-twooing of the owl I saw swooping in to the trees in the earlier darkness.

This would be the most idyllic spot for a romantic picnic and star gazing with your one and only. I shudder. I don't want to ruin the moment thinking about Scott or romance, so I take a chilly breath in and watch the sad thoughts go by, replacing them with the sound of the owl and the rustling of the pines in the wind.

I put my pen to the paper and don't pause to concern myself with conscious thinking. I write, and I write some more. I dare to write my deepest wishes, the scenes I can envision playing out in the beauty of this spot and the magic that nature can hold. It occurs to me that while, yes, a romantic night for two under these stars would be quite something, it's incredibly special and beautiful by myself too. As I take in my surroundings once more, I don't feel so alone.

The sky is much lighter when I next look up. Gone is the inky grey and black, replaced by a fabulous orange and pink, and I have but a few pages left in my notebook. My body, though now I notice it feels cold, is not tense. My shoulders are at ease, my eyebrows relaxed and my feet like feathers on the ground, delicately resting on the pure white snow.

Writing gives me that release and I remind myself how lucky I am to love my job and to be working for a company that I adore so much. I smile as I fold my notebook gently to push it back inside my pocket; I need to get back and finish this script. I stand from the stump and do a little star jump to encourage the blood back to my feet when I hear crunching to the right of me. In my calm state, I don't worry, I simply hold still not wanting to scare whatever animal it might be with my crazy jumping, if I am trespassing in its home.

Two giant snow boots come into view attached to my dad who steps into the clearing, holding two Christmas mugs. I can smell rich black coffee and a vanilla tea. Dad hands me the mug full of burning-hot coffee and I take it gratefully, with a smile.

'I thought you might have turned into an icicle by now,' he says with a playful smirk. Wrinkles form at the corners of his eyes as he takes a sip of his tea, his bluey-green eyes assertive and on me.

'How did you know I was out here?' I ask, holding his gaze and knowing full well that my dad would always know where to find me. I was twelve the first, and only, time I ran away. My parents and I have always had a special bond and I never truly went through any awkward phase where I hated them. To me, my dad was the coolest person in the world. He took me to concerts, let me listen to music that other parents wouldn't let their kids listen to and I never felt trapped or like my parents wanted me to be, dress or act a certain way – not like Madi's did. As long as I was kind, did well in school and acted with love, there wasn't a problem.

So, it had been a bit of a shock when I left a note one Friday night telling them that they were the worst parents in the world and that I had run away. Because I had never done this before, they didn't have a record to go off, a pattern to follow. I could have been anywhere. But an hour into my having run away my dad found me in the most hidden-away part of Hyde Park.

If I remember correctly, I'd actually forgotten why I was mad by the time he had turned up. My dad always looked so cool in his ripped black jeans and vintage tees and faux leather jacket, that I greeted him with a wide smile. He had looked at me and said, 'Nice choice, I used to come here a lot too.' And that was pretty much the end of my grumpy years. I think a kid had got to me at school that day, picked on me for having dirty hippie parents and a dad who made soap for a living. I believed the kid and I let him get to me. I didn't care to be laughed at. But when my dad walked into the alley looking like a dadlier, but still incredibly cool version of Jim Morrison, the memory of the kid's opinion had vanished in a matter of seconds. My parents had taught me better than that – if it wasn't constructive or kind then I didn't need to listen to other people's opinions.

'Remember that day when you were twelve and ran away? Well, I still got it,' my dad replies. He's right, he hasn't lost an essence of his cool since that day and I smile into my coffee that he is thinking about the same thing I am.

'This place is beautiful, Dad, but even more so this time of year. I can't believe it's taken me this long to visit for the holidays.' I look around taking in the rising sun hitting the bark of the trees, making the snow sparkle. Dad looks around too, with a fond smile on his face, then his eyes come to rest on my face once more.

'Are you going to talk to me, kid, or would you like your space?' my dad asks, always so considerate of my needs.

I can't remember how long it's been since my dad and I had an honest to goodness heart-to-heart and that pains me a little. Since my last visit, I've made time for quick phone calls and the odd Skype call, but I haven't really made them a priority. Standing in front of my dad now, I don't know how I've got through the last two years without his guidance and wisdom. Maybe that's why I'm in this predicament I find myself in now with Scott and my lack of enthusiasm for work or anything in life.

I look into my dad's blue-hazel eyes, which match my own, and the sparkle that is reserved for me is still there. Mum tells me he has had that since the day I was born, and it has never faded. I can't lie to him. With my dad, the wall I have built over the past year comes crashing down. It's not me, it's not who I am. I'm not a guarded person, I'm more an open book. I wear my heart on my sleeve. The closed-off and reserved person I am becoming is starting to scare me. Under the covers of my bed, hiding from the world, is not where I want to spend the rest of my life.

'I'm struggling, Dad.' The words come out surprisingly calm. My dad's face wrinkles, but his olive complexion, grey stubble and kind eyes make me feel safe and free from judgement. He puts an arm through mine and starts walking between the trees. My toes are grateful for the movement. The thoughts inside my head have been distracting me from how cold I have been getting. I take another sip of coffee and with the blood now pumping through my veins, my body is warming up again.

We're walking in silence and I'm getting lost in the sherbet-pink-coloured clouds that are disappearing into the baby blue sky that is peeking through the canopy of oak.

'I'm here to listen,' is all my dad says and it's all I need. I pull my attention away from the falling snowflakes, from watching them glide through the air and nestle on the blanket of snow below and I take a cool breath in. It's the first time I'm going to speak out loud to someone other than Madi about what's happened between Scott and I, and even though it's my dad an unexpected terror washes over me. It's unpleasant and not warranted. This is my dad, I tell myself, but the terror remains stubbornly in place.

Suddenly I'm scared that my dad might scold me for doing something wrong, or that he will give me a disappointed look for being a bad wife and not being strong enough to get over this whole ordeal. I feel like a failure; my shoulders droop as we walk. I want to run away, to throw my mug across the snowy path. The battle between conflicting thoughts in my brain is immense. A strange mix of emotions is stirring in the cauldron that has become my stomach, a dash of guilt, a drop of humiliation, a sprinkle of worthlessness and a splash of am I a terrible person if I open my mouth and speak badly of Scott? It's all there and it's all uncomfortable. Scott's words were 'It's your fault.' Would my dad think it was my fault too?

My dad squeezes my arm that is linked through his, as though to let me know it's OK and with this small act of love, the flood-gates open. I turn to him, heaving heavy sobs. My shoulders are moving up and down, my back is hunched over and my face buried in my dad's thick, soft jacket. My knees are shaking, doing their best to hold me up while small cries escape my lips in intervals, between breathless gasps.

A good five minutes, maybe more, go by before my tears start to slow down. I step back, wiping my eyes and dripping nose on my puffer jacket. My dad slowly releases me, only letting go when I make eye contact.

'Kid, listen to me. I want you to stop putting pressure on yourself to get over it. Our hearts all heal at different rates. Put your mind at ease and let it absorb all these emotions. The struggle comes from trying to deny them.' His words come out gently, with his usual laidback charm. He wraps an arm around my shoulder, in a half sideways hug, and kisses me on the top of my head. Then we fall into step again.

'But, sweetheart, can I ask that you do me a favour?' he asks. My tears have subsided now. I'm feeling a sense of calm simply listening to my dad – a man I can trust with my heart and soul. I can feel the good energy emitting from him and it's rubbing off on me. I know that my dad staying calm is not by accident; the energy is all his doing and for my sake.

I nod in response.

'Stop punishing yourself, kid. It's easier said than done, I know, but have you been meditating like we taught you?' He gives me a sideways glance, his features soft. No expectations are formed in a furrowed or raised brow, which makes me feel safe to open up.

'I haven't, no, and what do you mean stop punishing myself?' I ask curiously.

'Replaying all the hurt, his actions, his words. You can do nothing to change them, my love. They are your past, but they are not your present. I ask that you try and meditate on that.'

I look up from my snow-dusted boots and see my parents' house up ahead. With no more coffee left in my mug a chill seeps through my thick clothes and into my bones. I've been out here for some time now. There is an essence of forgetting time when watching the sky change colour; blossoming from a mysterious black to a sad grey, to a bold and fluorescent orange and pink, to a clear and peaceful baby blue. I'm not ready to go inside just yet. Between the sky and my dad's words, the dull throbbing of my heart is becoming more upbeat. I understand what he is telling me.

'Sugar, the universe only provides moments in life that we need. It may be time to rediscover yourself and chisel away the blocks that society has built around you, without you knowing. London life is so fast-paced, even marriage sometimes. It's easy to forget who you are when you're caught up in it all. Thirty is a funny age. I can only suggest you meditate on this time of re-creation.'

I squeeze my dad's arm and take in his words as we come up to the deck. Away from the shadow of the trees the light of the crystal blue sky engulfs me. I sit in one of the wooden rocking chairs and stare out across the skyline, my mind swimming in and out of words my dad has said and total quiet.

A few moments pass when atop the table I notice there are two mugs, one with coffee and one with tea, and two slices of Mum's cinnamon loaf. I can smell its inviting aroma. Mum must have seen us wandering the grounds. We grab the fresh mugs and I'm grateful for the warmth it gives my palms and fingers.

'Thank you, Dad,' I say offering him a smile that I know reaches my eyes. 'I've missed you. I needed that,' I add, understanding his message and feeling a million times better having heard it.

'Ah, the universe knows this and that is why you're here,' he replies with a small smirk and a wink, before sipping his tea and sitting back in his chair.

I contemplate his response. He's right; the universe was pretty smart bringing me here. I'd put up a front for so long, pretending that I was fine without my parents, but the universe knew better. A moment passes, then I let out a chuckle. The universe and Madi are strangely alike.

Chapter 7

The cold tingle in my cheeks and the tip of my nose has been replaced with a warm flush, thanks to Mum's endless coffee refills and cinnamon cake, which has a healthy dose of flavourful spices weaving their way through the foundation ingredients and are enough to give me a powerful kick. By the time we walk back into the house, the sun is well and truly out for the day and lighting up the sky. It's still early and stunningly peaceful around the house and outdoors as the sun blazes through the wall-to-wall windows that make the living room slash kitchen area one of my favourite rooms in the house.

I had gotten so comfy in the confines of my office, my cosy nook of a writing space over the years, but since we got here to Colorado, I have fallen in love with being able to absorb the sunset and sunrise each day from every angle. There is no escaping it, almost like it is forcing me to look up and experience it, eager for attention after I'd neglected it for so long.

It's difficult not to notice that the house now smells like Christmas. A sweet vanilla and cinnamon scent mixed with citrus and cocoa arises from the biscuits that are cooking in the oven. I smile as I start to peel off my layers of clothing. The fire is roaring, the flames making the tinsel garland above it sparkle, and when

I look over to the dining table, it's covered with colourful bowls filled with every kind of sprinkle you can imagine: hundreds and thousands, silver balls, crunchy snowflakes, Christmas trees and chocolate slivers and curls.

A fresh batch of Christmas-tree-shaped cookies rest on a holly-patterned plate in the centre of the table. My mum smiles at my open-mouthed gawp as I take in the scene, the winter wonderland she has created. She walks by me bearing another tray of cookies, this time Santa-shaped, and I give her a hug that nearly causes a few Santas to topple to their demise. She kisses the top of my head and in a smooth, swift move places the Santas on the table out of harm's way.

Then she turns back to me offering a bright smile and a piping bag bursting with red icing. She doesn't ask about my three-hour foray into the forest or pry into what I was talking about with my dad, because that's how cool my parents are.

My dad is busy in the corner hanging up our coats, then he joins us at the table where Mum naturally and ever so softly grazes his forearm in a loving manner. She hands him a piping bag filled with vibrant purple icing, no doubt coloured using beetroot. My parents have been vegan since I was a baby, but they never forced it on me, allowing me to make my own decisions. My mum is a fabulous cook, her dishes so vibrant and full of earthy flavours, and my dad's not bad either – he can make a mean meaty mushroom burger. I never had reason to complain when sitting down to home-cooked meals. Over the years though, I found myself cooking to meet the tastes of Scott and my friends or to accommodate the lack of time or desire to be in the kitchen when swamped with deadlines. Just the smells of my mother's biscuits has me licking my lips and longing to don an apron and have her teach me everything she knows.

I wrap an arm around each of my parents and plant a kiss on their cheeks, then take a seat at the table. At that moment I hear slippers shuffling along the wooden floorboards. Madi enters the room with a yawn. Her usually perfectly coiffed locks are on top of her head in a messy bun, flyaway baby hairs sticking out every which way. She is bundled up in her black and white polka dot dressing gown, her bare face still glamorous-looking, her skin bright and radiant.

'Am I dreaming?' she asks sleepily, putting her hands on my shoulders and leaning down to kiss my dew-dampened hair when she reaches the table. Both my parents chuckle. Dad takes a seat and Mum goes to check on a batch of cookies still baking.

'No, you're very much awake,' I reply, as my eyes wander over the decorations cluttering the table. I don't know where to start. I pick up a Santa and resist the urge to take a bite out of him before I decorate him. It proves difficult, as he smells of cardamom and nutmeg.

'This place smells like heaven,' Madi announces as she takes a seat next to me. She picks up a star-shaped cookie and I watch as it hovers dangerously close to her plump lips before finding its way to her plate. It's my turn to chuckle. I scoop up a handful of silver balls to the line the rim of Santa's hat and get to it.

'Last Christmas' by Wham! hums from the stereo. My mum joins us at the table with a pot of tea and I lose myself to the rainbow display of mouth-watering treats spread out before me on the table and the laughter and love that surround it. I'm transported back to those early years in school when it would be a thrill to hear the teacher say that we would be decorating biscuits for a bun sale. The teacher would bring out the icing sugar, bowls and spoons and the typical British decorations that were strawberry laces and dolly mixtures and I would get lost in the creativity that sprouted when giving a kid rich tea biscuits and their own bowl of sticky icing.

I'd like to think my decorating style has a little more finesse now, than simply seeing how many colourful dolly mixtures would fit on to one rich tea.

Three hours later I'm sprawled across the L-shaped couch, Madi's head resting on my thighs and crumbs littering my woolly jumper. *The Holiday* is playing on the TV and the log fire is still ablaze, its woodsy smell keeping not just the room warm but my heart too.

'I think we needed this,' Madi notes.

I nod in agreement. I've eaten too many cookies – one of each design, and there were five in total – to make a more enthusiastic gesture.

'It's nice to appreciate the magic of the real world, when we spend so much time creating imaginary ones,' she adds.

I smile politely though my eyebrows furrow slightly as I take in Madi's words. I hadn't thought about it that way before, not really. I often used my real life as inspiration for my stories, sure I used a whole lot of imagination too, but Scott was the fairy tale that made its way into many of the scenes that I injected into scripts. But sitting here with Madi, my mum having created the most magical morning, I realize Madi is right: this isn't for a script, it isn't material for my next film, it is life.

There is magic in life that doesn't require photos or shares on Twitter to make it real. It doesn't need to be made into a film where the not quite so perfect bits, the burnt biscuits and the sloppy icing, are edited out to make it more of an ideal fairy tale; it is a real fairy tale and it isn't happening behind the lens of a camera only when someone yells action.

I am in charge of writing my own story and who said it couldn't be a fairy tale? I guffaw a little at my last thought. OK, so my current situation doesn't scream fairy tale, but who said fairy tales couldn't have lumps in the snow? My stories so far have come from me unconsciously going about life. I was happy, I was in love and I was jotting it down along the way, editing out the bad bits, fast-forwarding the rough parts and elaborating on the good to make the perfect rom-com. What happens if I stop, take a step back and consciously pick up my pen to purposefully make the moments happen; if I go after the story, squeezing the most out of life and love every day instead?

'What's tickled you, Harp?' Madi asks, tilting her head up at me. Her blue eyes shimmer from an organic and natural sugar candy cane high.

'You're right,' I say.

'Go on.' She smiles.

'I've been documenting my life, being inspired by things that have happened, but not really controlling what's happening to me. What happens if I take the lead and make stuff happen? If I write it before it happens so to speak?' Madi sits up and my legs instantly tingle with pins and needles. 'Write the life I want to lead, and I don't mean literally write it, I mean live it.'

'I like the sound of that, babe. Oh, the lives we lead between the pages. I'm pretty sure my last leading lady got more action in two pages than I have in the last two years.' She snickers, then her eyelids droop and she gives me an apologetic look at her choice of words.

I turn my attention back to the TV just as Kate Winslet tells Jasper where to go and I suddenly feel full of gusto, which I'm thinking is mostly false bravado coming from the icing sugar and cookies that I have consumed, but I'm running with it nonetheless. The little old man is right: it's about time I stop being the best friend to the woman in my scripts and start being the leading lady in my own damn life.

I have shed too many tears in the last year. I am running dry. I've been allowing Scott and his girlfriend to make me feel like less than nothing, like I didn't matter, like rubbish they can just toss aside. Colorado has given me nothing but beauty in the past three days alone and I want to soak up every drop, not for the big screen but for me.

'Get ready, I have an idea,' Madi announces, springing up from the settee. 'Come on, chop chop, wrap up warm. Go.' She shoos me away, waving in the direction of my room as I catch her bounding over to my dad and whispering something in his ear. I can't read her lips, so I have no idea what to prepare for. After all those biscuits, I'm not sure I'm up to more than sitting on the couch consuming Christmas movies for the afternoon. I could be a leading lady from the couch, right? Madi catches me snooping.

'Oi, go get ready, Harp,' she shouts with a mock stern voice. What was I saying earlier about trusting my best friend?

*

When we get outside, the afternoon sky is a vibrant icy blue blending with feathery fluffy whites. I've got several layers on under my new thick snow jacket, as advised by Mads. The air is crisp and threatening snow flurries. I'm not quite sure what the plans are for the afternoon other than leaving my worries in my bed, my work brain at the house and to do what Madi tells me to do.

So far, so good. Kind of. My script is in dire need of my attention, but I still can't bring myself to confess that to Madi. I just have to keep my worries to myself so Madi can have some fun and then I promise myself I'll get it done.

I am loving my new yellow snow jacket that Mum and Dad surprised me with. I was able to open it early due to them conspiring against me with Madi about today's plans and saying that we would need them. They bought one for Madi too but in a very retro pink. It suited Madi to a T.

I was doing what I was told and felt cheerful as a ball of sunshine in my new attire, plus it was keeping the cold at bay, and I may have gobbled up another Santa as I left the house; so wins all round this morning, as long as I didn't think about my script.

We are trekking up the icy path, heading in the same direction as the previous day but suddenly we take a detour as we get closer to Main Street. I can't see much up ahead other than mountains, a zip line, a ski lift and the occasional log cabin.

'What are we doing, Mads? Where are we going?' I ask, curiosity getting the better of me. I'm not even sure if she can hear me with the breeze picking up the higher up the mountain we climb. She keeps walking and I keep following behind. My thighs are starting to burn with all the giant steps in and out of the deep snow, but my own buttocks could do with the exercise. I've not been sticking to my morning yoga since my marriage took a downward dog.

'We're nearly there,' Madi yells, turning back to check if I'm keeping up. I am . . . barely.

The cabin that had looked to be the home of a small ginger-bread man five minutes ago now looms large as we step up to it. It wasn't the tiny hut I had thought it to be but a giant lodge consisting of a café, a shop and what looks to be a reception area. I gulp as it dawns on me what the plan for the afternoon is.

I wonder how quickly I can roll down the mountain before Madi notices I've gone. I haven't even realized that I am mumbling to myself and shaking my head until we reach the automatic sliding doors and Madi is looking over at me with a huge grin on her face and a mischievous twinkle in her eye. She enthusiastically loops her arms through mine and leads me through the doors, sealing my fate.

Inside the wooden lodge is a stunning Christmas tree decorated with gold and silver baubles and red bells that twinkle in the light from the glowing fire that is burning next to it. There is a white angel nestled on the top and ornaments shaped liked crackers, presents and miniature skiers dangling from each branch. It's charming and distracts me from plotting my escape route.

In front of the fire is an inviting vintage sofa. I could most certainly rest up here and hang back in this cosy nook while Madi hits the slopes and I could finish my script without her knowing.

'Don't even think about it,' Madi informs me following my gaze to the comfy plush cushions. The smell of eggnog hits my nostrils. It's the perfect office for my writing brain to curl up in and write the day away. But I'm not supposed to be thinking about writing and I can't let Madi know I lied to her about my edits. I've still got time; I will get it done. I'm mentally working out the hours that I will need to complete it; coming up with a timeline in my head when Madi speaks again.

'Get your head out of script writing. What did you just say about living life? You're done for the holidays; we're having a break, Harp, and we're already booked in. There's a homemade Baileys hot chocolate in it for you at the end.' Madi lifts one of her arched eyebrows suggestively.

I can't help but smile, despite my half-hearted 'uh' of protest. She got me with the bribe of her hot chocolate. Madi and I aren't huge drinkers, but a drop of Baileys in her hot chocolate gives it that extra luxurious touch.

'Madi and Harper?' a voice calls out from behind us, making me jump. We both swivel around on the spot and are greeted by a tall, drop-dead gorgeous woman, with piercing blue eyes to rival Madi's. She reaches us and we both choke out a hello. Upon closer inspection she is even more beautiful, wearing very little to no make-up. Her cheeks are flushed red from the cold and she has a pearly white smile.

'How you doing, ladies? I'm Hayley. So, is this your first time snowboarding?' the goddess asks. I blink as the sudden realization of what Madi has signed me up for hits me hard in the chest. I nudge Madi, who seems as much in awe of this cool being in front of us as I am, and she lets out a laugh. I do not.

Hayley looks at me and offers a sweet smile. The anxiety is clearly etched on my face and she can probably smell the fear. Gusto, Harper. Leading lady, Harper. I remind myself.

'Stick with me and you'll be fine,' she says, waving her arm for us to follow her. 'Your lesson starts in ten minutes and we have an hour,' she adds, tapping her clipboard with a pen. 'First things first, we need to get you geared up.'

I offer a hesitant nod back while Madi is still sniggering to the side of me. When I glare at her, her face falls serious. I'm keeping one eye on Hayley so we don't get lost, and one eye on Madi as she opens her mouth.

'You've wanted to try snowboarding for the longest time, Harp. Now's your chance and I've got your back. I promise,' Madi says, giving me a squeeze around the shoulder after having composed herself, finally.

'You wouldn't happen to be Jerry's kid from Sugar Magnolia would you?' Hayley asks, referring to my mum and dad's shop, as she starts placing helmets and goggles on the counter before us.

'I would be, yes,' I say softly, concentrating on my breathing. Madi is right. I have always wanted to try my hand at snowboarding, but I would have preferred the option of doing it without the possibility of ten Santas making a reappearance.

'This should be second nature to you then, kid, your dad's a natural,' Hayley adds with a wink. Of course my dad is a natural. He's been skateboarding since he could walk. That talent of his, however, did not get passed down to his only daughter. I hold back this information from Hayley as she is looking at me expectantly like she is excited to see what I am capable of.

I send out a silent prayer to the universe that maybe somehow, on snow, I'll get the hang of it much better. At the same time I thank the universe that at least I am wearing leggings so there is a good chance that this time if I fall trying to come off a ramp, I won't flash the skate park, or in this case ski resort, my knickers; you couldn't get me out of my beloved lace long skirts when I was a teen, even when I was on a board. I learnt my lesson.

Chapter 8

There is no denying that I don't quite take to the snow like my dad and my hopes of somehow being better at snowboarding than skateboarding are dashed pretty quickly. I have landed on my arse more times than I care to count since I stepped onto the slope. The bruises on my bum cheeks that tingle and pulse each time I move give me a good idea. The apple has very clearly fallen miles away from the tree – which Hayley notes. At this point all I can do is laugh as I take my umpteenth tumble.

By now I'm not so scared of the fall and am loosening up. I dare say, I am having fun. Madi can currently take the title of my father's honorary daughter as she is getting the hang of snowboarding a lot faster than I am.

'Remember, bend your knees and follow the flow of the board,' Hayley repeats, sounding very like my mother and her 'follow the flow of the universe' speech, but sterner and bolder. She helps me up to my feet and doesn't let go of my shoulders until I'm steady on my feet. The frosty wind has frozen my eyelashes at this point. I'm afraid I'm going to see icicles falling from them, but adrenaline is coursing through my bones. When Hayley lets go, I follow the groove of the snow, bending my knees into the board. I get a good three metres before inevitably face-planting the snow again.

Madi and Hayley both come floating over to me, as teenagers and adults alike swoop down the mountain with ease. I swear I can see a few infants too, but I hastily look away before my self-confidence takes any more of a beating.

Madi and Hayley are doubled over laughing at my expense. Madi collapses on top of me, her board getting tangled up in mine as she's snorting between gasps of air. That last fall had been a doozy.

'You guys should come and ride with me and my girls. You could do with some more practice and I'm afraid your hour is done,' Hayley says, her American accent thick and velvety. She gives me a teasing smirk. She looks like a badass angel with the light of the sun casting a halo glow around her helmet.

I roll my eyes at her and shake my head, mock offended, then shove Madi off me with difficulty.

'Is that a challenge?' I ask, accepting Hayley's helping hand up.

'It most certainly is,' she replies. I'm in love with this woman's no-nonsense attitude and sweet demeanour, and only a touch jealous of her snowboarding skills – and I've only known her an hour. She pulls me to my feet, and I wobble. She grips hold of me tight with one hand while helping Madi to her feet with the other and now I'm envious of her strength – hoisting two grown women up out of the snow.

Once Madi is standing, Hayley bends down to unbuckle my boots and recommends I walk, pointing in the direction of where we are heading. Madi manages to hold in the fit of giggles I know are bursting at her seams and Hayley shoots off down the slope smoothly, sliding into the flow of other skiers and snowboarders speeding down the mountain. We're both watching her go; it's hard not to watch this woman. She's like Wonder Woman on snow.

We eventually peel our eyes away and Madi leans over and unbuckles her own boots.

'Are you not going to go with Hayley?' I query as I pick up my board and start walking. Madi follows suit.

'I admit, I'd follow that woman anywhere but the thought of you disappearing into a snowbank never to be seen again – well, I don't think I'd ever forgive myself.' She snorts and I shove her, making her drop her board.

We finally catch up with Hayley who is standing with a group of women, all of whom are beautiful in their own unique way. There's Em, whose hair is whiter than Madi's; she's wearing leopard-print earmuffs and fierce winged eyeliner. Madi immediately beelines for her, inspecting her wings and asking her how she gets them so perfect.

Then there's Ariana, whose black curls are barely contained under her rainbow beanie, her dark skin glowing in the sunlight, a natural highlight glistening off her cheekbones in the dewy mountain air. Her smile is warm and welcoming.

When I reach Bella, she pulls me in for a hug. She has brown braids tucked into a woolly hat and a scarf pulled tight around her neck. Her pink glossed lips are smiling brightly, causing dimples to appear on her rosy cheeks.

'Hayley tells us you need a little hand,' Bella says as I sit down to buckle myself up. 'Oh God, has she told half the mountain to watch out for me?' I say, giving Hayley a pointed stare. She simply shrugs and smirks.

'Well, you listen to her and you'll be flying down the slope like a pro in no time,' Bella says, giving me a hand up once I'm all clipped in.

Bella keeps hold of my hand as I gear up into position, trying to balance out my body weight on my board and doing my best to copy Hayley and the rest of the gang in their stances. I imagine this is how I felt as a baby learning how to walk. I'm grateful to the other girls for their patience, while I silently curse Madi for being so good. I get distracted for a minute as I watch her elegantly guide her board after Em and Ariana while Hayley and Bella keep close tabs on me as I start to move.

When I dare to look up and take my eyes off the bright snow

on the ground, the mountains are quite spectacular. I'm not going very fast, so I observe the children all looking like snowmen in their giant snowsuits. Some are riding down the mountain on sleds and some doing significantly better than I am during their ski and snowboard lessons. The mountain is alive with laughter and everyone is encouraging and supporting each other. Distracted, I begin to wobble again.

'Stop looking down,' I hear Hayley shout, from the left of me.

'Keep your head up and only look forward,' Bella says, from my right. I wonder for a moment if she's giving me life advice or snowboarding advice. Right now, I feel they are one and the same.

With some trepidation, I still my wandering head. When I look up and only forward the wobbling ceases. I focus on where I'm going, and the board miraculously follows my line of vision. I reach the bottom where the girls are hollering and cheering and realize I have succeeded in getting all the way down the mountain without causing further harm to my backside.

It has only taken a million and one attempts, but I'm taking it as a win.

*

There is more laughter and lots of chatter inside the café. It's like no café Madi and I have ever been to in London before. Each booth has its own fire pit in the centre with tea lights adorning the window ledges. The low, light wooden beams are decorated with the most magnificent holly garlands and mistletoe, but you can still see each grain of wood and tree carving in their design. We have all offloaded our equipment and stripped off our heavy snowsuits and are crowded into a booth by the kitchen. As Hayley works here, she takes the lead in ordering what she feels we need after an afternoon on the slopes.

When a tray of crackers, chocolate, marshmallows and mulled wine is brought to our table, I think I'm officially in love with

Hayley. I take a sip of the cinnamon, nutmeg and citrusy mulled wine and it instantly warms my bones.

I smile dreamily and thank her for a wonderful afternoon.

'This tastes incredible,' Madi gushes from opposite me in the booth. Em is sitting next to her toasting a marshmallow, which causes a sugary sweet aroma to hit the air. I didn't think I could stomach more organic or processed sugar today after this morning's cookie exhibition, but as the aroma wafts my way my stomach growls with want.

'Jake adds a splash of whiskey to his mulled wine for extra punch and flavour. You'll get to know Jake – he's a complete goof-ball, but one hell of a chef. He runs this place, so you'll want to be in his good books,' Em reports with a wink. So that explains how it's going down so smoothly, I think to myself feeling the colour rise in my cheeks.

'So, how long are you girls here for?' Bella asks, while layering a piece of chocolate onto a cracker.

My hands are wrapped around my mug and I'm savouring the delicious drink before tucking into a marshmallow. They look out-of-this-world scrumptious.

'Until just after the New Year,' I answer merrily, the whiskey hitting the spot.

'We're visiting Harper's parents for the holidays. We've never been for Christmas before, but this place is fabulous,' Madi coos as she pops a crispy-looking toasty marshmallow into her mouth. I watch her as she closes her eyes in ecstasy and licks her lips. 'Oh my God, what is that? I've never tasted a marshmallow like that before.'

The girls all laugh, and Ariana wiggles her eyebrows. 'Jake knows what he's doing in the kitchen.'

'And out of it, if the smug look on your face is anything to go by,' Em says, her tone teasing as she looks at Ariana and winks. Ariana blushes, but shrugs confidently leaning back into the booth. 'I take it he's as good between the sheets as he is between the pots and pans?' Em adds after a pause, ensuring more laughter.

71

Ariana doesn't answer; instead she takes a bite out of a fluffy pink and white marbled marshmallow and smirks coyly, like the cat who got the cream.

'I'm liking the sound of this Jake,' Madi says, reaching out and offering a high five to Ariana, who happily slaps Madi's hand.

'Your parents are really cool,' Hayley says kindly, changing the subject. She's nursing her own mulled wine, taking tentative sips, which I think is probably a good idea. I take note, as the whiskey and wine have already given me a light buzz and I hold off on the last few sips. With Madi and I not drinking often, it doesn't take much.

'Thanks,' I reply, caving in to what I believe to be s'mores. I pick up a cracker and copy Bella, placing a piece of chocolate on to it. Then I attach a marshmallow to the stick I have been given and hover it over the flames, twirling it between my fingers and watching as the flames make the pink mallow bubble and burn and turn golden.

'Is it just the two of you or do you have partners here with you?' Bella asks. Her mulled wine is gone, I notice. The question catches me off guard and my marshmallow promptly falls off my stick with the nervous jerk of my hand. I can feel Madi's eyes on me. Only now does it occur to me that I haven't thought about Scott for hours.

My focus on the slopes, the tingling bruises on my bum, the adrenaline in my veins and the banter and laughter with the girls have all completely distracted me from dwelling on things. I've felt more alive and joyful this afternoon than I have done this entire year, but the weight of Bella's question casts a shadow over that joy, momentarily threatening to take it away.

Fortunately for me, the other shadow that hasn't left my side since Scott did steps in to save me from mumbling through an answer and having to ruin this amazing day.

'It's just the two of us. We haven't had a girls' trip in forever and thought it was about time we treated ourselves to one. Plus, like you said Hayley, Harper's parents are the coolest. They practically raised me, and we were due a visit!' Madi sings chirpily as she sandwiches a golden marshmallow between two crackers and a piece of chocolate and hands it to me with an 'I've got you, keep your head up' smile.

I receive it gratefully, aware that Hayley is watching me. I simply smile at her too and take a huge bite of the s'more. The marshmallow melts on my tongue in a silky explosion of texture and flavour. It's incredible. The chocolate is happiness on my lips and I nearly groan with pleasure.

'Jake has a lot to answer for,' Em notes. OK, so maybe I did actually groan out loud. We all erupt with laughter once more. My whole body feels light and loose and it's a welcome break from the tension that has been gripping my muscles for the past few weeks.

'How are things going with you and Jake?' Bella asks Ariana with a slight slur of her words. Who topped up our mulled wine? My glass is now brimming, and I hadn't even noticed. How strong is this wine and how much whiskey did this Jake person add to this thing?

'It will sound corny, so don't laugh, but everything about him is delicious,' Ariana says, breaking her own plea as she giggles into her mulled wine. Em and Hayley snort. Madi whistles and Bella claps her hands excitedly while I raise my glass.

'Cheers to those who are getting some,' Madi toasts, causing a few heads to turn in our direction. I'm partly conscious that the occupants of our table are growing sufficiently tipsy. The other part of me hasn't felt this giddy in a long time so I'm more than happy to celebrate with our new friends and I clink mugs with Madi.

'Speaking of getting some, have you said yes to Colt taking you out yet?' Em asks, turning her attention to Bella. Bella flushes purple. Her pupils grow wide in the light of the fire.

'Colt who works at the market?' Madi and I ask in unison. Bella smiles with a faraway look in her eye.

'Yes, that's him,' she says with a hiccup.

'He seems really sweet,' I say, trying my hand at toasting another marshmallow.

'Yes, he was lovely when we met him the other day at the market, and he makes the most amazing waffles,' Madi says, adding her two cents.

'He is lovely.' Ariana sighs. 'He's one of the finest bachelors left in Breckenridge and he's been trying to win this one over for months, but she won't let herself be wined and dined,' she adds, tilting her head in Bella's direction.

'He may be nice, but Bella can date in her own time. She doesn't need a man to be wined and dined,' Hayley pipes up. Her tone is light, a small smile on her face, but when I catch her eye, I sense that there is hurt behind their ocean-like blue.

'I couldn't agree more,' Em says brushing her knuckles against Madi's as they touch their glasses in another cheers.

'I appreciate everyone's sentiments and I do like him, I just want to take my time, that's all,' Bella informs the group, her voice coming out sweet and a little shy suddenly when it comes to talking about her own love life. I get the feeling Bella is the youngest in the group.

Hayley puts her hand on Bella's. Her brows are furrowed with concern. 'There is absolutely nothing wrong with that. Ignore this lot – there's no reason to rush anything,' she says.

Bella looks up, the cheeky glint in her eyes back from before, when we were discussing Ariana's love life, is back. 'Besides the fact that he is ridiculously hot and every time I see him, I want to kiss him.'

Hayley playfully shoves Bella's hand away and rolls her eyes. I nearly choke on my marshmallow and the other girls all make a variation of wolf whistle and whooping sounds. I can barely keep up with the dips and dives of this conversation but it's certainly keeping me entertained.

I'm nearing the end of my second mug of mulled wine and

the boozy marshmallows have given me a warm happy glow when Bella decides to take the attention off her and generously pass it over to me once more.

'Has anyone got you feeling lustful under the mistletoe this Christmas?' Bella asks innocently, picking at a cracker and nibbling its edges.

I look over at Madi but find her and Em deep in hushed conversation and her eyes are blurry from one too many mugs of whiskey-infused mulled wine. I'm on my own with this one. I drain the last dregs of wine and strangely enough feel my back straighten up and a weight being lifted from my shoulders. The idea of sharing my story with these girls doesn't seem so daunting. 'I split with my husband a year ago and am taking some time to focus on myself,' I say and then exhale a deep breath. Surprisingly, I don't feel scared by my admission, I feel liberated as I say the words out loud. It beats putting on a brave face and keeping a secret. I don't like secrets. Secrets meant that people got hurt. I gulp as I think of my white lie to Madi over finishing my script, but I still have time. If I can sneak off tonight and get it done, it will be a lie no longer and there will be no need to upset Madi.

Em pulls her attention away from Madi to me and the other girls are staring at me, eyes wide. Hayley I'm sure has tears in hers. But I don't want her to feel sad for me or for them to pity me. I don't want to feel pathetic and helpless anymore. If I'm pathetic and helpless who would want me? Nobody would want me, and Scott would be right to run away from someone so weak and fragile. I want to be like Hayley. I want to be confident and fierce. I want to be able to snowboard and look like Wonder Woman while doing it, not Bambi on ice. I'm done with feeling sorry for myself.

'I found my boyfriend of three years in bed with one of his clients seven months ago. They'd been seeing each other for weeks,' Hayley says, then downs her mug of mulled wine. When she looks up and her eyes meet mine, we both burst out laughing. Be it the mulled wine, the fact that my brain has exhausted thinking about Scott or the fact that I want to scream out to Hayley that it's her idiot boyfriend's loss and that she's better off without him, I don't feel so terrified in admitting my failure. In fact, by the laughter barrelling out of me, it's safe to say I needed this release.

'Here's to the dicks; may we spot them, keep away from them and be rid of them fast,' Em choruses. I'm too far gone in a state of marshmallow-infused bliss to pay attention to the disapproving stares that our table is getting, though I am relieved that there are no kids around this evening.

Chapter 9

Madi is still snoozing when I wake up. She fell asleep in my room last night after we got back late from our evening of mulled wine and marshmallows. I feel my stomach twist anxiously as I realize I missed out on another day of editing and my deadline is now tomorrow. I groan, roll over and fight the cold as I peel off the duvet. It must be early as the fire in the living room usually sends heat through the entire house when Mum and Dad get it going in the morning. I quickly pull my dressing gown on and slip my feet into my slippers. I head in search of coffee, or maybe I'll have tea this morning. Like my dad I was a tea drinker until late nights finishing scripts meant that coffee had become a habit; a necessity to get me through my day. This morning I fancy a non-caffeinated tea.

My parents aren't up yet, which explains the lack of the fire. When I enter the kitchen, my eyes scan the room and stop on the vintage-record-style clock resting against the mantel. It lets me know that it's four-thirty in the morning, a little earlier than my normal wake-up call. However, today I have energy in my veins that is eager to be put to use. I'm not in the mood to stay indoors. I think I'm becoming addicted to fresh air in my lungs and need my fix.

Through the giant windows I can see that last night's blizzard left a heap of fresh snow and that snowflakes are still coming down. I get a tingle of excitement in my stomach. The sky is deep blue, but there is a dusty orange sneaking in on the horizon. I set about boiling the kettle and carefully selecting my tea for the day. I choose a ginger tea for its energy and focus and when the smell rises in the air I smile. I take my mug and tray over the fireplace and begin loading the grate with logs. I light the kindling and let it work its magic.

Then I sit back and watch the baby flames grow as I sip my tea. The flavours excite my taste buds in the same way the snow gives my stomach butterflies. A rush of joy floods through me as I daydream over the last few days in Colorado. Suddenly, just what I need today pops into my head. Maybe if I get this out of my system I can come back later with a clearer head, readier to tackle my script.

I jump up and carry the tray back to the kitchen before returning to my room. Madi is snoring; jet lag and whiskey most likely screwing with her body clock. I throw on my winter thermals, wash my face, brush my teeth and shove my relatively neat hair under a woolly hat. I then trudge back through the house, pausing to write a note to let everyone know where I will be and inviting them to join me later should they wish.

*

It's only when I'm nearing the top of the mountain and the ski lodge is in view that I even consider it being closed at this early hour. The slopes do seem awfully quiet.

But I persist anyway, thinking the walk will do me some good, then breathe a sigh of relief when I get closer and see the lights on in the reception. My stomach bubbles with a mixture of excitement and nerves as it suddenly dawns on me; 'what the hell am I doing here?' I'm not exactly a natural on a snowboard and my bottom is still very much recovering from the many bruises I accumulated yesterday, so why did I think this was a smart idea?

I walk into reception and it's clear why the slopes are quiet; everyone is crammed in here. I instantly start to sweat under my many layers as I try and navigate myself through the flocks of people, all of whom I notice are wearing numbered bibs. The Brit in me is apparent as I use the words 'sorry' and 'excuse me' constantly as I squeeze past people, some twice the size of me. When I reach the desk, beads of sweat are trickling down my forehead unattractively, I fear, when the guy who greeted Madi and I yesterday in a friendly manner, greets me today with a quizzical and awkward look.

'Sorry, the slope is closed for tournament practice this morning. It will reopen to the public this afternoon,' he says before getting pulled to the far end of the desk to hand over more bibs to yet more people.

I turn to face the crowd and look to the entrance of the café, feeling deflated at my failed attempt at pushing myself out of my comfort zone. I should be grateful that the tournament saved me from my own stupidity at coming up here alone and possibly getting hurt doing something that could be dangerous when a person doesn't know what they are doing. Maybe it was the universe telling me to go and grab a hot chocolate, pull out my notebook and pen and actually get some work done. That is probably a better idea.

'Not so fast, you're with me.' My eardrums prick up at the familiar voice. I look around and see Hayley waving at me from over by the Christmas tree a few people in front of me. She's standing with a group of people all wearing vests that match hers. She is wearing a number, so I can only assume she is entering the tournament and that this is her team. I make my way over to her, all my bravery from before evaporating, my notebook tickling my chest reminding me that it is there and ready to come out.

But I have no time to think about that now. Hayley pulls me in for a hug and introduces me to everyone.

'Hi, nice to meet you all,' I say slightly overwhelmed by all the professionals I am sandwiched up against.

'This is my coach, and these are my teammates. They're in the competition too,' Hayley informs me in a chirpy tone. My face must be a picture of confusion as Hayley explains, 'Sorry, today's the start of the Dew Ski Tournament. One of the biggest ski tournaments in the world. We get to practise this morning and then the competition will start Boxing Day, to you Brits. It gives outsiders a fair chance to get used to this mountain range. I take it you didn't know?' Hayley asks, raising her eyebrows and chuckling at my bewildered expression.

'Wow,' I say. 'That's really cool. I best get out of your way then and leave you all to practise. Good luck,' I mumble as I nod in everyone's general vicinity and start backing up. 'Good luck. I'll come back Boxing Day to cheer you on.' I smile at Hayley and do a weird bow.

'Hold on a minute,' Hayley says. 'Did you come up here on your own free will?' She looks around, which I take to be her wondering where Madi is. 'To snowboard? By yourself?'

I can already tell what Hayley is plotting and what I had originally thought to be a bold and marvellous idea on my part, one that I had been ready to give myself a gold star for, now seems like a terrible plan. Unfortunately, Hayley doesn't seem to agree. She has a distinct sparkle in her blue eyes. Yes, Hayley is right. I had intended to come here and snowboard by myself, but the universe had other plans for me when it created this tournament, therefore it is leading me away from any broken bones. But I don't need to tell Hayley any of that.

'No, no, I just needed a walk and somehow ended up here. The mountains look so pretty . . . I was just wandering,' I stutter and start to back up again. It's hard to make a quick getaway with all the bodies around me. I'm barely a few inches away from her when Hayley takes one stride forward and casually places her arm around my shoulders, that teasing smirk back on her beautiful face.

'I don't believe that for a second,' she whispers in my ear, before saying aloud to the group: 'Harper's come all this way to snowboard and snowboard she shall. She's on our team this morning.' Then she winks at me.

OK, universe, our plan is back on. It's time to step out of my comfort zone and try not to mortify myself in front of hundreds of professional skiers and snowboarders. I gulp.

*

I'm currently revelling in a new record I have set for myself; I have been snowboarding alongside Hayley for the past forty fir trees, three drop-offs on the ski lift, and I have yet to trip, stumble or eat snow. The feel of the wind whipping in my face, the smell of pine trees and the sound of my fellow skiers swooshing by – as they are going a tad faster than me – is exhilarating. Every bone in my body is alive, albeit aching and screaming, but alive.

The bottom of the hill is in sight. We're zooming towards it, Hayley a board length in front of me. I'm watching her as she glides smoothly along the snow, her knees slightly bent, completely at ease on her board. When we come to a stop, I simply gaze at her in awe.

'You're incredible,' I say enthusiastically, adrenaline pumping through my veins. Hayley slows down and falls back into line with me. She tilts her head in my direction, so I can just make out her blue eyes twinkling through her goggles. She pulls her scarf away from her lips, puckering them in thought, as if she has just put lip gloss on.

'I can say the same about you.' She pauses, looking at me inquisitively. I feel there is more she wants to say. After a moment she opens her mouth again. 'You said you and your husband split a year ago, but I feel like there's more to the story of you finding yourself again. If you don't mind me asking, what happened?' Hayley asks. After her admission around the table the previous night, I know she is someone that will understand my pain, after finding her boyfriend cheating on her; more importantly, I feel like she needs me to open up, and that we can help each other.

I lift my goggles, blink back the bright white of the snow and take a deep breath. 'We were married for six years, together for eight. We were lovely and settled in a beautiful house, with great jobs, but apparently, I wasn't giving him all he needed. I found out he'd been having an affair a few weeks after he walked out claiming he just wanted a break, and that was that really. I had fought for our marriage up until that point, but the affair was too much. When I called him out on it, I realized that I was the only one fighting, that he wasn't sorry I'd found out and didn't care. I stopped reaching out to him after that. I never did get all the answers. He never looked back. I guess once it was out, he was free to move on and be with the woman he loves.'

Hayley is quiet as she listens to my story. Surprisingly, the words don't sting as much as they used to when I speak them, and I feel my shoulders rise and fall with a shrug; it happened, it's OK, it's in the past now. It doesn't seem as bad with my current view and happiness zipping through my bones from the run we've just completed.

Hayley contemplates my words for a moment, coming to a complete standstill on the small platform before the hills dip and trail off again winding around fir trees and pines.

'How did you get over him?' she then asks. My mind had been miles away from Scott while racing down the slope, which is one of the reasons I wanted to come up here today. When I'm snowboarding, I feel free, but this isn't so much about me; this is about Hayley and how I can help her.

I let out a low but considerate laugh and touch her elbow.

'Honestly,' I start, 'I'm not entirely sure I'm over him, or maybe I am over him but it's a touch trickier to get over the marks he left behind, if that makes sense? The anxiety, the nagging insecurities, they tend to plague me when I least expect it, but hey, I'm getting through it every day that's for sure. Do they get you too?'

Hayley reaches down and unclips her boots from her board. I follow suit. We're stood in a precarious spot and could be bowled over by swooping skiers if we're not careful. As though we're crossing a road, we look behind us and when it's clear, trudge over towards the trees lining the edge of the slope; there, we lean our boards against a thick pine.

Hayley sits first, removing her goggles before resting her elbows on her knees. I don't push her to speak, I simply take a seat next to her letting her know I'm here when she's ready. I have a feeling Hayley is a lot like my dad and that she saves herself for a few people; that's probably why they get on so well.

'They sure do. Uh, it's been seven months now and I can't seem to shake the vision of finding them together in our bed, but admittedly the image does get fuzzier each day.' She pauses, dusting a little snow off her boot. 'And it's not him I miss, it's myself. Those doubts and insecurities you talk about, they just come out of nowhere when I least expect them. I think maybe because the whole thing was so utterly random and caught me off guard, I'm so fearful of being happy – like what else is going to happen?'

I huddle up closer to Hayley, so we're sat with puffy coats crinkling as they touch. That randomness and being caught off guard, I know too well.

'Honestly, it sucks,' I say and then pause trying to find the right words to comfort Hayley. I push around some of the tiny snowflakes that have settled on my thigh. 'It's going to take time, hon,' I start again, feeling too inadequate to give advice; having to resort back to Madi and my dad's words of wisdom for guidance. 'I guess the best thing you can do is not dwell on it. You're out here living your life; inspiring people, making them forget their worries for hours and making them believe that anything is possible. Hey, you got me standing upright on my board after

83

one day – that's a pretty big accomplishment.' I nudge her gently; she smirks.

'I love it out here. I've been coming up to these mountains since I could walk,' she says wistfully gazing out across the landscape where a wave of skiers and snowboarders flash by us. 'Teaching people and watching their love for the slopes grow, it's what I live for. You know, you've got some natural ability in you, so you shouldn't doubt yourself too much. You weren't that bad.' She playfully nudges me back and shoots me a side-glance with a cocked eyebrow. I laugh and shuffle in the snow, my bum starting to feel the cold through my jacket.

'You know, just because he didn't see your worth it doesn't mean others – those you teach, the friends around you, your family, me – don't see it,' I say, noting the passion in her eyes when she talks about the mountains and wanting so badly for Hayley to know how awesome she is, yet knowing full well there's only so much I can say; she will have to find that belief within herself. I tilt my head to the clouds asking the universe for a moment of forgiveness as I'm aware I'm being a little hypocritical, giving advice to Hayley that I need to work on myself.

'Thanks, Harper. When you put it like that it all seems so trivial, he was one person and I'm surrounded by so many rad people. I don't want him to control my feelings and emotions anymore.' She wrings her hands together. I put my arm around her shoulders.

'I know you don't. It will get easier. I think you're doing an amazing job and I think if you keep living and creating new memories and moments, the less those insecurities will affect you. I'd like to think time is a great healer, but time for everyone is different. We're not all going at the same pace,' I say, squeezing her shoulders and reciting my Dad's words. I look out at the plumes of white clouds, grey shadows looming in behind them and for a moment stop hating myself for my struggles. I didn't bounce back a week or a month after Scott's departure. I'm dealing with the aftershock a year later and that's OK; it doesn't mean I'm not healing; I'm just doing so at my own pace.

'I feel like I'm sat talking to Mother Nature or Father Time,' Hayley teases, her smirk more prominent now. I can see her blue eyes are glassy but don't doubt she's too proud and stubborn to release her tears.

'What can I say? I am one with the universe; wisdom flows through me – it has to when you've got parents like mine.' I laugh, crossing my legs and pretending to meditate, which scores a laugh from Hayley.

'You've got a great family, you know. Your mum and dad are awesome,' Hayley notes and it's her turn to shuffle in the snow; we've been sitting for a while now. The cold is starting to seep into my clothes. I wonder if Hayley is immune to it.

'Yeah, I got pretty lucky when Mother Nature was assigning parents. What are your parents like?' I ask, while getting to my feet. I shake out my legs trying to get some feeling back into them and blow on my hands. Hayley looks up at me her ocean blue eyes murky, contradicting the smile on her face as she stands up with great enthusiasm. Once on her feet she faffs around with her board, brushing off the snow, like she is having to think hard about how to answer my question or whether she actually wants to. Throwing her board on the ground, she clips one foot in.

'My dad's pretty cool, a bit like your dad but less broad moun-tain man and more scrawny can't-play-sports-to-save-his-life, but he's always on the front row cheering me on in competitions and has been since I first took up snowboarding,' she tells me nonchalantly, before pushing her board along the snow, edging towards the slope once more. I pick up my board and follow her; I'll clip in when I'm on level ground. 'My mom's not around much,' she says with a shrug, squinting her eyes over me with a smile before covering them up with her goggles.

I sense there's more to that story, but don't want to push. I have the feeling letting people in is not something that comes

85

easy to Hayley so I'm grateful for all that she has shared so far. I'll be here for her if she ever wants to talk about her mum. I give her a small nod to let her know this and bend down to clip myself onto my board.

'Do you and Scott have kids?' Hayley's question takes a second to reach me while I'm hunched over, blood rushing to my head trying to push the last clip down over my big snow boot. It momentarily catches me off guard and makes me wobble unsteady, but Hayley reaches out and grabs my shoulders to keep me from falling.

Just like with Hayley and her mum, I haven't shared that part of my story; the part that is filled with fear over the future and more specifically over if I will now ever have kids of my own.

I stand up, feeling a rush of dizziness when I do. Before I can come up with an answer a flock of numbered bibs and neon Nineties colours whizz past us in a blur. That's a story for another day, I think to myself. I'm having too much fun this morning to want to knock on that fear's door.

And besides, getting to talk to Hayley and hear part of her story has given me strength; I don't feel so alone. Instead I feel a sense of something bigger than myself, something more to work for than my own needs. It makes me feel empowered and gives me a sense of worthiness. A moment of unity passes by before we both push our boards onto the platform towards the edge of the run. We've said what we're able to today and my spirits are lifted.

I shake my head to answer Hayley's question and nod towards the slopes.

'I'm very glad you came to Colorado,' Hayley shouts over to me from underneath her scarf. I'm grateful that she seems to get me and hasn't pushed the kids thing.

'Me too,' I reply, taking hold of her hand as we shuffle to our next take-off point.

Within seconds of hitting the slope my body has warmed up. I'm sweating under my many layers and embracing the sting of the occasional snowflake that hits my cheeks at full speed; they're not so gentle when coming at you with force. The bottom of the slope comes into view and I stretch out my arms to my sides like an eagle spreading his wings ready to soar. Hayley must copy me as her hand reaches out and grabs mine. I chance a look at her and within seconds of taking my eyes off the path I can feel my board wobble and know there's no coming back from it. I clip Hayley's board and before I know it, we're tumbling the last leg of the slope like one giant neon yellow snowball. By the time we come to a stop there's no air left in my lungs for laughing. I can't feel my face and I'm certain Hayley's knees are digging into my ribcage.

When the whooshing sound calms down in my ears, I can hear Hayley belly laughing by my side.

'Harper, get your hands off my butt,' she chokes through her laughter.

*

By the time lunchtime rolls around I am famished. I'm walking back to the lodge with Hayley and her team, and feel triumphant. The tournament might as well have been today for me. I feel victorious. I'm breathless, I can't stop smiling and my backside is bouncing along with glee for I did not fall on it once; luckily, getting tied up with Hayley cushioned my fall, because today I took my grandest spill yet, but with my butt having not made contact with the ground I'm not really counting it as a fall. However, I feel as though the apple might have rolled its way back to the tree and hope that my dad reads the note I left and heads up here, so I can show off my new skills, by which I mean completing the majority of the course, not the spectacular nose dive I took at the end.

My wish is granted when we walk into the reception area and spot not only Dad but Mum, Madi, Em, Ariana and Bella as well.

'Hey,' I say as I run up to them all trying to hug them all at once, making Mum and Dad chuckle. I can see in Mum's eyes how happy she is to see me beaming, like my old self again.

'Dad, the snow is rad today – the slopes are so smooth,' I exclaim, buzzing from the adrenaline.

'Did you just use the word *rad*?' Madi asks, grinning at me. I feel my cheeks flush – so maybe I'm a little dizzy from adrenaline and hunger. My brain feels light and the professionals have been using that word all morning and without getting too ahead of myself, for a brief second in time I felt like a pro.

'It slipped out,' I say to Madi, with a shrug, my face creased from embarrassment. 'Did I use it in the wrong context?'

'No, it suits you,' Madi replies, putting her arm around me and following the others walking into the café. 'I couldn't be prouder. Em says she got here about twenty minutes ago and wondered who was killing it with Hayley. She saw you coming down the mountain and says she couldn't take her eyes off you, you were doing so well.' Madi squeezes me and I touch my head to her shoulder, accepting the compliment and feeling grateful for the rush it gives me. If she didn't see the fall, I'm not going to mention it. 'She said she almost fainted when she realized it was you,' Madi then adds before bursting out laughing when I pick my head up so fast and gasp, giving her an evil stare.

'Hey, I wasn't that bad,' I say, trying to stand up for myself as Madi takes a seat next to Em in the booth and I shuffle in next to Bella.

'You certainly weren't rad,' she notes with a teasing wink. I throw my goggles at her but Em catches them before they make contact with Madi's nose.

'Harper, hon, please don't hurt Madi,' Mum pipes up from the end of the booth next to Hayley, which elicits sniggering all round, even from Dad. Is it possible to act like a sophisticated adult when around your parents? I seem to have retreated to that teenage girl they always looked after.

'I hear you did awesome on your board this morning,' Bella tells me while scouring the menu. 'Hayley's an amazing teacher. I knew she'd have you up to speed in no time.'

My stomach rumbles as I look over all the delicious-sounding dishes, but when I home in on the veggie burger, I know that's what I would like, so I rest the menu down and lean back against the cushions of the booth.

'She's incredible and thank you, it was a lot of fun,' I reply. 'I much prefer flying down the hill on my board and not on my butt – it makes for a more scenic view.' Bella laughs. 'It's definitely good exercise, which is what I need. I haven't done much as of late,' I say casually. I don't want to talk about why, but it feels good to be focusing on what I need to do and actively seeking out more positive ways of getting back on track with my life.

'Snowboarding is fantastic exercise, great for exercising your mind too. I think people forget how important fresh air is for the body and the mind. It's a way of life here. I'm so happy you came,' Bella says, excitement and sincerity in her voice. She's right: I'm so often locked away inside writing at my laptop that I don't make time for outdoor activities anymore.

'What are you both doing tonight?' Em asks after we order our food.

I automatically look over at my parents and they both meet my gaze with a smile.

'We'll extend curfew just for tonight, kid,' my dad says mock seriously, causing me to laugh out loud. I shake my head at my childlike behaviour. I guess old habits die hard and all that.

'You heard the man,' Madi says, nodding her head in my dad's direction and raising her glass. We were sticking to water today, no whiskey-infused mulled wine for us before hitting the slopes again later. I want to maintain my bruise-free record for the day, plus it's not actually allowed.

'I do an outdoor midnight yoga class once a month – you're welcome to come along if you're interested?' Em informs us.

'I'd love to,' I say without hesitation. 'Count us in,' I add as Madi opens and closes her mouth with a smile. Today the universe is answering my calls. The adrenaline starts to pump through my body at the thought that I will get to do yoga tonight – and under the stars. I can't wait.

'Will you be there too, Bella?' I ask, turning to Bella next to me, her brown eyes wide. Since I met Bella her eyes always seem alight with wonder, and now I feel my own matching hers.

'Not tonight – I have Poppy and Evan with me. But you're in for a treat; Em will blow your mind,' Bella says with great enthusiasm. Madi chokes on her water and I can't help but smirk. I avoid eye contact so as to not make anything awkward in front of my parents; no matter how close and open both Madi and I are with them, talking sex around the table is not something either of us want to partake in. I chance a side-glance at Em and notice her blush. I'm pleased that she doesn't look horrified, instead bearing the same mischievous glint in her eye that is currently present in my best friend's.

I turn my attention away from thoughts of matchmaking and back to Bella. 'Who are Poppy and Evan?' I ask, hoping I don't sound too nosy.

Bella seems delighted by my question and turns to face me, putting her knee up on the bench so she can fully engage. 'They are the most beautiful little things. I look after them from time to time when their foster carers are in need of a break. I've been doing so since they were two years old and they've just grown so much. They're four now and a lively pair. Oh, you'll have to meet them, they'd get a kick out of your British accent,' Bella says, reaching for my hands. The passion in her voice makes something stir in my gut and a shiver of goose bumps cover my arms.

Before I have time to ask another question, our food arrives and Bella turns to dig in. My stomach grumbles its gratitude to the server and I automatically bring a chip to my lips and chomp on it while my brain is processing what Bella just told me. The others are all tucking into the food, happily in conversation with one another when I crouch down and lower my voice to Bella. I'm not quite sure why I don't wish for the others to hear my question.

'You're a foster carer?' I ask, curiosity and intrigue bursting inside me.

Bella swallows a bite of her halloumi burger, then looks at me. Her eyes remain bright but there is now something in them that again connects with whatever is having a field day in my gut – understanding, love, support, I can't put my finger on it, but my heart is skipping a couple of beats a minute as I wait for her to answer.

'I am, yes. Well, not a full-time foster carer. I'm a respite carer, so I look after the children whenever their main carers need a rest. Poppy and Evan's foster parents are having a Christmas dinner party, so the kids are coming to stay with me,' she answers and slowly turns away to take another bite of her burger. Although I'm starving, I'm not ready for my food yet. I have more questions.

'What's that like?' I ask, pushing a chip around on my plate, not wanting to freak Bella out by staring at her while she eats.

Bella wipes her mouth with a napkin. 'It's lovely. We play, we do activities, we just have loads of fun. There is quiet time too—' she laughs '—but it's just about giving them love and taking care of them the best I can to get them through this transitional time in their lives.' She stops, and a small smile appears at the corner of her mouth. She places a hand on my forearm. 'I'll bring them around tomorrow afternoon, and you can meet them,' she says softly.

The fluttering settles in my gut and I turn to demolish the food before me all while my mind is acknowledging each fear I have faced today; trying my hand at snowboarding again and opening up with Hayley and now engaging in talk of kids. OK, so I've not quite admitted my desire to have them but I'm asking questions and don't feel the need to cry. It's a brilliant start. Staring

91

into the golden-brown chips before me, I smile – a smile that crinkles my nose and makes dimples form at my cheeks. Then my mum's mantra pops into my head: I am the sun, the moon and the stars. Is the universe speaking to me?

I lean back in the booth, twirling a chip between my fingers and catch Madi's eyes. She's looking at me, grinning, her blue eyes all-knowing.

Chapter 10

I feel a hand nudge against mine as it tugs at the blanket I have wrapped around me and I make to shove it away. Stretching my arms out to the sides of me, my palm makes contact with pouty lips, a nose and perfect cheekbones. I shove Madi the blanket snatcher more gently until she groans. She is attempting to rattle me awake with one hand, yet she remains lying next to me, grasping for more blanket, looking snug, making no attempt to move herself. She eventually swats my hand out of her face and announces, 'We must get up, it's nearly midnight.'

At her words, I throw off the blanket causing Madi to roll off the couch onto the rug with a light thud. I hear a very matter-of-fact 'ouch' before she slowly rises from the floor and walks sloth-like to the door where I am now holding out her pink ski jacket.

'Come on, Mads, it will be fun. I haven't been to my yoga classes for ages and I've missed it so much. I can't believe Em is a yoga instructor.' At the mention of Em, Madi's pace picks up, and we are soon out the door. Thankfully the sky is clear and the forecast said there should be no more snowfall for the rest of the night. It's still difficult to navigate the mountains in the dark, but the Christmas lights adorning every house help to light our way.

Dad pointed out which paths we would need to take when we

walked home earlier after an incredible time on the slopes. I'd impressed my dad with my newfound snowboarding skills and walked around with a spring in my step all afternoon. I need to will some of that spring back into my step at such an ungodly hour. Madi and I are definitely not night owls, but the cold air is helping to keep my tired eyes open. It doesn't take too long before we reach our destination.

A little bit further into the pine tree forest is a clearing. I can already make out people gathering together, and mats being raised into the air and then brought back down to be placed neatly on the snow-covered ground. It hasn't occurred to me before now that I've never heard people talk about doing yoga in below-zero temperatures. Hot yoga yes, cold yoga, not so much. Can this really be good for you?

We walk closer and I see torches illuminating the yoga circle. However, the trees have begun to thin out and in their place are what look to be hot tubs buried in the ground. I gasp.

'Pretty, aren't they?' Ariana says, coming out of the shadows and into view. A tall and very muscly gentleman is standing with her. They both have towels thrown over their shoulders and are wearing tank tops. Ariana has toned arms and looks incredibly svelte in her yoga pants. I suddenly feel overdressed in my giant ski jacket.

'This place is gorgeous,' I agree, slightly breathless. 'Where are we?' I ask, unable to help myself. I feel like I've stepped through a portal and fairies will be making their grand entrance anytime now.

'It's aptly called Pine Springs – we're surrounded by hot springs, you see. The trees are our way of keeping this place more sacred for the locals. You can find hot springs all over the place in Colorado and they attract tourists like sugar attracts bees. It's nice to keep something for ourselves and have some privacy,' Em explains, stepping out from behind the mountain of a man with Ariana. I don't mean to judge but this man seems more like a professional bodybuilder than a yogi.

I take my eyes off the muscly man with short brown hair and bright green eyes and listen to Em. She too is wearing a tank top and yoga pants. I hesitate for a second, worried that I am going to freeze to death the minute I take my jacket off, yet I can already feel the beads of sweat forming on my brow.

'It's beautiful,' Madi replies, looking around and taking it all in. I notice two small fires up ahead and the steam is billowing from the springs. I feel as though I'm in a sauna with the amount of clothes I am wearing.

'Everyone here is really friendly; it's only a small group, but you can stick with Ari and Jake if you'd like. We'll be starting in a minute,' Em says.

Jake gives us both a handshake and a cheery hello.

'It's lovely to meet you, Jake. We've heard nothing but great things and your mulled wine is exceptional,' I inform him when he shakes my hand. OK, so I know Jake is a chef, but he has to moonlight as a wrestler because the man is huge. I can't picture him doing the warrior pose. I can suddenly feel my face getting hotter and hotter. I need to find a spot and be rid of this heavy jacket and my furry snow boots.

'Ahh, Jake. The yoga would make sense, given the things that Ariana has told us.' I can't quite believe Madi just said that out loud, but then again it is Madi. I daren't look at her. Jake looks at Ariana and winks. Em has her arm around Madi's shoulders and hasn't batted a single eyelash.

'All about flexibility. Can't let her do all the work, have to do my bit too, hey.' Jake's voice is deep and playful. He puts his arm around Ariana and pulls her close to him in a suggestive manner.

'Amen to that,' Madi says, while Em shoves Jake and adds in a teasing tone, 'None of that during the class please.' Ariana simply tuts and kisses his cheek before finding her mat.

Em and Madi stay close while we're talking, an elbow touching the other's, hands brushing, until it's time for Em to take her spot front and centre and Madi and I find ourselves an empty space right in front, not far from the fires. I finally free myself from my ski jacket, but I'm still wearing a long-sleeve top. Madi is wearing her cropped red gym top, one that complements her Fifties pin-up look to perfection. Her hair is wrapped up in her favourite polka dot headscarf and out of her face. It's hard not to notice Em clear her throat when Madi steps up to her mat and starts to stretch, her black yoga pants clinging to her figure in all the right places. I really, really hope I don't faint and plunge into a hot spring because I can't guarantee that either Madi or Em would be able to peel their eyes off each other to notice and rescue me.

I hasten to spin my loosely braided hair into a topknot on my head, so I don't get tangled in it during the yoga poses and then I begin to stretch. My body instantly loosens up to the movements I make, recognizing each one, happy for its reintroduction into my life. The tightness in my chest evaporates as Em calls out each pose and guides us through. I close my eyes and can faintly hear the bubbles of the hot springs and the hoot of an owl in the distance. I stretch into cobra position and exhale my breath, releasing the negative energy stored in my bones.

Occasionally I feel a slight chill as the breeze whips through the steam and the heat of the fire making my body tingle. But my mind is focused on my breathing and feeling the strength in my muscles as I hold each pose to Em's count. I'm sweating from head to toe.

As we move from one pose to the next and I find myself lying on my back, I open my eyes and, in an instant, they are filled with moisture. My breath catches as the golden stars twinkle down at me. They are alive and sparkling. I feel as though any second they could shower down on me, sprinkling me in tiny specks of gold dust there are so many of them. It looks like a bag of glitter exploded in the sky. The moon is clear and bathing our circle in its pearly glow. I feel like I've stepped out of who I was and have become someone new under its watchful eye. The toxins flowing through my veins, all the negative, draining thoughts that have been sinking their way into my skin, sucking away my good vibes, are perspiring off me. I close my eyes under Em's instruction and focus on my breathing once more. I watch my thoughts swim by, homing in to the bubbles, the slight rustling of the pines and the group's gentle breathing.

I've not felt this good in forever. I open my eyes again and the tears return. The view is out of this world. I can vaguely hear Em announce that it's the end of class, but I don't wish to move. I want to sleep under these stars. I want the moon to watch over me. I lie still with my hands on my stomach feeling it move up and down with slow and concentrated breaths. It's been a while since I've been this connected to myself, since my breathing has worked with me and not against me. I want to savour it.

I don't know how long Madi indulges my need. I can only assume she is now wide awake and deep in conversation with Em somewhere. When I finally do roll on to my stomach, only getting caught the once on the rebellious strands of my hair that have escaped my topknot, everyone is gone except Em, Madi, Ariana and Jake.

I blink myself back to reality before Jake's face comes into view. He's bending down in front of me with his arm outstretched and a broad handsome smile on his rugged face.

'So, what did you think?' he asks. I take the offer of his hand and he gently pulls me to my feet. I nod my appreciation of this kind gesture before replying.

'It was incredible. I've never done anything like this before; it's invigorating,' I say, somewhat breathlessly. Bella was right: Em blew me away.

'Despite what the others might say . . .' he starts, his voice softer now, almost shy – looking at him I notice him blushing ever so lightly, or that could just be the heat from the hot springs. '. . . The yoga helps with the aches and pains of being hunched over a kitchen counter and being on my feet for such long hours. The view is a welcome change from the sterile kitchen walls, I must admit.' I release a breath, relaxing now, safe in the knowledge that the conversation has veered away from any talk of flexibility. Jake must read my face as he laughs when my brow unfurrows.

'I know how you feel, except I spend all day hunched over a laptop and there's a perfect indentation of my butt in my couch . . .' Jake raises his eyebrow and now it's my turn to blush, but he laughs and glosses over it, for which I am grateful. The only butt he should be thinking of is Ariana's. 'Stretching does wonders. I used to do classes regularly back home, but this is literally a welcome breath of fresh air,' I say, looking around and taking in the magical feel of my surroundings.

'You're the writer, right? From London?' Jake queries, patting his face down with his towel as I try to tame my mane in another bun, but fail miserably. My bobble isn't strong enough to hold its weight.

'I am, yes, so as you can imagine I don't get many views like this on the daily; it's more brick buildings, looming towers and traffic – some of those beautiful in their own way, but this is more up my alley,' I reply with a laugh.

'Who's up your alley?' Em's voice questions from behind, making me jump. Jake rolls his eyes and reaches over my head ruffling Em's bleach-blonde hair. I turn around and catch the cheeky glint in her eye. She doesn't seem fazed by Jake's behaviour, she simply blows away the hair that has fallen in her face, like she's used to it, like it's routine with them. 'We're going for a dip – are you two in?'

'Sure,' I say. 'Your class was amazing, Em, thank you for inviting us.'

'No problem, I'm glad you could make it. We're two hot springs to the right of that pine,' she replies, turning to point at one of the giant trees. I squint; they all look the same. I shove my feet in my boots in a rush to follow her, as she punches Jake in the arm and adds, 'Don't get lost,' before briskly walking away.

Jake doesn't register the punch to the arm. His bicep is five times the size of mine and all defined muscle. I'd be surprised if he felt it. 'She's punched me countless times over the years. I'm numb to it now,' he says, seemingly reading my mind. I chuckle, grab my coat, and start walking in the direction Em went in. Jake walks alongside me.

'You and Em remind me of me and Madi. I can't quite believe Mads has met her match in the bold and feisty department,' I say glancing at Jake with a smirk.

'Argh, well, Em has been my best friend since we were three, and bold, she has always been,' Jake tells me through a laugh. That would explain their easy-going attitudes towards each other. 'There's not much we keep from each other and yes that means I get to hear way more than I'd care to hear at times, but I can't pretend I don't feel honoured that she comes to me.' His green eyes sparkle when he talks about Em. He has his hands casually tucked into his short pockets as we walk; this mountain of a man so casual and chilled. I let out a laugh.

'I like her,' I say with a nod.

'So, what's your story, Harper?' There's something about Jake that makes me feel safe, like I can open up and he will listen. 'Erm, well, this time last Christmas my husband left me, and then I found out he had been having an affair. I'm here in Colorado to find myself again or possibly re-create myself, I'm not sure. Maybe a mixture of both.' I breathe out and realize we have stopped walking. Jake has his hands on my shoulders; he's leaning down to look me in the eye.

'I'm sorry to hear about your husband. That is a dick move.' Jake's tone is calming and kind. I can feel my heart rate slowing down, having not been aware it had picked up with my confession. 'How is the finding yourself going?'

He still hasn't broken eye contact and though I have some fear making me want to retreat in on myself, he challenges me to keep my gaze. I squint my eyes in thought, then glance around at the trees and the snow-covered ground. 'I'd say it's not without its ups and downs, but it's going well. I love it here. Madi was right to suggest we get out of London. It took me a year to do it but now I can see why I needed it so much.'

'I'm glad to hear it. There's so much natural beauty here – you will find what you're looking for,' Jake says, pulling me into a hug. 'And truly, I really am sorry to hear about your husband – on behalf of me and my fellow men, I'm sorry. He sounds like a coward.'

It's a welcome feeling to be cared for and I relax in his hug for a moment. In his hug, I feel calm, like he's a big brother protecting me, the same way he would Em.

'Thanks for that and for the confidence booster,' I say, genuinely touched. 'There's certainly a lot of love out here. You guys are lovely,' I add as Jake drapes his arm over my shoulder and we start moving again.

'Of course. We're surrounded by love in many forms every day – friendships,' he says, moving his arm away from my shoulder and gently shoving me like I'd seen him do with Em. I chuckle. 'Family, the love we have for our work, for nature and don't forget the most important love of all that's inside you and you must harness every day.'

'What's that?' I say, as we reach the hot spring chatter is emanating from. I can make out three heads amidst the steam.

Jake stops and turns to face me while leaning down to take off his shoes. I notice yoga pants lying around. It's like a teenager's bedroom with clothes strewn along the snow.

Jake prods at the middle of my chest. 'The love you have for yourself.'

'Come and love yourself in here,' I hear Madi shout out. The steam clears, and I can see all eyes on us. Ariana's black curls are bouncing atop the water. She's smiling lazily with her head tilted back against the spring's edge. Em is absentmindedly playing with Madi's hair while wiggling her eyebrows at me and Madi is giving me a once-over.

'You're wearing too many clothes,' Madi shouts. Jake winks at me in a way that makes me feel part of the group. He strips down to his boxers and jumps into the spring to hoots and hollers from everyone inside. Ariana reaches for him. He towers over her for a moment as she admires his six-pack with her fingertips, then he sits beside her and peppers her face with kisses. From knowing the man for only a little over an hour I'm impressed by his ability to be incredibly manly yet not afraid to engage in talk about love and emotions. I look forward to getting to talk with him more; I like my new friend.

The way I grew up, I rarely had time to be self-conscious about my body or give thought to it being anything but beautiful, thanks to my mother. I was the baby running around the garden naked, then attending festivals with my mum and dad where not a lot was left to the imagination regarding the outfits of those in attendance. I've never cared too much for bras – still don't – and being naked is never a problem. But with the moon glowing up above, this night feels different. Peeling off my layers feels like so much more. I feel more vulnerable than I have ever felt yet powerful because of it. I feel free from judgement from both my friends and myself and there's a raw and honest vibe in the air.

My toes curl when they touch the snow, snapping my whole body into the present. This night has been magical. I don't want to forget that or the way I felt during the yoga class, or when I looked into the eyes of the moon from my mat. I want to remember the power the stars gave me and the kind words that Jake spoke.

I stand up straight and pull off my long-sleeved top first. I'm wearing one of my favourite lace bralettes with no padding, the one that always makes me feel sexy and like myself. For a moment I completely forget that anyone is watching and take a second to embrace the freedom and confidence I feel stripping in the great outdoors. That is until Madi yells, 'Get that sexy body in here.'

Seeing me strip, she's gone into full best friend support mode; I love her a little more.

I release my hair from the half bun on my head and it cascades to my hipbones. Away from the fires I feel the freezing nip of the morning air and make a dash for the hot spring, to the sound of cheers and a wolf whistle – thanks, Madi.

I'm laughing when my toes touch the burning water, sending a rush of heat to my cheeks. It's like a fire has been lit inside me. 'Where've you been hiding this one?' Em says, tapping Madi's shoulder while looking me up and down.

'I tried to get her to snowboard naked, but she was having none of it.' Madi shrugs, winking at me before poking Em in the ribs and saying, 'Oi, she's mine.'

I let out another laugh from my core and shake my head in Ariana and Jake's direction. They're both laughing too. Seeing them sitting together, Jake's arm draped around Ariana's shoulder, I decide they make such a stunning couple. Her petite frame fits snug against his broad chest; they look content.

'You two should be on the cover of romance novels,' I say, smiling excitedly. The heat of the water soothes my bones and my mind.

'This one's camera shy,' Ariana replies, stroking Jake's jawbone adoringly and giggling up at him.

'Oh please, he just doesn't want to be outshined by you,' Em pipes up, flashing a wicked grin at Jake.

'You know me too well,' Jake responds, matching Em's grin and splashing water in her direction.

Their easy banter is endearing and very much like mine and Madi's. It brings me great comfort and lulls me into a sense of peace. I rest my head against the hot spring, watching my hair as it floats up around me, then I look to the dreamy night sky. The yellow stars are flickering and the moon still watching over us. We're in the middle of nowhere yet I feel safe. Jake is right: I'm surrounded by love. I have the love of my best friend and my family. I love my job, this place and my new friends. I just need to work on that love for myself.

Stripping down in the middle of a forest and being happy with what I see is definitely a start, I think.

Chapter 11

In contrast to how I felt beneath the relaxing water of the hot springs, my body is now restless. I can't find a comfy spot in my bed or settle into a position. My mind is ticking over as panic fills the creases in my worried brow. It's Christmas Eve. Am I out of time? It's still dark outside, the moon is setting, and the sun hasn't yet made an appearance, so my room is far from bright, I can't see my chest, I can only hear its rattle and feel it rise and fall with apprehension.

I decide sleep will not be on the agenda tonight, or should I say this morning – we got back from yoga at 2.30 a.m. With the peace the yoga had blessed me with I'd have thought I'd have drifted off the second my head touched my pillow, yet I am unusually wide awake at this late/early hour. Knowing the reason why, I quickly rush around to the bench under my window ledge and grab my laptop bag, carefully retracing my steps so I don't trip and fall, and switch on the lamp by my bed as I climb back under the warmth of my duvet.

I've not been typing for more than ten minutes when my door creaks open. The low light from my bedside lamp highlights Madi walk in rather spritely carrying a tray – the aromatic smell of lemon tea fills the room.

I see a cafetière, a pot of tea, a plate overflowing with pancakes and syrup, a small bowl containing an apple, banana, grapefruit and perfectly ripe peaches, a bar of dark chocolate and some leftover Christmas cookies. My stomach growls its approval of the delicious spread before turning over with an uncomfortable lurch at the thought of Madi realizing what I am doing. I tilt my laptop nervously to avoid her seeing my manuscript on the screen.

'Mads, it's three-thirty in the morning, what are you doing?' I ask softly, grateful for the incredible breakfast spread and provisions but a tad confused at how awake she is at this hour.

She places the tray next to me on my bed and gives me a coy grin with an eye roll.

'I could feel your agitated aura from down the hall. Now, get it done Harp. I love you.' She replies, kissing the top of my head before leaving me alone with my tight deadline and all the snacks a writer could ever need.

I can't help but chuckle and let out a joyful sigh as I load my fork with pancake. How did Madi know I hadn't finished my edits and why wasn't she mad? I love her, I really, truly adore her.

I take a bite out of the buttery pancakes, loaded with natural syrup, as my eyes adjust to the gleaming white mountains that even in the dark glisten and sparkle under the moon's glow.

I stare at my laptop on my bed and my joy is replaced by the nerves that threaten to overwhelm me as I worry I won't be able to get this script over the finish line. I take a sip of coffee, the taste automatically snapping me into writer mode. No, I am not going to let the nerves win. I hear my mum's voice in my head: 'You are the sun, the moon and the stars.' I feel Madi's supportive kiss tingle on my forehead. And I remember how I felt during midnight yoga mere hours ago; how my body felt strong with each movement, the wave of power that wove its way through my bloodstream and how in control I felt of my own well-being. Jake had pointed at my chest, like ET, like there was a magical glow in his finger, urging me to pay attention to the love in my heart that I not only had to give for other people, but that I had to give to myself.

The velvety rich coffee slides down my throat, warming up my insides. I squint at my laptop now, giving it the evil eye to show it who's boss. I'm Harper Hayes; my maiden name rolls off my tongue and a thrill washes over me. Madi had taken to using it but I haven't used it in years. I'm a writer. I write romance and I'm bloody good at it. I nod defiantly, then quickly take another bite of pancake. I lean down, grab the fork and pop it in my mouth, careful to not drip syrup on the floor or my white dressing gown, then I'm back to my evil glare, I can do this. I have plenty of love in my heart. In fact, I have more love in my heart for my family, my friends, my work, and yes, even myself, now that Scott isn't hogging the majority of it.

*

I'm staring at the screen only two hours later, my fingers hovering over the keys, my tongue savouring the melting chocolate in my mouth. I fancy washing it down with some vanilla tea, so I reach over and pour myself a mug full to the brim. The pot has kept the tea lukewarm and the delicious flavour refreshes my taste buds the minute it passes my lips. Feeling wholly deflated after reading through my script and making notes, I finish the cup of tea, scuttle off the bed and wander into the bathroom to wash my face. I always feel better once I've washed. This will ensure my eyes feel more awake and readier to look at the bright lights of my laptop screen again. It will give me the right boost to tackle the more lovey-dovey moments that need tidying up in my screenplay.

Looking into the mirror while I dab at my face with my towel, I see that my hair looks matted and dull. It's been tied in braids, up in a bun and stuffed under beanie hats and helmets so much this week and I haven't cared to maintain it too much recently. I get the scissors from the bathroom cabinet and tie my hair into a long ponytail. I gather the ends and snip an inch off. I'm not about to do something drastic and cut it short – despite Scott's occasional suggestion that I have it cut and styled, I love my long hair – but a small trim might encourage it to grow a little faster. I then retrieve the conditioner from the shower and pour a healthy amount in my palm and slather it all over my head. I cover my hair and note that I probably should have taken my robe off. There is now conditioner all over it with short strands of freshly cut hair sticking to it.

I wash my hands free of conditioner, peel my robe off and pull my pyjama top over my head. I get stuck at the top and end up with a mouth full of soap as my hair flips over into my face as I try and make the head gap wide enough to not scrape all the conditioner off as it goes past.

I'm standing naked in front of the mirror looking like a troll with my hair spiked up on my head. My eyes start scanning over my body, over the stretch marks on my hips, the freckles on my left collar bone, the tattoo of a tiny arrow on my inner right bicep that Madi and I both got when we were twenty; then my eyes catch the small heart tattoo on my wrist, the one I got for Scott. I'm frozen for a moment, my eyes threatening to glaze over until . . .

'Harp, what are you doing?' Madi's voice snaps me right out of my trance. I hear her clattering about with the teapot before she appears at the bathroom door.

'Hey.' I smile, feeling vulnerable and bare yet completely safe and myself. I don't need to cover up for Madi or hide any part of me.

'Hey,' Madi replies, smiling back. She leans against the doorframe. Her blonde shoulder-length blunt cut is shining and glossy, with a pink headscarf keeping it out of her face. Her blush is a baby pink complementing her nude lips and she's tied a pink sash around her basic white long-sleeved skater dress today. She looks beautiful. I have a feeling I can attribute part of Madi's glow this morning to Em, as well as the fact that she is up and perky at this hour on barely any sleep.

'I might be procrastinating,' I say with a laugh looking from Madi and back at myself in the mirror.

'You think?' Madi retorts, with a raise of her eyebrows, as she glances from me back over to my bed where my laptop is paused on a Zachary Levi video and not my current jumble of a manuscript. She sighs softly and walks over to me. Her hands move to my shoulders as she stands behind me. She's looking at me now through the mirror. She sees all I see, and she has stood by my side for the past twenty-seven years.

'I'm not digging this script, Mads, it's just not flowing,' I say into the mirror.

'So, what are you going to do about it?' There's a slight flicker of a smirk at the corner of Madi's primrose pink lips that is cheeky and challenging. She drops a kiss onto my shoulder as I pout in thought.

'Come on,' she encourages when I don't respond, grabbing my nightie and helping me to pull it over my head; avoiding my Poppy-the-troll-style, full-of-conditioner hair.

I'm lost in thought, as Madi guides me to my bed. I'm trying to come up with my next move. The script isn't what I want it to be. And the fault does not entirely lie in the fact that my heart has turned to coal and that I hate the mushy stuff (hate is such a strong word). I really don't, not deep down, it's that it's missing feeling.

We get to the bed and I'm yet to speak. I mull over in my brain what I need to do. I know Madi won't let me off easy. She already forgave me so quickly and kindly over lying to her about my script being complete, so I must think of something clever that won't let her or myself down.

'I can't fault your taste,' Madi says, Zachary Levi getting her approval as she climbs on to my bed and clicks the play button on my laptop, pinching a piece of apple from the fruit salad that lies on the tray with the fresh tea she has just brought me, as she does so. 'We can watch one more Zachary Levi video and then it's back to work, babe. OK?' she adds, giving me a determined smile as she brushes my conditioner-covered hair out of my eyes.

I stare at the scene before me – Madi snuggled up next to me, food lovingly prepared for me – and I take in us both giggling at bloopers from Season One of *Chuck*, and think of all we have done here in Colorado, and a lightning bolt of love surges through me. I kiss Madi on the head before shoving her off the bed. She falls not so gracefully with a squeal and throws a pillow at me once she's upright. I apologize to my best friend and the beauty that is Zachary Levi for crossing him off the screen and pulling up my manuscript instead.

'I'm going to rewrite it,' I announce. 'My leading lady is so much more. She doesn't want to be swept off her feet or stuck in any sort of love triangle – she has better things to do,' I finish, a beaming smile now etched on my fresh face.

'I'm out of here,' Madi says, clapping her hands together and giving me a proud and confident nod.

I glance at the clock on my bedside table, grateful to the moon for keeping me awake; my script is due today and with the time difference in England I need to hurry. Lara wanted this script Christmas Eve-it's Christmas Eve, I'm running out of time.

But it's still early here, only 5.35 a.m., which makes it 12.35 p.m. in London. Even though I'm cutting it fine, if I buckle down and focus, I might just pull this off and still make it in time to meet Poppy and Evan with Bella this afternoon.

*

Nearly eight solid hours later, I reach over to the bedside table and take a giant swig of refreshing tea. Then I uncurl my legs from a lotus position and stretch them out in front of me, twiddling my toes as I reach my arms in the air and make the same movement with my fingers. A lot can be said for Zachary Levi's dazzling smile and for having a best friend as incredible as mine, because I think I've completed my script. I tilt my head from side to side loosening up my neck. Gone is the damsel in distress. Gone is the shy, insecure leading lady. In fact, gone is my original story. 'That's not how this story ends,' I say out loud to myself as I click save.

'No broken-hearted damsel in distress,' I repeat, jumping off the bed. The floor cools my warm toes. I can see the sun bold, bright and magnificent in the sky through the sheer curtains. I pat down my robe and go to brush a hand through my stiff, still full of conditioner hair and repeat my mantra while trying to remember what day it is. Sometimes my scripts have that kind of effect on me, plucking me out of the real world and plonking me back in it disorientated; today I feel that's a great sign, I love this new version. My script is finished. I let out a huge sigh of relief that is mixed with genuine delight.

Allowing myself to be so exposed earlier when I faced myself in the mirror, alongside Madi's interference, finally knocked some sense into the part of my brain that kept looking back. With all the advice from Mum, Dad, Madi, Hayley and Jake, I really needed to listen to it, listen to myself and act on it. Once I did this, the words started flowing.

I fire off an email to Lara praying that even though I know it's spectacularly late- I usually have my scripts with her at nine am on deadline day not nine pm- that it will still count, and she won't be too mad at me. Within minutes my laptop pings with a reply.

'*You just made it! Have a good Christmas, Harper. X,*' it reads. I let out a delirious laugh.

'Oh, thank you, universe,' I whisper. 'Thank you, Madi,' I add making to tidy up the tray and neaten up my bed from where I have been sprawled out across it.

I catch my reflection, just faintly, in the glass behind the sheer curtains. I feel new. I look new. The woman I see is no longer a wife, no longer Scott's. She has felt pain. She has felt humiliation.

She has felt hopeless. But it is to be no more. The sun is positively luminous, the snow is glistening, and life goes on. I rush into the bathroom and rinse off the conditioner in my hair. It feels silky smooth as I leave it to dry naturally and pull on my festive red jumper, a pair of thick tights and my long navy skirt. It's Christmas Eve at my parents' house and I couldn't feel happier to be here. Better yet, I have managed to complete my script before 1.30 p.m., which means I can still catch up with Bella today and meet Poppy and Evan.

Chapter 12

The smooth base of the sled slides over the snow with ease. I'm shooting down the small slope at some speed. 'Arrrrrrgh,' 'Woohoooooo,' I'm shouting at the top of my lungs, a smile plastered on my face. If I had any cares or concerns right now, I might be worried my dimples are going to freeze and become a permanent fixture on my face. The same could be said for my bright red elf-like cheeks. Could windburn be a blush replacement?

We come to a bumpy stop at the bottom of the short slope. 'That was fun, can we go again?' Poppy pleads, her pretty brown eyes open wide. Her nose resembles Rudolph's and her voice comes out cute and sweet. I can't possibly say no, and I don't want to.

'I'll race you to the top,' I say and receive a giggle and shout of 'yay' in return as she turns and runs up the slope towards Bella and Evan. It takes me a minute to scoot off the sled, my puffy ski jacket still quite new and rigid and my skirt getting wedged underneath. I can hear Bella laughing at my struggle and when I look up to scold her, she gives me a thumbs-up and throws her head back to continue her mocking.

I make it to the top and Evan, with his piercing brown eyes, immediately tugs on my jacket. I bend down so I'm at his level. He is quieter than Poppy, who had no trouble jumping on my knee and getting straight to playing with my hair, when I met up with Bella at the café and she introduced me to the twins earlier. Evan has stayed close to Bella while I've been sledging with my new partner in crime, Poppy, for close to an hour now.

'Harper,' Evan's sweet voice starts. 'Can we have a race?' His face lights up when he completes his question, like the excitement overcomes him leaving no room to be shy.

'Of course, we can have a race,' I reply, causing him to clap his hands together. He then grabs Bella's hand and says, 'Come on, Bella, we're having a race with Harper and Pop.' Hearing his nickname for his twin sister melts my heart. I'm frozen watching him as he pulls Bella onto their sled. A little hand taking hold of mine brings me out of my trance and I look down and see Poppy smiling up at me.

'Come on, Harper, we're going too slow. We've got to win the race,' she says, like butter wouldn't melt.

'Ooh, yes, quickly, let's go,' I say, as Bella and Evan are in position watching us climb onto our sled.

'Are you ready, Harper?' Evan asks, when I sit down and shuffle back to make room for Poppy. 'Are you ready, Pop?' he asks his sister and again my heart tugs at the loving way he says her nickname. She's his home, she's probably been his only constant in his four years of life and somehow, I can feel it when he says her name.

I wipe away the water that is quickly prickling my eyes, just in time to grab hold of the rope on the sled as Poppy and Evan both scream, 'Go!'

We're flying down the children's slope, which is part of the play area at the back of the ski lodge. It's full of sleds and doughnuts, giant connect four games and slides. It's an absolute treat, one that I'm enjoying just as much as the kids.

We're flying down the hill and again laughter is barrelling out of me as Poppy and Evan cheer and whoop. Be it twin magic or fluke, Poppy and Evan's outstretched feet hit the barrier at the bottom of the slope at exactly the same time. This causes them to jump off their sleds, with way more speed, agility and energy than either Bella and I, and hug each other giddily while congratulating each other, with: 'You did it, Pop, you were so fast.' 'Good job, Evan, that was really fast.'

Before the waterworks can begin again, I get a snowball to the side of my face. The twins erupt with giggles and shouts of 'arrrgh' as they run away from Bella when she starts to chase after them, snowballs held aloft in each hand.

'I'm going to get you back for that one,' I shout at Bella and clamber up off the sled, quickly adding it to the pile of sleds ready for other children to have a go, before running after my group.

'I'd like to see you try. Snow is my forte. I thought rain and grey clouds were London's specialty,' Bella retorts with a snort and a wink.

*

Two hours later and we are all snowballed, connect-foured and hide-and-seeked out. We're tucked away in a booth with a fire pit, which now has a grid around it to keep the kids safe, and we are warming up with hot chocolates – whiskey-free, Jake assured us.

While Poppy and Evan are busy counting out their marshmallows and recounting their brilliant and successful attempts at covering me in snow while I made a snow angel, I chat with Bella.

'They are delightful,' I say wistfully. Being outdoors was again refreshing and playing with the children had been revitalizing. I'm aware that my emotions have been all over the place as of late. I know I'm on dangerous ground getting so attached to these kids, and allowing myself to entertain ideas of having kids right now is absurd but I can't help it.

'Talk to me,' Bella says gently before dunking a biscuit into her hot chocolate.

I look away from the twins and into Bella's warm brown eyes. A small sigh escapes my lips.

'I'm scared to want kids,' I finally say after a minute or two. I feel at ease talking to Bella even though I have only known her a short time. Her manner is encouraging and non-judgemental, like Hayley, so my words find their way into the open.

'How do you mean?' Bella asks, giving me the chance to unload my thoughts and herself a chance to fully understand me before giving me advice.

'Well, I wasn't so scared before, you know when Scott and I were together. Back then it was exciting. We talked about it so much, talked about baby names and nurseries and the wonder of growing our family and I knew I wanted it; I knew I wanted to be a mum. I could boldly say it, knowing that I had this wonderful means of it becoming a reality, that Scott would be an amazing dad and I was lucky to have it all.'

Bella reaches out and takes my hand but doesn't speak.

'But now, now I don't have that. I don't have time to date people, to figure out if they want to marry me and have kids with me ten years down the line. I'm thirty and I'm scared because I wanted it and I thought soon I would be having it and now it's gone.' My lips are trembling. I look out the window, at the snow-covered mountains and the crowds that are still gathered after this morning's tournament practice, worried that if I look over at Poppy and Evan I won't be able to keep my emotions in check and that I'll break down in front of them. It's not something I want them to see.

Bella waves over a server as I focus on my breathing by spotting Hayley whizzing down the slopes and taking to a jump on her board. She does a backflip and lands without a wobble. I smile and turn my attention back to Bella, who has acquired colouring books and crayons for the twins.

'I sense there's more?' Bella says softly, gently patting my hand. I look down at my hot chocolate and prod at the marshmallow watching it then bob up and down.

'I feel selfish; like I'm a bad person. Is it wrong of me to be spending so much energy and time thinking about kids when I'm on my own? How could I purposely want to bring a child into a home with only me to provide for it and take care of it? There will be financial strains, emotional needs to be met for both the child and me. What if I'm not strong enough or capable or simply can't offer the child enough?' I reveal the inner workings that have been on replay in my mind over the past year, making sure to whisper so the kids don't hear me. I'd never want them to grow up and speak such silly words. I'd never want them to think they alone weren't good enough or capable of anything, because they will always be worth it, yet the thoughts continue to sneak into my brain.

'Honey, you are not weak or incapable. I understand when we go through bumps in the road that our insecurities come to light; words people may have said stick around for longer than we'd like and how others have made us feel can poison our insides and interfere with our confidence. But you're growing from all these things, there's lessons to be learnt in all of them. Now, you know what you want, you care about something so much that of course you're going to be scared, it's just testing you. But it does not mean you are selfish.' Bella pauses and takes my hand in hers.

'I happen to know that Poppy thinks you are a princess. She's mesmerized by your hair and your kindness and Evan over there thinks you are the best racer there is. They adore you; you've got so much to give. You must start believing that. Families come in all different forms and, Harper, having a kid is not quite the vision we think it is in our heads at first but we learn as we go. We all make mistakes and that's OK – please don't be afraid of making them,' she adds, squeezing my hand.

Bella proves to be a great motivational speaker and listener as she keeps hold of my hand, assessing me without judgement. She takes care to choose her words and it's this care that helps them to get through to me.

'You are right, you know? When I think about it, it feels wonderful to know what I want, but extremely terrifying at the same time,' I say through a chuckle. 'I think I've held an ideal vision in my head for so long about what my family would be, what it would look like, that accepting anything different; offering a child anything less than what I deem perfect, it feels wrong,' I admit. Bella squints her eyes at me and leans forward on her elbows.

'We can put a lot of pressure on relationships, on ourselves, on our dreams and put them all on pedestals without realizing it. Though it's great to push ourselves and reach for perfection, there comes a time when you realize it's all in your head. You have the power to find the beauty in everything, Harper, in all the imperfections, in all the bumps and twists and turns. Those pedestals sometimes make us think that a situation we didn't plan or envision is wrong and ugly, when in fact it turns out to be the most right and magical,' Bella finishes, squeezing my hand again for further reassurance. Her words hit me as hard as the snowball she threw at me earlier – so painfully hard; Bella has a strong arm.

I feel brave enough to glance at the twins, though my eyes are threatening to switch on the water sprinklers, and I don't want them to see me cry. Poppy and Evan are colouring away, sharing crayons and huddled over their drawings, nattering to each other in what I believe must be twin language. I can't make out what they are saying, but it's a beautiful thing to witness. All the while Bella's words are buzzing around in my brain. Here I am talking about being a single mum, worried about what I can offer when Bella is sat in front of me, a single carer to Poppy and Evan, who both never planned for a childhood in the foster care system, but whose smiles are beaming back at me bright and beautiful.

Bella is giving them all the love in her heart and it is more than enough for these two gorgeous creatures.

I know I'd like a child and though I'm not quite sure which avenue I'd like to go down right now, I believe when the time is right, I will be strong, and I will be capable for that child. Even in my weaknesses and my vulnerability that child will know love. I stifle a yawn as Bella and I lean back in the booth and finish our hot chocolates, a comfortable silence creeping over our conversation. With her last words, I had nothing more to offer than a small nod and a smile, which she returned in understanding.

After a few moments I notice that Bella's eyes are glassy as she looks out of the window. It's not lost on me that for someone who's been on this planet five years less than me she just imparted some heavy and knowledgeable wisdom on life. My stomach turns with the thought that she has been hurt in such a way that has afforded her this knowledge. When Jake walks over to top up Poppy and Evan's hot chocolates and is rewarded with giant cuddles from the both of them, I can't help feeling a pang of protectiveness over Bella and curiosity draws the next question out of my mouth.

'What made you get into fostering?' I ask, lightly, sensing this may be where her knowledge comes from. I place both mine and Bella's empty mugs on Jake's tray, waving away his offer of a refill, Bella does the same and watches Jake walk away with a grateful smile on her face before she turns her attention back to me. I notice her eyes seem far away, lost in distant memories. I don't push her to answer and am prepared to change the subject, for fear that this whole conversation has brought up a past that is causing pain to my new friend. I'm about to tell her that she doesn't have to tell me if she doesn't want to, when she speaks with a smile at her lips.

'Don't you even dare think of keeping your feelings to yourself,' she says first, reading the apology behind my eyes. My throat suddenly feels less restricted. I offer a small smile in return.

'Life is about connecting with others. If you don't share your feelings and experiences, how are you supposed to connect and find those souls that were meant to find yours?' she adds before taking a bite out of her peach and cinnamon muffin. The velvety cake brings the colour back to her eyes, making them full and rich once more. I feel as though Bella has chosen to avoid my question, so I simply nod, holding up my vegan carrot muffin in cheers and to say thank you.

After a short minute, she leans back in the booth, releasing my hand and looking at the kids colouring. I follow her line of vision and get lost in watching them do their best to colour in the lines. For four-year-olds, they are doing a brilliant job.

'I love my parents because they are my parents. It's that label that keeps them in my heart despite them not living up to my expectations of what parents should be. They were young when they had me, still in their teens, so I can't blame them for not knowing what to do with me. They had their whole lives ahead of them and they deserved to go out and live it. They did well for a while. I remember being packed up in their mini camper van going on trips, but a crying baby and diapers to change couldn't have been easy on the road. I was four when I was put into foster care and seven when I got a new family. They visited with me for a while after my initial placement, but I think it got to be too much; for them because the further they travelled the harder it was for them to stick to meetings, get back in time for events, and for me because I couldn't understand where my parents kept disappearing to. I think it became easier to think of the happy times we shared and focus on what I had and not what I didn't.'

I'm staring out of the window, again not wanting the twins to see my face. I'm crying, tears streaming down my cheeks. My hand is over my mouth to stop the short gasps from escaping and it's taking all I have not to jump over the table and embrace Bella. She spoke in a hushed whisper, so Poppy and Evan couldn't hear much. At moments during her recollection, her voice became wobbly with sadness, yet her face remained light and she kept her eyes on me. I had broken eye contact almost instantly when the tears rushed my face.

'It's OK, Harper, it really is. I had an amazing childhood with my new family. They never made me feel like a burden and I did everything a kid should be doing, always playing, always laughing. My new parents were always there with support, encouragement and love, but of course I've struggled over the years. Like you, no matter how great my new family was I had a picture of the old one in my head, would go to sleep at night dreaming of the perfect moment my parents would come back and get me, feeling a little empty that I wasn't good enough or that my new situation wasn't real, that it was all a lie. I stopped believing I was lovable and couldn't accept life for what it was. I stopped laughing for a period, but my new parents never gave up on me; they just continued to shower me with love. Other children came to the house for respite fostering and I got to learn their stories and mine didn't seem so bad. We were all there for each other and that became all that mattered. Looking after them, I started to see my worth, what I could offer, who I could be and here we are today,' she finishes with a bright smile and reaches out to play with Poppy's hair.

I quickly and aggressively wipe away my tears with the sleeves of my top, not wanting to upset anyone with my outburst, but I am in awe of Bella. I'm trying to find the words to help her, to support her, to thank her for being so amazing, but I'm struggling to get them out.

'And listen,' Bella starts, leaning across the table, 'I didn't tell you all that so you can feel bad about yourself or to make what you're going through seem like nothing. I say it because all the things that you are feeling now, I've felt them too. I wouldn't say I'm over it; it's more about continually getting through it each day. I go weeks, months even, without thinking about it and then boom, one day something will catch me off guard and

119

I'm a mess, but that's OK too. That just brings new lessons. You will grow from this. I understand your fears and your desire to have children but try and let go of your expectations or maybe the way you have been picturing it all these years with Scott. Life might have a different plan for you right now.' She leans over the table, half standing, and kisses me on the forehead like a protective mother. I close my eyes to feel my heart burst with an overwhelming sense of gratitude for this woman.

'Right, toilet break, you two,' she announces scooting out of the booth and shuffling Poppy along with her as she edges out, walking like a crab between the bench and the table, leaving me to digest the conversation we have just had.

I recall the conversation I had with Hayley the other day and how we discussed the idea that it isn't about getting over it but getting through it each day, and it made sense again when Bella said it. I can't just snap my fingers and make my insecurities go away – they are there but it's how I use them, how I listen to them, that will make all the difference. I look over the mountains and watch the numerous snowball fights taking place between friends and families. I gape at the skiers and snowboarders taking to the skies as they double backflip off the jumps in the distance, as I tap my nail against my mug to the same beat of the song playing over the speakers, throughout the café. My face feels sore from the cold winds earlier and from the tears I so harshly rubbed away moments ago but connecting with Bella just now felt special.

She is right: opening up releases something inside us and helps us connect to those around us. We are not perfect and it's these imperfections that make life meaningful, that make it real. I feel like I was meant to come to the mountains, that I was meant to find this unique group of women, who are all teaching me something about myself, helping me rediscover who I am.

Chapter 13

The Breckenridge sky is nothing but clouds of light grey, threatening snow, so the four of us – me, Dad, Mum and Madi – are currently out in the garden at the back of the house attempting to get our very early morning task of chopping wood completed swiftly to beat the blizzard, which I'm hoping will come and go this morning so we can at least spend some of Christmas Day out on the deck breathing in the Colorado air.

'Line it up, Mads, that's it. Keep your eyes on that line of focus and swing,' Dad calls out from a safe distance away from Madi and her swinging axe. I've got my own stump with my own small log waiting to be halved resting on top of it. I'm heeding my dad's instructions too, with it being years since I've done this sort of activity, as I study my log, looking for its breaking point. I keep my eye on the small crack in the wood, raise my axe into the air and bring it down with all my might. The log splits in two and I automatically jump up and down in the air, feeling incredibly proud of myself. My mum is busying herself collecting more logs but pauses to clap at my achievement. I look over to my dad and he is grinning proudly from ear to ear.

I stop jumping when I notice Madi with her tongue sticking out, her eyebrows scrunched up, staring fiercely at the log before her. I don't want to distract her. Memories come flooding back of the one time Madi helped me release some teenage angst when my mum was out at the shop. I grimace. It was rare for my parents to get angry, but that day my mum had been fuming when she arrived home to find me with my head wrapped up in a bandage that had been white to start with but quickly turned crimson the moment Madi had put it to the two-inch slice on my forehead.

It had been my fault. I had been teaching Madi how to hold the axe and where to place her weight, when I'd got too close. The axe was a touch too heavy and when I thought she was going to lift it up over her head and take her swing, she instead dipped it back slightly to regain her grip, catching me right above my eye. Why I thought it a good idea to stand behind her, I will never know. I was young and dumb in that instance. It had taken weeks of grovelling for my parents to forgive me and let me anywhere near their workshop again.

My dad catches me looking over at them and winks at me as he takes another step back. I smile. Madi swings her axe with a Wonder Woman roar, which makes me chuckle. She too cracks the wood in half. 'Did you see that? I did it. Whoa, that felt good,' she says, stretching her arms above her head as much as her pink ski jacket will allow.

'I did, you did amazing, and I'm still in one piece,' I say, nudging her gently. She shoves me right back and we both start laughing. Mum places new logs on our stumps while Dad collects the halves and loads them into a basket by the deck and we both resume our positions. We manage to fill the basket before snowflakes start to descend from the heavens in heavy clumps. The wind is starting to pick up; it's hard to keep my eyes open. My shoulders are sore and heavy from all the swinging, but I suddenly feel like a child and don't want to go inside when I hear Mum's shout.

'I think we have enough logs for the next two days and it's safe to say that the blizzard is starting earlier than expected.' She looks at the sky and waves us in before grabbing one side of the basket and helping my dad lift it up the steps and next to the sliding doors that open to the living room right near the fireplace.

I tilt my head skyward and get a face full of snow, some of the bigger icier chunks sting my cheeks as they graze them and fall to the ground. My body feels alive with this morning's exercise of chopping wood. I want to stay outside and brave the elements, not wanting to lose the adrenaline that is pumping through my veins. But it's my dad's turn to try and wrangle the child within me.

'Harper, get your butt inside; the wind is picking up. These blizzards are no joke,' he shouts. As if to prove itself, a gust of wind howls around me and gives me no choice but to head inside as it pushes me towards the decking where my dad grabs my hand and helps to pull me up the now icy steps.

Inside, Madi is helping my mum load some fresh logs into the fireplace, so I take off my coat and replace my snow boots with my fluffy slippers and set about making tea and coffee. My mind is buzzing, replaying each wood chop and how powerful each one had felt. My lungs are full of the crisp snowy air and I feel rejuvenated.

Back inside, the house feels like it has been sprinkled with magic. I get that giddy Christmas morning feeling in the pit of my stomach – the feeling I used to get as a child. The multi-coloured lights spiralling around the Christmas tree seem extra bright while the peace signs and more hippie Santa ornaments wearing sunglasses twinkle under their glow. The fire crackles giving a sheen to the wrapping paper covering the few presents lying in wait in front of it as I make myself comfy on the rug under my favourite turquoise knitted throw.

It doesn't take long before Madi is slipping under the blanket with me, my parents joining us to kick off Christmas morning with a little gift giving. When I pause to take in the wondrous scene, I think of Bella's words, and how she spoke of perspective and removing expectations and ideals. I could never have predicted this Christmas after the heartbreak of the last one, yet here I am living

123

in the moment, taking in each minute I am given, surrounded by my heart and soul. All the events that have taken place have led me to this, to being with my parents on Christmas morning again after far too long, and I wouldn't change it for the world.

Madi hands me a present – which snaps me back into the present (rather apt) – and I take it from her and place next to me. I'm more excited for Mum and Dad to open theirs and so sit up on my heels to reach for Madi's and their gifts.

We're now all holding a present encouraging each other to go first, looking at each other expectantly. Madi jumps in, ripping apart the polka dot wrapping paper I so carefully wrapped her present with.

'Oh, my goodness, they're gorgeous,' she expresses as she lifts the lid off the box and finds a pair of vintage white and mint two-tone saddle shoes. I spotted them back in London in a charity shop window a few months ago and they had screamed Madi. With their kitten heel and scalloped detail, I knew they would go with most of her wardrobe. Mum and Dad both have their hands resting on their presents watching Madi and I with adoring gazes. Madi begins to faff about trying the shoes on while I wave at my parents and urge them to open theirs.

They both laugh as they dive in, Mum more elegant than Dad when it comes to tearing the neat tissue paper. I savour the moment of watching them, with the backdrop of the snow falling behind them outside and with the warmth of the fire blazing, their features – every expressive wrinkle and laugh line – important marks indicating the life they have lived and the love they have given. Unable to wait until they have finished opening their presents, I reach out and envelop them both in a hug; one arm around my mum and one around my dad. They are the gift I want to receive each and every Christmas and my most favourite one of all.

*

Mum loved her crocheted scarf with moons and stars weaved into the stitching, which I picked up from the Handmade holiday market, and Dad got a kick out of the Grateful Dead vinyl wall clock that too came from an incredibly cool stall at the market, which crafted some exceptionally creative and inspiring pieces out of old vinyl.

Madi is walking around wearing in her new shoes while the smell of roasting vegetables fills the kitchen and living room as Mum and Dad prepare Christmas dinner. I'm making myself (kind of) useful if useful means writing down my mum's recipes so she (more like me) doesn't forget them (she's never forgotten a recipe) in my new one hundred per cent recycled notebook. It has two arrows, like mine and Madi's matching tattoos, emblazoned on it in delicate ink. It's gorgeous, my homemade gift from Mum and Dad, and it instantly made me want to write.

With my brain fuzzy and warm on new beginnings and appreciating moments, writing down Mum and Dad's recipes is the first thing that springs to mind, as I know I'm going to miss them so much when we get back to London. My diet has improved tenfold since coming to Colorado and I feel better for it. I've been getting back to my roots (quite literally), eating tons of root vegetable dishes and vegan staples from my childhood and I'm determined to keep it up when I get home.

When I'm certain I have enough notes and scribbles, I go to turn the Christmas music up, then tie my stunning cream lace headband, my gift from Madi, around my head to keep my hair out of my face, before taking Madi's hands and dancing around the living room. The rest of the afternoon plays out with much of the same: swooping in and out of the kitchen to help my parents, eating, dancing and chatting away. Em pops in sometime in the evening to wish us a 'Merry Christmas' and stays for one of Madi's famous hot chocolates, at which point we are all stuffed, and the dancing has subsided and been replaced by the Pegasus channel.

It's been a whole day and a half since I sent off my script to

Lara and getting lost in the moment means that I haven't had much time to think about what she thought. As the Pegasus channel launches into this year's Christmas premiere, I can't help the tingle of excitement as I wonder what next year's Christmas premiere might be.

Chapter 14

Through the window the sky is lighting up with a multitude of colourful fireworks, letting me know that it's 9 p.m. and Breckenridge is ready to party. Fortunately, the third announced blizzard of this week only lasted all of half an hour this morning and the sun made an appearance earlier this afternoon. I grab my faux fur fleece teddy jacket and make my way into the living room. It's peaceful in the house. The fire is blazing and brings a flush to my cheeks. There is no movement. I can't place my parents or Madi. Another crackle of fireworks burst into sprinkles in the navy sky, grabbing my attention. I look out on to the deck and see everyone huddled around the fire pit, heads tilted up to the party above.

Madi spots me walking towards the sliding doors; her eyes light up. I see the golden fireworks dancing in their crystal blue. She waves at me and quickly assesses my outfit; her eyes look me up and down. She smiles broadly as I step into the chilly evening.

'You look beautiful,' she gushes. I've opted for my navy and white polka dot dress with long sleeves and lace trim, with a pair of thick tights and brown boots. I feel more like me than ever. The days that followed Christmas Day were nothing short of inspiring: getting to spend more time on the slopes, witness Hayley come second in the Dew Ski Tournament, persuading Em to fit in another midnight yoga class and getting to dine around the table with my parents and lounge on the couch with Madi. It has been utter bliss.

'You too,' I reply. She truly does. Tonight, Madi has opted for no winged eyeliner. Her face is sporting a no-make-up make-up look with a simple gold glittered eye shadow, rosy pink blush and rouge lip to match her fitted red pencil dress. I edge closer to the fire pit, already needing the heat from the flames as my mum and dad turn around and notice me. They had been too busy gazing up at the fireworks while hand in hand. I smile as I think about how much I adore my parents.

'Hey, kid,' my dad says, pulling me in for a big squeeze.

'Hi treasure,' Mum says, getting in on the cuddle. This makes me chuckle.

'This is beautiful,' I say, when they release me. Madi hands me a tall glass of something bubbly. I happily take it.

'It kicks off the New Year festivities every year, kid. They know how to party out here,' my dad explains, his face crinkled with a contented smile. 'Madi tells us you're heading to see the torchlight parade and to meet up with your friends. Enjoy Colorado, honey, it's truly magic at this time of year,' he adds, dropping a kiss on my forehead. I close my eyes and breathe in the familiar scent of my father, the man who is always there to catch me when I fall. The man who looks burly but has a heart of gold, who I have only ever witnessed being an utter gentleman to Mum. I told myself that I wouldn't cry this evening, but my eyes become foggy. I take a sip of cooling wine and blink back my emotions.

'I will, Dad,' I manage before Madi takes my hand and twirls me around, giggling.

*

'Oh my God.' I gasp. My breath is coming out in short bursts. If I thought the fireworks were spectacular, they are nothing compared to my current view. From where I stand sandwiched between Hayley and Madi, we look out over the colourful torches that are illuminating the mountains and the people who are gathered to watch the breath-taking scene. The trees look to be silhouettes and even with all the people about there is a sense of peacefulness as everyone watches in silent awe, the winding trails and swirls of red sweeping down the mountain. The moment has me on the verge of tears for the second time this evening.

The cold air fills my lungs, but the whiskey Jake brought with him is keeping my toes warm. An eruption of shouts and hollers break my reverie as the finale of powerful gold and red fireworks explode in the starry sky and people begin to move around. Hayley takes my hand and our group starts shuffling but I'm not ready to leave the view behind just yet. I feel safe here, safe watching the stars twinkle, watching the giant trees dotted along the mountain sway ever so delicately in the breeze. The footprints and the tracks in the snow have been dusted over with a fresh layer of snowflakes. Everywhere looks crisp and smooth, natural and untouched. It's calming but also gives me the feeling that anything is possible. Tomorrow the snow will be marked, marked with possibilities, adventure and experience from footprints, skies, snowboards and paw prints. Each night it will be renewed for a new day.

That feeling of newness hits me again, square in my chest. I cough as I take in a lungful of air. It's a good feeling but one that is mixed with self-doubt and fear.

'Are you OK?' Hayley asks. She is still holding on to my hand; the others have started walking towards Main Street. Hayley doesn't push me to walk after them. I know how much she loves these mountains too.

'I'm both ridiculously excited and terrified,' I reply, taking my eyes off the red and green torches and turning to look at Hayley.

She catches my eye and her face changes from concerned to a soft side smirk.

'Remember your first day on your board?' she asks. I nod and squint back over the mountains reminiscing about that day nearly two weeks ago where I very nearly chickened out of partaking, but instead gave it a shot and proceeded to spend an hour falling on my arse, covering its surface area in bruises.

'How could I forget?' I tut playfully and shake my head. In the distance I can see fireworks whizzing into the sky as parties are getting underway in homes. It truly looks like something out of a fairy tale with the Christmas lights glowing on the gingerbread cabins.

'It was daunting because you had never been on a board before. Everything is scary before you start.' She shrugs; my eyes find hers again. 'It's not going to be easy, Harper, but if you can pick up snowboarding in a week, I have faith in you. You're stronger and more capable than you think. You've just got to hop on and face that fear head on.' With that she tugs my hand and starts running after the others. It's not easy to trudge through the snow in snow boots let alone my dressier boots. I'm laughing and out of breath before I can gather my thoughts around Hayley's advice.

Before we reach the others, I tug gently on Hayley's hand. 'You doing OK?' I ask, a little out of breath.

Hayley spins me around in the snow, her radiant skin glistening under the moonlight.

'I am positively great.' She beams, her signature smirk tugging at the corner of her lips. 'You have been a breath of fresh air for me, Miss Hayes. I'm going to miss you when you leave,' she adds, watching me twirl.

'I can say the same for you,' I reply, shoving her gently towards the others.

'What was keeping you, slow coach?' Madi enquires, throwing her arm around my neck, her other hand holding Em's. Main Street is packed with people chatting away, throwing their heads back with laughter, and dancing along the path to the music that can be heard coming from every bar.

'I'm a breath of fresh air, apparently.' I wink at Madi and Hayley pushes me gently inside an unassuming club with a small black rectangle sign above the door that reads 'Cecilia's'. The party is already in full swing. The room is neon purple and I see a sort of stage and a pole past the fully stocked bar with rows and rows of interesting-looking bottles, before I'm thrown into the foray of dancing Coloradans; Madi, Hayley, Em, Jake and Ariana at my heel.

'Will Bella be out tonight?' I shout over the noise to Ariana.

'No, she's got the kids tonight,' Ari replies with a swivel of her hips. Jake is standing close behind her taking orders from Em and Madi. Jake points at me and makes a drinking motion. Before I can answer my brain flits to my mum, and I start rattling through my mind the list of beverages I know to be vegan. Something about spending time with my parents these past two weeks has made me want to reconsider my choices. Since I have been in Colorado every day has felt like an epiphany. I feel like I'm taking control of my body, taking control of my choices, taking control of my life.

Jake sends a lopsided smile my way and ruffles my hair. 'I'll just take water please,' I say. He looks momentarily shocked – it is a night for celebrating after all and I have enjoyed my fair share of infused treats this holiday – then he winks and retreats to the bar. Hips connect with mine, hands wave in front of my face, the music is loud, and the vibe is electric. I don't want to get tipsy tonight. I want to be present, to experience all of it and let go without alcohol in my system. I'm aware that I've relied on it a little more recently but taking my dad's advice of meditating and spending time in the glorious outdoors, I know I don't need it to open myself up anymore.

Three dance anthems later and I'm holding on to my fleece, making it a part of the rhythm and my dance moves. I'm sweaty and feeling invigorated. I like it in here but as I catch a glimpse of the clock on the wall, I realize I don't want to celebrate this New Year indoors surrounded by people. I want to be outside in the snow watching the sky as it changes colour, wispy clouds drifting through it and disappearing off into a new beginning.

I don't want to disturb my party-going friends who are fully absorbed in the beats and rhythm of the music, so I sneak away when they're not looking. It's not difficult with the number of people bumping and grinding. My blood is pumping through my veins, heating up my skin, but the icy air stings my pores the instant I step into the snowy path. I throw my fleece over my shoulders and head towards the base of Peak Nine, where we were gathered not long ago. This time though, it's only the Christmas decorations lighting up the mountains and the odd pop and fizzle of fireworks shooting into the air, the torch lights dormant until next year.

I walk further up the peak, taking deep breaths in to give myself energy. I can confirm my dress boots are not cut out for snow. I wiggle my toes every few seconds to make sure they're still attached. The noise of the crowds and bands become faint as I come to a small mound on the mountain. From here I can see the silhouette of the ski cabin, the wires of the gondola and just to my right the giant forest of pine trees looming over the mountains, standing guard.

I swing my hands around myself and clap them together, fidgeting. I wish I had my board with me, there's something enticing about the untouched snow, the way it gleams at me, like tiny crystals teasing me, waiting to be disturbed by the action, the laughter, the footprints of all the locals and tourists.

The moon is full tonight, like a giant wheel of Parmesan watching over me. I don't think I'm ready for Mum and Dad's total vegan lifestyle yet after all, but maybe I can incorporate some changes. I know I want to start looking after my body better, but I'm not sure I can give up my cheese. Do people really live without cheese? I smile at the moon and stop myself salivating over the thought of its deliciousness.

The horizon looks like one of those backdrops they use in movies, strokes of onyx black with hints of deep navies, a splash of baby blue and a drop of purple. The snow on the ground is pure and fierce but somehow delicate and fine. I sit down hoping to ignore the frostbite to my bum long enough to ring in the New Year with such a powerful and sublime view.

I hear a crescendo of thumping music from afar, mixed with a few hundred voices yelling numbers into the air. I look at my watch; the small silver face and the ticking hand let me know that I'm a minute away from New Year.

I feel strange but can't put my finger on it. I feel so far removed from where I was last Christmas, last New Year. I have learnt so much this year and feel like I'm leaving behind a part of me that I don't recognize anymore. I want to go forward as a woman who doesn't crumble at someone's actions and words. A woman who can be strong and brave and most importantly love herself despite the one person she loved more than anything in the world deeming her unlovable and unworthy of loyalty and truth. I'm stepping into a woman who wants to give all those things to herself.

My bum tingles, indicating the wet snow has seeped through my dress and my knickers, but I'm determined to tough it out. The countdown is getting more raucous. I look up to the heavens, close my eyes and breathe. Five, four, three, two, one . . . I inhale deeply and slowly open my eyes to the New Year. The moon and the mountains look the same but deep down in my soul, I know everything has changed.

Chapter 15

All I can hear is the sound of fingers tapping across our keyboards. A pot of steeping gingerbread tea rests on a tray between Madi and I, piled high with plates of biscuits left over from our trip to Colorado. My mum sent us home with a goodie bag that I have never been more grateful for; though I have her recipe, mine haven't quite turned out as well as hers.

We've been pitched up like this all afternoon on either side of Madi's couch, laptops on our knees. Madi is working on a short for Pegasus while I'm hashing out some ideas for my next original script. I love doing edits and rewrites for other writers, but my dream is to write originals and since my trip to Colorado I have been taking this dream more seriously. I haven't heard back yet from Lara about my first original that I sent off over the holidays, but I have been keeping my fingers crossed that it gets green-lighted. It would be my ultimate dream come true as a screenwriter.

In between notes for plots and characters, I've been talking a lot with Bella, learning more about becoming a foster carer and the options that I have. The likelihood of having my very own children right now is slim. I don't want to rush into another relationship – it's actually the furthest thing from my mind – but meeting Poppy and Evan opened my eyes. It felt like a sign. Now that I have relinquished certain ideals and expectations, I realize I have other options to make a difference in a child's life. It's a huge deal and would be a big step considering I don't even have a place of residence anymore. There's a lot I need to figure out both practically and mentally before I bring a child into my home. In my heart, I know it's what I want to do, but I need to know I can give the child my all. I am both incredibly excited and nervous about it all but have been meditating every day, like my dad told me, to keep in tune with my new path as well as remembering the conversation Bella and I had, reminding myself that it's OK to make mistakes and be scared, but that can't stop me going after what I want.

Meditating is certainly helping me to stay in tune with my emotions and to keep my composure as with a house up for sale and divorce papers out in the world you'd think Scott would be conversing with our lawyers but he's not responding to anything right now.

My lawyer hasn't heard a peep from him since the papers were sent two months ago when we got back from Colorado. I've deleted him from social media, so I have no idea where he is or what he's doing. I've been in touch with a solicitor and set up a meeting in the coming weeks, but they have yet to get a confirmation from Scott either.

I'm somewhat torn between demanding answers and getting in touch with my lawyers to see what more they can do, and simply letting things be and having faith that they are doing everything in their power and following protocol with Scott's silence. It's better for me to focus on other things as I've come to find that in taking care of myself and focusing on the good in my life, I don't wish to speak to Scott. It's like he's this toxic entity that I don't want to surround myself with.

I nibble my biscuit thoughtfully, choosing to let thoughts of Scott and lawyers drift away for the afternoon. I have more pressing things to worry about when I witness Madi giggle like a schoolgirl at her screen.

'How's Em?' I ask, intrigued as to how their budding relationship has been going since we got back to London and knowing that giggle can only mean she and Em are engaged in conversation. On New Year's Eve they were inseparable, and I have never seen Madi so happy and carefree around someone other than me. I'd hate for her to think she can't be excited about falling in love because of my current situation. She gives me a side-eye and takes a tiny bite of her biscuit. 'Madi, talk to me. Scream, shout, jump up and down on the spot and be in love. Don't you dare hold it in because of me,' I say sternly, making my eyes big and tilting my head to drive home how serious I am.

Madi shifts to look at me again and waves her biscuit in the air. Even with no make-up she looks like a Fifties pin-up. Her blonde fringe frames her structured face boldly and beautifully.

'I'm not, Harp, I promise. I know you better than that,' Madi responds. Her lips form the smallest of smirks but her eyelids droop. I can see she's a little torn. It's my turn to be patient and let her speak at her own pace. 'Em is awesome but we're taking things slow. Neither of us ever thought about having a long-distance relationship before so for now things are what they are. We talk but there's no pressure, though we've both made it clear that we're not really interested in seeing other people and if that situation did arise, well, then we'd let the other person know.'

I squeal despite Madi's more matter-of-fact and solemn face. It only takes five seconds before she lets a squeal slip too. We both grin at each other like we know the secret to what my mum puts in her tea (I wish) and mirror-image each other stuffing our remaining chunks of biscuits in our mouths.

'That sounds very mature and rather wonderful,' I say through a crunch. 'I have to agree with you that she is pretty awesome. I miss everyone,' I add, swallowing the scrumptious biscuit and thinking of Mum and Dad, their house, our new friends. I miss the fresh air and the slopes as I guiltily look around and realize Madi and I are falling into our usual writer hibernation mode. 'We should just move to Colorado,' I say, watching Madi as I do so.

She kind of shrugs, her lips pursed into a thoughtful pout. Does she think I'm crazy or does she think I'm just joking? Am I just joking?

'How's your research coming along for fostering? How's Bella doing?' Madi asks changing the subject. A wave of disappointment washes over me. Was I really feeling that serious when I mentioned moving to Colorado? Had I been expecting Madi to jump on board and agree with me? Or maybe at least just discuss it with me? But really what is there to discuss? We can't just up and leave London. We've lived here our whole lives. Our work is here, our network, our friends; well, Scott's friends, it turned out. I can't put wishy-washy thoughts in Madi's head and get her hopes up over being with Em with just a throwaway comment. I shouldn't have said it without thinking about it properly first.

I follow Madi's lead and ignore my own absurd comment and focus on answering her questions.

'Bella's doing great, thank you. I think she might even be thinking about saying yes to Colt and actually going on a date very soon,' I reply. Thinking of Bella makes me forget my unreasonable disappointment from moments ago and instead excitement bubbles in my gut. Madi feels it too.

'Oh my gosh, that's so exciting. Oh, I love her, and they would just be so cute together.' Madi expresses her approval. I grin in lieu of using words to express my happiness for Bella; she deserves the world.

'And, I'm booked in for a meeting with one of the social workers in a few weeks to get the ball rolling. I've been reading as much as I can on the different types of fostering and what it can entail, and I think this is something I'm meant to do, Mads.' I feel content and enthusiastic about my decision; a decision I've made all on my own.

'I love you, Harp, and I think you are amazing,' Madi says, picking up the last biscuit and snapping it in half, handing me a piece.

'I love you too,' I reply, taking the biscuit.

'We're in this together, you and me,' Madi adds. I tuck one leg

137

up under the other, my laptop balancing on my knees so I can adjust to see Madi better without twisting my neck awkwardly.

'Always have been and always will be,' is my response, to which Madi holds up her half of the biscuit. I meet her halfway and we cheer with our cinnamon crunch, before promptly erupting with laughter. A ping from my laptop draws me away from my best friend's mesmerizing eyes and infectious laughter, and I notice an email appear from Lara.

I had been getting anxious over not hearing from her after sending in my revised draft over the holidays two months ago. I'm never usually this nervous but after cutting it so fine and struggling with edits for my first original script – having been given only a short extension to rewrite it – my stomach is in knots. Deadlines are vital in this business. If my boss hated it, she can simply pick another movie or get someone in to rewrite my words or cast it aside to the unwanted pile and forget I ever pitched it.

I keep my fingers crossed that the love she had for the original spec means she won't give up on me so easily. My heart starts thudding in my chest as I read her cheery *Hello Harper* – at least I hear it in my head in a chirpy manner. I have worked with Pegasus Entertainment and Lara now for nearly six years. I've built up a professional yet relaxed rapport with her. She has a friendly manner and is always the epitome of fun meets sophistication each time I meet her at the Christmas parties every year. Her emails always read warmly, which has the ability to calm me down and make me want to do the best job I can for her. In all I'd say that she is the kind of cool boss that I would hope to be, if I ever had the desire to be the boss of a company.

I continue reading.

I hope you had a lovely holiday. I apologize for the short delay in getting back to you. I'm pleased to inform you that your script has been picked up for production and that explains my brief absence. Things are always moving so quickly as you know.

*Attached, you will find the provisional outline of the direc-
tor's plan, in addition to meetings and filming schedule. I'd
love you to join us on set if you can. Can you let me know
as soon as possible?*

'Great job with this one, Harper. You should be proud.
I personally think it's gorgeous.'

My chest heaves and I feel a trickle of tears escape my eyes
before I can stop them. I'm grateful that today they are happy
tears. *Really* happy tears.

'Harper?' Madi simply says my name to encourage me to
share whatever has just made me cry. I rub my eyes in disbelief
and read over Lara's words before opening my mouth to Madi.

'I just got the green light,' I say, slightly incoherently. My
tears are becoming heavier. I'm blubbering. Life has caught me
by surprise and I'm somewhat in shock. In this moment right
now I have my amazing career, incredible parents who looked
after me over the holidays and who poured so much love into
my heart, I have my ideas and dreams for the future that will
(hopefully) include making a difference in others' lives and I have
a ridiculously beautiful and loyal best friend who has put up with
my ups and downs for the last year and two months and who
just jumped up off the couch, spilling the dregs of teas from the
bottom of both our mugs. I'm happy. I am *really* happy. What
do my mum and dad always say about the universe providing
you with what you need? Oh yes, that you must trust in what
it has given you and allow it in, allow it to lead the way. I have
been given yet another moment to be grateful for, yet another
reason to believe and trust the universe and it feels invigorating.

'Time for a break and I think some hot chocolate to celebrate,'
Madi announces, marching out of the small living room. I can
hear her start to bustle around the kitchen opening cupboards
and grabbing the saucepan. A wave of goose bumps washes over
me. I stare at the email and attempt to blink away the cloudy tears
before I can reply. I sigh to myself. This is it. My first completely

original screenplay has just been given the go-ahead for production. My mouth feels like sandpaper. Sure, I have been on movie sets before. I have the posters on my phone of the movies that I was signed on to rewrite and aid with. I was proud of those movies. I am proud of those movies. But to have my idea, my script, my characters to be loved enough to be given the chance to come to life, well I'm gobsmacked. It's a dream come true. It's what I have worked hard for since I was a little girl writing short stories in my bedroom late at night under my blanket forts.

'Did I tell you how proud I am of you?' Madi asks as she enters the room bearing two tall mugs of saccharine hot chocolate piled high with whipped cream. My eyes bulge at the sight of the sprinkles Madi has added on top. It's a rainbow delight. 'We're celebrating – we can indulge in a little sugar,' she adds with a wink as she hands me my mug. Since getting back from Colorado we have been working on changing up our diets and habits thanks to my parents' glowing skin and full-of-beans energy.

I've neglected my health over the past few years and my body hasn't agreed with it. My mind needs to be on top form too, so a little overhaul was in order. It's been going well so far: more water, less caffeine and a notebook full of delicious veggie recipes from my mum.

'Thank you,' I say to Madi as she joins me on the couch. 'How about we take these to the patio and get some fresh air?' I add, shuffling my laptop to the side of me and standing up, taking a slurp of cream from the top of my mug so it doesn't drip as I do so.

'Sounds good,' Madi replies, following my footsteps. I push open the double doors at the back of her living room that open to the modest patio. The sun is shining but there's a nip in the air. We take to the two wicker chairs Madi has next to a tiny table. I take a big gulp of hot chocolate and it instantly warms my insides.

For a few moments I want to be entirely present and enjoy the sunshine and scrumptious drink while I let the news sink in.

Chapter 16

It's been three months now since I filed for divorce and two weeks since my lawyer last contacted Scott. He has received no replies. It's frustrating to say the least but I have been far too busy to let it get me down. Moving on would be a beautiful thing. A year and three months have gone by and I feel ready to do so; if these finer details could just be sorted out swiftly and smoothly, it would be great. I've done a spot of house hunting, booked my foster care interview and tomorrow, bright and early, I'm off to the Cotswolds for the first day of shooting my movie. My script has been reviewed a few times over the past month and all on board are happy with its current read. I'll be on set in case any problems arise. If something isn't quite making sense or doesn't fit when the actors act out a scene, I'll be there to adjust when and if necessary.

It's always quite the thrill being on a movie set, getting to see actors at work and your words come to life. I get a small flutter of nerves in the pit of my stomach as I think about the adventure that begins tomorrow. This script means a lot to me. My screenplays in the past have reflected the joy of romance, falling in love with your perfect match or a dashing stranger, but this one, this one looks at love in a different light. The nerves heighten when

I think about Pegasus introducing it to the rest of the world this Christmas. Will the world like different? Will the Pegasus movie enthusiasts warm to a slight stray from their usual magic formula?

I fold my cardigan into my travel case and check everything over. Work-appropriate clothes: some fitted pieces, tailored cream trousers, collared blouses. I throw in a long skirt and ruffled dress too in case I get the chance to explore on my own, something I'm trying to do more of. I love staying at Madi's house and am beyond grateful to her for hosting me. It's not like I feel like I'm overstaying my welcome or anything – we're practically sisters and I know I would offend her if I thought such a thing – but I'm actually excited about escaping to the Cotswolds for the next three weeks. It will be the first time in a very long time that I am making a trip on my own.

With competent snowboarder being added to my list of skills and it being something I had on my bucket list but had been too afraid to try and now could tick off, it's safe to say that my experiences in Colorado have given me a new lease on life. In addition to a new outlook with work and my future goals, I want to enjoy each second of every opportunity I am given. I have been writing screenplays for as long as I can remember and I adore my work, but I want to push myself harder to get my work out there and challenge myself as a person and with new projects.

It has taken me a minute to get there but waking up on my own in my own bed has become something I thoroughly relish. Stretching out like a starfish, being able to recite my morning affirmations and start the day on my own terms makes me feel amazing. I'm looking forward to the new surroundings of a cottage-like hotel and to fully embrace my aloneness without Madi, even though just thinking about being without her for the next few weeks makes me miss her.

*

I manage to find my way on to the film set. The film trucks, wires and people hustling about letting me know I had found the right place. My quaint bed and breakfast is just a short walk along the river away – Bourton-on-the-Water, the Venice of the Cotswolds – and it's stunning. I almost didn't want to leave its confines this morning. But it's a glorious day, perfect for filming. The sun is high in the bright blue sky, no clouds casting shadows, and I'm looking forward to seeing my leading lady act out the scene where she bumps into a local farmer as she's herding chickens off the road and into her truck. It has elements of your classic Pegasus movie but with a twist. In her escape to the countryside my heroine meets three different women, all with unique jobs, all with diverse pasts, all incredibly badass – a shepherdess, who escaped to the country to get away from her parents' belief that she was nothing if she did not become a high-paid accountant. There's a dog walker, who ended up in the Cotswolds after finding out her fiancé was cheating on her days before they were set to say their vows, and a vegan pastry chef who fled her country due to a troubled family past who now owns a small B and B and her own vegetable garden. In these women my leading lady finds strength and inspiration.

OK, so maybe a little part of the friendships I had made in Colorado influenced my resurrected script, but it came from a new perspective of having taken a leap and my making the moments happen; choosing to open myself up, seeking out such incredible experiences like snowboarding and living the life I wanted to lead. In my time there, I didn't just let life happen to me. I consciously made myself present and in turn it was really those feelings of empowerment and learning from every person I met that I couldn't resist exploring in my writing.

I introduce myself to as many people as I can, not wanting to interrupt those who look frazzled and busy until I find Lara. She's usually around on the first day of shooting and then pops in and out for the remainder of the time. We exchange pleasantries before she offers me a seat behind one of the many large camera rigs.

143

'This is a beautiful story, Harper. I'm eager to see it come to life,' Lara says encouragingly. I smile, grateful, unable to stop my eyes from wandering around taking in all the action. The scenery is stunning, evergreen, with blossoming flowers and farm animals dotted about, it's just how I pictured it in my head. Picturesque and idyllic, just the place my leading lady needs to be to escape her hectic city life. I hear a beep and a shout, which I know to mean 'quiet' followed by a loud 'action'.

I twist my head automatically in the direction of the director and instantly my blood runs cold. I feel it draining out of my head, away from my heart. My heart is crashing in my chest, trying to get the blood to pump back to it. It's him. It's my husband. Well my ex-husband, but technically still my husband because he hasn't yet signed our divorce papers. I really can't hyperventilate and have a panic attack right now.

I jump out of my chair, not looking back to see if my boss has noticed me missing and I dash to the nearest trailer.

'Oh goodness, Harper,' I mumble to myself; I check the coast is clear once inside the trailer and close the door behind me. I steady myself by holding on to the small kitchenette counter. 'You are the sun, the moon and the stars,' I say airily, trying to lighten my own mood in this silly situation. I am a grown woman. I fan myself with my hand; my face feels flushed and rosy. 'Please don't do this now, you're better than this,' I say to myself as I pace up and down the tiny living area. Involuntary shakes have decided to take over my limbs.

'Scott's here and that's OK. I can just stay clear of him. I don't need to go anywhere near him.' I shake my hands to try and wriggle off the nerves, feeling slightly claustrophobic in the confines of the cosy trailer.

'And if I do bump into him, it will be fine. I can just say hi, hello. I hope life is treating you and your girlfriend well or maybe, maybe I can just get it all out, shout and get angry and tell him how mean he is.' Uh, I wish Madi were here. 'No, I can do this on my own.' I turn my back to the living area and look out of the window over the sink.

'Why didn't Lara tell me that Scott would be here? Probably because it's no big deal to anyone. Come on, Harper, his affair is last year's news. Everyone has moved on and so have you,' I say, shaking my head, watching the busy crew members fight with a tangled cable through the plastic window. I brush a wobbly hand through my hair.

'Maybe I'm the only idiot who believes in true love and the sanctity of marriage and I've been a fool all along. Maybe affairs are as common as proposals these days.' I tug at the collar of my chiffon blouse, feeling flustered and thrown by my contradicting emotions.

'Oh, really, Harper, don't do this; think of all you have learnt. You still believe in love and you're happy now. He's happy now. Life is good; you're in a better place. You've got this, I've got this, I can do this,' I say more forcefully to myself. I don't want to be this person. I'm not this person. This has all just been a knee-jerk reaction, a bit of a shock to the system that's all. I'll go back out there and I will be fine. I nod.

'Scott sounds like an incredibly shitty human being, if I can be so bold as to give my two cents. If it's any consolation I think you've got this too.' I snap around and am greeted by a warm smile and empathetic eyes. I don't know how long I stand and stare before I inhale deeply and finally smile in return, but it feels like an age. But the man doesn't rush me. Before I know it, a light laugh escapes my lips. I raise my hand to my forehead.

'I'm so sorry for barging into your trailer. I had a moment of panic seeing Scott and . . .' I pause, annoyed at myself for talking about Scott. I really don't want to think about him; today has just thrown me off guard.

'You needed a place to hide?' The man finishes my sentence, raising an eyebrow to see if he got it correct, but his words are gentle.

'Yes. But that just seems ridiculous now. I sincerely apologize for bursting in here and please understand I have no intention of bad-mouthing my husband. I didn't mean for you to hear that,' I say, edging closer to the door.

'I don't believe for a second you are bad-mouthing your husband, but I couldn't say that if you were, I could blame you. I apologize for overhearing. Please, if you need a moment longer, sit down and make yourself at home,' he replies, gesturing to the small couch. My heart is still palpitating rather erratically, so I smile and take him up on his offer.

'I won't be too much longer,' I say confidently, the air finding its way into my lungs more normally now.

'There's no rush. Can I get you anything? Would you like some tea?' the man asks, filling up the kettle. He's tall with chestnut brown hair and piercing grey eyes nestled behind black-rimmed glasses. He has a kind way about him and I feel comfortable in his presence. I don't feel like he is just being polite, I genuinely feel as though I don't need to rush. I appreciate him greatly in this moment; biding my time before I face the inevitability of seeing Scott again.

'That would be lovely, but I'll have to pass. I mustn't be too long in case they need me. Thank you for the offer though,' I say softly. Patting under my eyes to ensure no stray tears have ruined my make-up. I tug at my oversized faint mustard cardigan before my eyes drift around the room. They land on the kind man once more, who I notice is looking at me. He seems at ease in his plain white T-shirt and blue jeans. Trying to rack my brain over my script and who this man must be cast as has gotten me stumped, which makes me laugh and distracts me from thoughts of Scott.

'I'm Harper,' I say with another chuckle and hold out my hand. 'I wrote the script, so I'm just on hand in case they need anything changing if it doesn't sound quite right.'

'I'm Dean, it's a pleasure to meet you, Harper.' He smiles genuinely, reminding me of Madi when she looks at me and really sees me. It momentarily takes my breath, that I'm struggling to steady, away. I miss Madi and I've only been away from her a few hours. I could do with a friend after today's unexpected turn of events. I want to be strong but seeing Scott for the first time in months has knocked me for six. I'll be OK in a few minutes, I tell myself. Under Dean's watchful gaze I find my breath and feel it returning to it's more regular rhythm and my mind clearing.

'And what do you do, Dean? Forgive me but I'm trying to place you in my cast of characters. There are no male heroes involved and I'm having a hard time picturing you as the local dairy farmer.' I look him up and down.

He copies me, looking himself up and down and stating, 'If I was an actor I would be offended.' He laughs. 'You really don't think I could play a dairy farmer?' He smirks playfully and my eyes crinkle with laughter. It's a nice release and eases the tight tension in my abs as the laughter barrels out of my belly.

'I'm sorry, I'm sure you could play a dairy farmer – you'd be the best one,' I tease. He raises his eyebrows and purses his lips in a mock-cocky fashion.

'Why, thank you. But, no I'm not an actor. I'm kind of hiding out here too. My sister is playing your wonderful pastry chef. She had me tag along. We're making a trip out of her crossing the Atlantic for the first time for a movie, but I'm not inclined to get in the way today,' Dean says. Before I can ask where in America he and his bold accent are from, there is a knock at the door. I jump up, worried that I've been unprofessional disappearing from set like this when a beautiful brunette who I saw earlier in front of the camera barrels in with a beaming smile on her sun-kissed face.

'There you are. Are you not coming to watch me?' she says mock exasperated at Dean, her smile not faltering.

Dean holds up his mug, bearing coffee not tea. 'I need some caffeine in me if I'm to watch you perform all day,' he says slyly through a wicked grin. 'This is Harper,' he adds, gesturing towards me. The woman shakes her head.

'I'm so sorry, where are my manners? I didn't mean to ignore you. I just wanted to grab this one before my next take. I'm Sophie.

Wait are you Harper Hayes, the woman who wrote this script?' she enquires, her voice coming out high-pitched and excitable. It's hard not to smile in this woman's presence. She has a positive aura to match her strikingly pretty face.

'That would be me,' I say, with a modest shrug, feeling my cheeks flush. 'It's wonderful to meet you, Sophie. I best get back to set. I'm looking forward to watching you work,' I say as I head to the door. I hesitate for a second wondering if I will be able to avoid bumping into Scott but somehow feeling that I'm strong enough to get through it if I do, thanks to my brief encounter with Dean and his kindness. A stranger has reminded me that there is love and beauty in the world. (I sound like my mother.) 'It was great to meet you too, Dean. I hope you both enjoy our side of the Atlantic.'

'It was great to meet you too and for the record I don't believe you're the only idiot left,' he replies raising his mug and tipping his head. As I walk away my lips curve into a smile, then I hear Sophie tell Dean off for calling me an idiot and another crack of laughter bursts out of me.

I make it over to the tent where I see Lara hanging out with other staff, cameramen, assistants, actors, while I'm trying to compose my giggles. With Sophie's arrival in the trailer I take it that they've called for a break to set up the next scenes. Before I can check in with Lara to see how things are going, I'm intercepted by the man I was hoping to stay clear of. I feel Scott's grip on my elbow as he guides me to the side of the tent by the catering table full of fruit plates. My blood runs icy. I close my eyes. When I open them, I register that this is no longer the man I loved, and I no longer feel weak in his presence. I hold my head high and imagine myself on the slopes with Hayley, wind in my face, adrenaline coursing through my veins, gliding along the snow, looking fear in the face. I zone in to how I felt then, how powerful nature ensured me that I am.

'What are you doing?' Scott asks abruptly. It comes out in a hiss; I'm not accustomed to this harsh tone from him. 'Could you just give me a break, Harper? There's no need to come to my work. I thought you would be more civil than that,' he adds, his voice low. He doesn't want to make a scene apparently, which comes as a bit of a shock considering how much he and his girlfriend have enjoyed splashing their relationship across social media – or so my 'friends' have told me.

The words are not forming in my brain quick enough to respond, so I stand stock still, once more looking like a goldfish in front of my husband. Did he just ask me to give him a break? To cut him some slack? I tug my arm fiercely out of his grasp. I don't want him touching me.

'Look I've seen the papers, I've seen the emails, I've just been busy with work. If a divorce is what you want, then we can get a divorce.' He tries a gentler approach, trying to soften my stone jaw with what he must think to be a kind gesture – that he will give me what I want. He wants sympathy for working hard and he wants to be the gentleman and give me what I want, because it's me who wanted a divorce?

I can actually feel my blood boiling; it bubbles under my skin. I'm uncomfortable. Being this angry terrifies me. It's not in my nature. *You are the sun, the stars, the moon,* I think to myself, picturing my mother's calming face.

'Just don't make a scene,' Scott then says glancing around the tent. I don't follow his gaze. Right now, I'm not interested in how this looks to anyone else. I'm not worried about making a scene. All the hurt, the anger, the confusion and frustration of the last year reaches its peak. I have given Scott a break, sat back over the last year and a half waiting for his response about the divorce and the house, an apology even, but it's my turn to let go now. It's my turn to move on. How dare he say he's busy, too busy to sign divorce papers, too busy with his new life, his new girlfriend, to allow me to move on. I'm not waiting any longer for him to move his pawn on the chessboard. I have a life to live. I'm done with taking one step forward and two steps back.

149

I smile a shaky smile at first but then it grows bolder as I breathe in the fresh country air and feel the sun kissing my cheeks. I bloody love the outdoors and need to spend more time in it.

'Scott. I think it's perfect that we ended up being on this movie set together.' I'm about to say more when Scott interrupts me.

'Well, I don't. This is ridiculous. There's no need for you to be here, just go, Harper. I'll deal with the papers soon.' Of course, Scott wouldn't think I have any reason to be here. If how he has treated me this last year is anything to go by, I'm anything but a person of importance. He looks around anxiously, a pleading look in his eyes like he's dismissing me and urging me to drop it with so many people inside the tent in close proximity. At that moment Lara calls out to me, giving me reason to turn away from Scott's callous glare.

'Harper, we need you, hon. We have a question about this next scene in your script.' She nods in my direction and waves me over to where she needs me. I wave back, grateful for the distraction and breather from Scott's aggravating words. I turn back to Scott with more determination and confidence and the desire to do what I should have done a long time ago: stand up for myself.

'Scott, I have every right to be here. You see, it's my script. I wrote this movie. My first original movie and I'm so damn proud of it. Maybe you can learn something from it if you pay close attention.' My voice is stern, a little shaky around the edges, but confident. I don't look away from Scott's eyes. 'You have the divorce papers, which is great, now I'm here you can get them signed and hand them over to me tomorrow morning. The solicitors are sorting the house so if you need to speak to anyone you can go through them. I am done here. I am so finally done.' I squint my eyes as I think whether I have anything more to say to Scott, any other important information that needs to be addressed, but I think that should cover it. I'm aware that all eyes are now on us. I didn't mean for my words to come out so loud but they sure felt good to say; like a weight has been lifted from my chest.

I go to step away, but hesitate, giving myself a moment to take in Scott's features: the blonde hair I used to love running my hands through, his bright eyes that used to light up when they saw me, those lips that made my stomach flutter. My confidence wavers when I go to step away. This is it. I'm putting it all behind me. The man speaking just now, the man standing in front of me, is not my Scott and I have to acknowledge that. There's no warmth in his eyes, no consideration of how I'm doing or what this has all been like for me. It's all about him. We're not in this together anymore. That stopped the minute he built a relationship with another woman behind my back. Though I know my emotions are the least of his worries, I go to speak them anyway, for myself.

'I'm not angry with you, Scott.' The few words leave my lips before all the things I thought I wanted to say, the speeches that months ago were floating around my brain wanting to burst out, simply fizzle away. I side-glance to the sunshine, full and orange above the green fields and catch sight of Sophie and Dean. Dean's fists are clenched. My lips curve into a small smile; Madi would like Dean, I can't help but muse. He has a protective look on his face, which is sweet since I just met him.

When I look back to Scott, a moment of euphoria hits me. There's nothing more I need to say to him. I have nothing to prove to him; the fight I once had to be right and tell him that what he did was wrong has long since passed. He doesn't need to know of the pain he caused me. If I have to tell him, it's not worth it and beside the point. And what did my dad say about my past not being my future? Nothing I say can change what happened and, in this moment, I know that that's OK, for everything that happened was meant to happen. The pieces of me that crumbled are being put back together in new and beautiful ways each day and I am loving the person I am becoming.

I walk away.

Chapter 17

In the distance I can hear the faint sound of sheep 'baaing' and right outside my window the birds are having a full-on conversation while the sun is rising, casting my hotel room in a peachy glow. I stretch out my legs and wave my arms above my head to wake myself and find myself smiling. I look around the room taking in the bare brick walls, the porcelain standalone bath in one corner, an egg-shaped chair in the other; which screams for me to curl up on it and write the day away or get lost in a good book. I affirm to myself that today is going to be a great day.

Checking my watch, I see that I have plenty of time for a hot bath, breakfast and a morning stroll before call time. So, I throw off the deliciously crisp and cosy duvet and get the tap running while I choose my clothes for the day.

The hotel bath is dangerous. I very nearly drift off to sleep relaxing back into the warm bubbles and perfectly curved nook that eases the stress in my shoulders and has my eyelids fluttering to stay awake. The sun rising over the lush green fields keeps me on task; the light bouncing off the morning dew enticing me. I want to be able to explore the quaint village before a day spent on set; the greenery being somewhat tarred by wires, tape and rigs.

My long mauve skirt with a crochet overlay tickles my ankles.

I pair it with a slightly oversized white jumper and manage to style my hair in a thick loose braid. With a dusting of blush, a swipe of gloss and mascara, I'm ready for breakfast.

On the stairs I bump into Sophie whose bare face and joggers instantly make me smile.

'Good morning, Sophie,' I chirp, excited to see her now that I'm feeling more myself and am not frazzled like I had been yesterday. Sophie looks up and catches my eye.

'Harper? Hi, oh good morning,' she says enthusiastically enveloping me in a hug. 'Isn't this place magical? Are you hungry?' she gushes.

We walk side by side down the small staircase that leads into a reception area that boasts fresh flowers, a brick fireplace, a floor-to-ceiling bookshelf and a heavenly smell of vanilla. I feel like I've stepped into Kate Winslet's cottage in *The Holiday* and might have to ring Madi and tell her I'm not leaving.

'It's stunning and yes, I was just heading for some breakfast. Would you care to join me?' I reply, receiving an eager nod and doe-eyed smile in response. Breakfast is served in a conservatory just off the cottage. It's absolutely gorgeous with the morning sunlight reflecting off the white linen tablecloths, pastel bunting and mouth-watering trays of croissants and bowls of fresh fruit. We take a seat by the large windows overlooking the vibrant courtyard and order coffee for Sophie and a lemon tea for me.

'So, how long have you been writing?' Sophie asks, resting her elbows on the table and her chin on her hands, showing great interest.

'I can't remember a time when I wasn't writing if I'm honest, but I started working for Pegasus Entertainment nearly six years ago now. It's mostly been rewrites and edits; this is my first original screenplay that has been picked up,' I tell her. 'How long have you been acting?' I ask, as the waitress places our drinks in front of us. I take a sip while I listen to Sophie.

'Oh, only since I turned twenty-one and moved into my own

place. My parents are doctors and naturally I was expected to become one too. It was frowned upon – my wanting to consider another profession. Don't get me wrong, we still talk, and I still see them, but Dean is most definitely the golden child,' she explains with a laugh. 'I watch Pegasus religiously. One might say I'm a little addicted . . .'

'One might say, or one does say?' I hear Dean's voice first before he reaches the table. When his eyes meet mine, he winks playfully. Sophie rolls her eyes.

'OK, I am a Pegasus movie addict,' she says with a 'what are you going to do about it?' shrug.

'That you are. Good morning, ladies,' Dean says. He looks a little sweaty, and his grey eyes are sparkling with a hint of ocean blue in the morning light. He's not wearing his glasses, which makes their colour pop more clearly.

'Morning,' I say, smiling at his cheeriness so early.

'Are you joining us?' Sophie asks. Dean doesn't make to sit down. He looks from me to his sister before I notice his cheeks flush.

'No, thank you for the invite but I best get cleaned up. Enjoy your breakfasts. I recommend the custard pastries,' he notes before nodding and walking away.

'If you want to know the best dessert spots in Colorado, my brother is your man. In fact, he'll find the best desserts just about everywhere we go. He has the biggest sweet tooth of anyone I know,' Sophie tells me with a giggle. 'Shall we?' she adds gesturing to the buffet table. I let out a chuckle and stand before I fully register what she just said.

'Colorado?' I question without actually managing to form a proper question. Her mention of Colorado piques my interest and I raise my brows.

'Colorado born and raised. That's where I auditioned for this role. It was only a few years ago I discovered Pegasus Entertainment had an office in Frisco and that's when I knew I wanted to try my hand at acting full time and tell my parents no more medical school. I haven't looked back since,' Sophie says loading her plate with toast and one of each pastry. I like her a lot and I can't seem to stop the odd stirring of butterflies in my stomach at the fact that she and Dean are from Colorado. I feel like I'm being sent another sign and I smile as I place a custard pastry on my plate.

'It's the first time I've ever travelled for acting, which is why I asked Dean to come with me, which probably makes me sound lame! But he's a protective older brother through and through. And in truth . . .' She pauses as we take our seats at our table and looks me intently in the eye. 'Don't tell him this – I just wanted him to get away for a bit and have a break. He doesn't often get holidays and when he does, he never goes far as he's always on call. It might be selfish of me when I know his patients need him, but younger sisters are allowed to be protective too and he has been looking exhausted recently. I kind of over-exaggerated how nervous I was travelling so far on my own.'

I smile at Sophie's words and because I have just taken a nibble of the custard pastry that Dean had been right to recommend. It's warm and full of flavour. I already know I'm going to need another one.

'I think that's incredibly sweet of you,' I say in response to Sophie's confession. 'It's lovely that you care enough to look out for him, and I think it's wonderful you get to spend this time together and celebrate your first acting job abroad. It does seem to be doing him wonders. He looked rested and well this morning,' I add washing my scrumptious pastry down with a delicate sip of tea.

'He's an early bird. He will have had his pastry and coffee with the sunrise and then hit the gym,' Sophie says, a loving infliction in her voice. I can tell she thinks fondly of her big brother the way she smiles warmly when talking about him. There's even pride in her tone when she's making fun of him. 'Oh my God, this pastry is delicious. I love England, I could just live here,' Sophie announces making me chuckle. I ponder the thought of us actually re-enacting *The Holiday* and my swapping places with her in Colorado. We sit a little while longer discussing the differences between traditional British cuisine and Colorado staples until our plates are cleared and Sophie rushes off to do her morning rituals before show time.

I decide I still have enough time to spare before I need to be on set and so make my way through the conservatory and out into the courtyard. The orchards and fields beyond the wooden gate stretch for miles and I can make out a dusty stone walking path along the edge. I fancy walking off the pastries and seeing where the road leads. The sprouts of daffodils and bluebells have me reaching out to trace my hands softly over them, their scents wafting up and filling my soul with appreciation for where I am.

The sun warms my face and I'm thinking I should have worn a hat to shield me from its rays. There's still a soft breeze blowing, making my light jumper and skirt combo the right choice, but sunglasses would have been a sensible choice too. It feels as though I have walked for miles through peaceful lands when I come to a paddock and find sheep grazing. They are the only souls about; their calm 'baas' speaking to me and making me feel welcome in their home. I lean against the log enclosure and say hello.

*

'I don't know if I could have done that; even if it was fake. I'd be too frightened to look at myself,' I say, scrunching up my features and shaking my head. Sophie, Dean and I are sat around a picnic table under a beautiful yellow umbrella at the village pub, a short walk from our hotel. It's where we have spent most of our evenings over the past two and a half weeks.

Sophie is regaling us with stories from roles she's played and extra work she had done in order to pay her dues in the glam (or not so glam if her recent anecdote is anything to go by) business of acting.

'I was totally numb by this point. We were shooting well past midnight and the worst thing was I couldn't even jump into bed when I got home at 3 a.m.; it took another hour and a half to peel the scabs and scrub the blood off me,' she says dramatically with hand gestures and all.

'I'd have been good playing a corpse by that point. I'd have been asleep on my feet by 10 p.m.' I laugh.

Dean takes a sip of his beer and shakes his head with a chuckle. 'But after all that you made the best zombie in the whole film,' he says and receives a playful whack from Sophie.

'No way.' I gasp with a cheeky smile, catching on to Dean's sarcasm and playing along. I have a feeling I know where this is going.

'Yes way! Four hours of make-up, having ice-cold blood thrown at me and layers of silicone attached to my body and they practically cut me,' Sophie says, flabbergasted, causing us all to howl with laughter.

The banter continues well into the evening but by ten-thirty I've consumed enough tea to fill a baby paddling pool and we make our way back to the hotel. We are responsible adults after all, and Dean and I are both aware that Sophie has a job to do in the morning that I'd like to think is a step up from her days playing zombies in indie movies.

I've enjoyed getting to know Dean and Sophie over the past few weeks. The chatter doesn't stop; what with tales of auditions gone wrong and Sophie's lively personality, there's never a dull moment. Dean doesn't share too much about his job and Sophie tries to keep the conversation away from his work; I can only gather that's to help him switch off.

Filming has been going smoothly from what I've seen. When I caught a few moments with Lara the other day, she divulged that both the director and producer were thrilled with how the screenplay was translating on camera.

I haven't seen Scott since he handed me our divorce papers

and each new day since has felt like a small victory; I'm putting him behind me.

After a quick dip in the bathtub (it's hard to resist its luxurious lure even when it's past my bedtime) I dive under the covers of my gorgeous fluffy bed and pull out my notebook. Ideas have been flowing for the new script I'm working on. And Sophie and Dean keep adding to my list of things to do and places to see in Colorado the next time I visit. The little voice in the back of my head that keeps suggesting a crazy, ridiculous move to Breckenridge has been nagging at me more and more. I haven't shared my connection to Colorado with Dean and Sophie or my thoughts on moving out there as I haven't discussed it with Madi yet. But with all Dean and Sophie have to say, that voice is getting steadily louder.

My new friends know that I have visited Colorado, but I have yet to tell them that my parents live there for fear that they will just give me more reasons as to why I should go. I miss my parents and I love their place in Colorado, so add in all the amazing places that Dean and Sophie have informed me about and moving seems the most reasonable and logical idea. But I can't possibly plan my life without Madi or discuss my dreams with others without consulting my very best friend, not least because it would include her in a massive way.

I fall asleep dreaming of snow-capped mountains, an office overlooking piles upon piles of the sparkling white stuff and how cool people from Colorado truly are.

Chapter 18

Today is the last day of filming. I'm up to my usual morning routine of telling the sheep my hopes for the day and my gratitude for the days and moments gone by when I hear a small 'excuse me' from somewhere behind me. I'd been so engaged with the sheep (they make great listeners) that I hadn't heard the rustle of the gravel.

When I turn around, I'm greeted by Dean's friendly face. The sheep I had been chatting to beats me to a good morning as it 'Baas' at Dean before turning its attention to grazing on the grass.

'What she said.' I smile, deciding my new friend is a girl. Dean gazes at the ground, one hand in his pocket, the other combing through his deep brown hair. His right cheek lifts into a small smile making a dimple form.

'I didn't mean to disturb you, I was just passing by and thought I'd stop and say hello,' he says a touch shyly. I appreciate that there is a softness to Dean that he doesn't try to hide. His confidence is prominent when he's around Sophie and he can be playful and tease me when he senses it's right to do so, whereas now he seems to understand my more mellow state and respect my alone time.

159

'Oh, you're not disturbing me at all. It's such a stunning walk and I don't mind the company,' I reply honestly. I gesture to the fence and turn around. Dean walks up beside me. We stand in comfortable silence for a minute or two. I study the daisies blowing in the morning breeze and pay close attention to the slight hum of a bird and rumble of cars in the distance.

'Dean, my mum used to tell me that the universe will provide you with what you need and that doors will always open for you if you take the time to look and be aware. Have you ever felt like something was right in your heart, but you've been too afraid to jump, like you just don't know how to get your feet off the ground?' My thoughts roll off my tongue without my feeling the need to edit them or worry about Dean thinking me odd. I focus on the sharp blades of fuzzy grass and speak without inhibition. Dean is quiet for a moment. I sense his eyes on me, but I close mine wanting to heighten my sense of hearing to really take in how he responds.

'It's like the universe is watching you, you can feel its eyes on you, and you know it's rooting for you, for something, and has a plan for either route you choose. It will help you get to your ultimate destiny but it's waiting for your next step, so it knows what it needs to provide you with next. I think it's OK to be scared to jump. I believe you will know when the time is right. The universe likes to shake us up and if we don't heed its message it will find a way to tell us more than once.'

It's my turn to watch Dean as he takes in the plumes of wispy clouds.

'You know, Dean, your words made a lot more sense than Shelia's,' I say with a grin; his words meaning more to me than he will probably ever know.

'Shelia?' his American lilt questions, his eyebrows raise.

I nod in the direction of my friend from earlier who has been peeking glances at me from behind a nearby shrub. Dean lets out a hearty laugh.

160

'Well, I'm glad I make for a better conversationalist than a sheep,' he notes, still chuckling, as he pushes his glasses up the bridge of his nose.

'Indeed, you do.' I nod, mock serious.

Sophie is a joy to watch from behind the camera. The utter love she has for what she is doing pours out of her whether the scene be a happy or dramatic one. She truly gives it her all. I feel proud to call her a friend. The day has been wonderful, starting out with the delightful conversation and stroll around the paddock this morning with Dean. He has a charming manner about him that he seems oblivious to and the way he carries himself so politely is endearing. It's easy to get wrapped up and lost in conversation with him and I found myself wanting to keep walking and losing track of time.

But the set life hasn't been so bad either. Watching my scenes play out has been somewhat magical and gives me the feeling of wanting to write forever. I'm grateful for this experience and the reinforcement that writing is what I'm meant to do and is where I find I belong. Everyone involved has been amazing and I have loved experiencing that teamwork from the crew and actors alike. It's made for a different work experience for me when I'm usually favourably isolated, in my own world writing.

I spoke to Mum, Dad and Madi on the phone earlier and they were all doing well and being their usual incredible support system, expressing how excited they are to see the movie trailers. I think once I see it playing on the TV it will be make it more real. The day wraps up in the early afternoon and by late afternoon I'm outside the hotel with my suitcase; Dean and Sophie are waiting with me until my taxi to the train station arrives. I've taken both their numbers, insisting that Sophie ring or message me if she ever needs anything and telling Dean to keep me updated on any more English desserts he comes across and favours. There is a certain mellow vibe in the air. I don't want to say bye to my new friends but I'm willing myself not to be sad. I believe I will see them again one day.

Sophie squeezes me in a tight hug and tells me to visit Colorado again soon and to be sure that I let her know so we can hang out. She's dying to meet Madi after I told her all about her; she'd also heard of her before too. Sophie certainly knows her Pegasus Entertainment trivia. Dean gives me a short gentle embrace and I feel something I can't quite place. When he takes a step back, I know I just want to register his grey eyes again before I depart; there's something in them that I am drawn to. Our eyes connect and I give him a short nod as my taxi pulls up.

On the train home I channel my dad and meditate on the last three weeks and my vision for the future. It's a vision I know now is up to me and my faith in the universe. I feel my growth and learning is allowing me to walk alongside my fear and let go of perfect planning. It's a vision that is etched in my heart and it will come to fruition should I listen to the signs and follow my instincts.

Chapter 19

I'm not sure if the clicks and creaks are coming from my bones or from the floorboards as I roll my back out with my foam roller, loosening my limbs for our yoga session. I feel spoilt after Em's yoga classes under the twinkly stars and fluorescent moon, but the whitewashed gym room is beautiful and serene in its own way. Our instructor always lights tealights and candles at the front of the room and dims the neon tubes to give it a subtler and more calming vibe. I like it and there's good energy flowing through the other participants tonight.

I stretch up into a cat stretch on my hands and knees and then push my back to the ceiling untangling the knots that coil around my spine from being sat at my laptop all day. Our instructor glides in. She's really a wonderful instructor, older than Madi and I and very serious in her approach, but I don't mind that. It usually gives me focus, but as she begins, I can't help my brain comparing her to Em. I dislike comparing people, but Em had such a relaxing and charming aura about her that my mind opened up and let go of its stresses for a whole hour. Now I find myself thinking, distracted as though I am shouting and bargaining with my worries and dreams to leave me alone for the session and it's anything short of relieving.

'Do you think Em would move here and be our private yoga instructor?' I turn to Madi and whisper with a teasing smirk playing at my lips. Madi coughs, and her elbows buckle under her downward dog pose. I stifle a giggle, not wanting to disrupt the class. 'Get your head out of the gutter, Mads, that wasn't an innuendo.'

I receive a shove for my chatter before Madi regains her composure and gets back into position. I roll out some of the tension in my neck as just thinking about our friends in Colorado puts a smile on my face.

'I miss them all, you know,' Madi whispers back. 'I miss your parents too. I guess life was moving so fast when they left and then it just became the norm them not being around, but I miss them.'

'I miss them all too. Do you think we could ever actually move out there, like leave London behind?' The question leaves my lips before I can stop it. I can't seem to help myself; my subconscious seems to be thinking about moving to Colorado a lot. The thought has crossed my mind more than once since we got back, especially after meeting Dean and Sophie, but it seems like such a daunting decision to make and after the last time I mentioned it and Madi didn't respond I had tried to ignore the desire. Could I really leave London behind; the place I have lived my whole life? Where everything is familiar, has sentimental value and feels homey?

I realize I'm now sitting cross-legged, looking at Madi, awaiting her response. This time I don't want to move past it, I want to know Madi's thoughts. Missing London seems neither here nor there in comparison to missing Madi. I could never move without her, so what she's about to say will put my daydreamer and wanderlust thoughts to rest for good. Madi unfurls out of her safety position and matches my cross-legged stance before replying, her eyes squinting telling me she's giving my question serious thought.

'Before Christmas I probably would have said no, but honestly I feel in a different place right now. Does that sound crazy? I mean I know you're the one going through the huge life change, but maybe we had both just settled into our comfort zones a little too much and this is what we needed to shake us up. I don't know, but I'd definitely consider it,' Madi says, her voice hushed. My heart feels like it performed a triple backflip at Madi's words. I'm not sure why I feel so excited. It's not like I'm about to jump on a plane and move to Colorado tomorrow, but something inside me stirs at the thought.

Lost in thought, it takes us both a minute to register the toes tapping in front of us. Simultaneously we look up to find beady, angry eyes glaring down at us. 'Sorry,' we say in unison. I am genuinely sorry. It's very unlike me to cause a disruption and disrespect the Zen in the room. But I suddenly don't want to sit or stand still in yoga poses, I want to race to the nearest coffee shop with Madi and discuss the possibility of us spending more time in Colorado.

I consider it being a pipe dream as I bend into triangle position. I mean I have a house to sell and I've just been approved for a foster care interview based on my living with Madi (Madi will be interviewed too) and her having a spare room for a child. I can't just flee the country. My mind is running through logistics while my heart optimistically ignores everything it's trying to tell me against the idea of running off to Colorado. Not forgetting my work is here, well, technically I can work from anywhere, but not tomorrow; tomorrow I must be at the office to look over clips from my film.

'What's going through that brain of yours?' Madi asks her voice low as she looks around to see that our instructor is now a safe distance away. 'I can feel your harassed aura from over here,' she adds, teasing. Her head is upside down and her cheeks are red.

'It just made me happy to hear that you don't think I'm bonkers for having thought about moving, that's all,' I reply. Strands of my hair are starting to escape my bobble, I try and blow them away so I can see Madi but flipping my head upside down once more in a downward dog manoeuvre causes my ponytail to fall in my face. My hair is too heavy to control by feeble blowing. I can't make out Madi's reaction.

'I'd never think you are bonkers, well, maybe a little when you mentioned it the first time. It all seemed a bit daunting,' she replies. 'But I've been putting some thought into it and things are changing, Harper, we're getting older. You've always taught me about growth, taught me to go after my dreams. You've always been the first to dive in with your heart so full and bursting with passion. I wouldn't have believed I could be a freelance writer or got a job with Pegasus if it wasn't for you having done it first. We took risks, but maybe we have plateaued just outside our comfort zones. If we'd never gone to Colorado, I never would have seen you snowboarding, and you've dreamt of doing it forever. When we were kids going on adventures was all we did, even if it was just in the back garden. You know I love writing, but you are right, you know, about what you said when we were in Colorado: we need to live our futures, not just write about imaginary people's.'

I flop back onto my mat, giving up my attempt and pushing into a headstand. I'm too wound up to relax this evening.

'I don't want to fear anything anymore, Mads. When I found out about Scott's affair, I felt weak, I crumbled. But I don't want to be that person who runs from fear. I want to face it, overcome it,' I say, my voice a low natter. I don't care about the odd heads that turn my way in warrior one pose, I need to get this off my chest. 'I'm not saying Scott trapped me or stopped me doing things for eight years, Mads, but so much of my brain was consumed with him, now it's like I have this empty space to fill and maybe this sounds selfish, but I want to fill it with all the things that scare me. I don't want to be the person who needs Scott. I don't want to only identify myself as an ex-wife. I want to explore and do all the things I dream of doing.

'Colorado was like some sort of magic potion that gave me a

166

new lease on life and these last five months have been so beautiful in growing and gaining a new perspective on life. From spending time with you, being on set with Dean and Sophie, and spending time with myself. I didn't think it possible for me to feel this good without a set-in-stone plan, but I feel incredible and I want to be more spontaneous and do those things that keep coming back to me.' The tension in my neck finally unravels as I release my words into the air. They give me a sudden thrill and I get an idea.

'Come on, let's go,' I say grabbing Madi's and my water bottles and my mat and nodding in the direction of the door. I remember where we are and anxiously look over to the front and receive a sharply raised-eyebrow stare from our yogi. I bow my apologies as I tiptoe to the door.

Out in the cool June evening I shake off the small beads of sweat on my forehead and throw on my tie-dye hoodie. Madi is keeping up as I walk quickly in the direction of the shops and cafés along Drury Lane. I stop outside our tattoo shop, the one where we got our matching arrow tattoos and which is home to a stellar artist whose work I adore – our friend Zac. I can feel the blood pulsating in my eardrums. Madi has more tattoos than me and hers are works of art. Mine are a lot daintier. Let's just say while I'm a fan of tattoos, I'm not an admirer of the pain.

My stomach flips over, and I suddenly feel unsteady on my feet. I think I have momentarily lost my mind. It usually takes me weeks, months even, to build up the courage to come here, not to mention the place closes in forty minutes, and it's highly unlikely Lily or Zac are free or would be happy to tattoo me with a moment's notice.

I duck in without overthinking and am met with a somewhat surprised yet warm and most certainly cheeky smile from Zac. Zac knows what I'm like when it comes to tattoos. I'm normally the one walking in a lot slower, cowering behind Madi, but not today.

'Harper, what's up? What can I do for you today?' he says,

swivelling around on his black office-style chair and putting away some inkpots he was fiddling with. I smile and nod at Lily who is busy with a client over at her station, before turning my attention back to Zac, who stands up and throws an arm over Madi's shoulder. They are both looking at me like I've got two heads and I assume waiting for me to chicken out.

'Hey, Zac, I'm thinking of something small, to symbolize this new time in my life and new adventures, think mountains, stars,' I say confidently, his kind features instantly relax me. Madi's face goes from quizzical, like she can't quite believe what I'm doing, to a beaming smile of understanding. Zac nods at her then at me and wanders over to his station. I follow him as he picks up a notepad and pats the bed, while Madi makes herself comfortable on a chair nearby. I take a seat, listening to the buzzing tattoo gun that Lily is wielding on her client and, shockingly, I don't feel terrified.

It doesn't even take him a minute and Zac produces a delicately drawn fine-line outline of four mountain peaks with a small moon to the right of the picture. It's gorgeous and exactly what I had been envisioning. 'I love it,' I gush.

'Where are we putting it?' he asks with a pleased grin as he stands up and sets about printing and acquiring his tools for the job. 'I can print a few sizes if you want to think about place-ment.' I know where I'd like it, but I must admit I'm hesitant. It's supposed to be painful getting tattooed on your ribs and I've come in here on a whim. I have Madi here to pick me up off the floor should I pass out, but I really don't want to pass out. I want to be able to do this.

I squint my eyes and pull my tie-dye hoodie over my head. I have a loose mustard-coloured tank top on underneath and a sports bra, which I suddenly realize needs to come off. I hop off the bed and signal I'll be back with my forefinger and make quick work of relieving myself of my too-tight sports bra in the toilets; I'm way more comfortable without it. Back in the studio

Zac looks me up and down with an expression that I can't quite put my finger on and holds out my choice of sizes.

I study them for a moment and then point to the piece that's no bigger than a fun-size Snickers. Zac tosses the unwanted tracing paper to the side as I lift my tank top to show where I would like it; on my right side maybe two centimetres below my breast. Zac bends his knees, leans back and touches the stencil to my skin. My cheeks heat, I feel lightheaded and worry that I am not brave enough to go through with this. I'm looking down trying to see what my tattoo will look like when Zac gazes up at me under his long lashes. A warmth spreads through me; a warmth I have not felt in over a year. I suddenly register that I don't believe it's the tattoo that's making me nervous anymore. Madi chuckles. Is it always a good thing having a best friend who's so in tune with your emotions? I ponder when she winks at me.

Zac moves his black and grey inked hands away once he is satisfied the tattoo is level, before clearing his throat and telling me to go and see what I think in the mirror. When I stand in front of the full-length mirror it takes me a moment to recognize the person staring back. I look strange – different – but in a good way. I feel like I have evolved from the person I used to be. With my top hoisted up revealing my skin with its stretch marks and scars and odd ink, it's like I'm seeing myself in a new light, from a new perspective. This body is for me. I won't be racing home to tell Scott what I've done, to show off my new tattoo to receive a disapproving glare or be after his approval of my body in order to love it myself. I love it.

'I love it,' I say out loud with a croak in my throat and pulling myself away from my thoughts, more determined to do this.

'Right, then hop on, Miss,' Zac says cheekily, helping me shuffle onto my side on the bed. I take a deep breath in. Madi squeezes my calf for reassurance.

'Relax, Harper. It will be fine, I promise.' Zac's voice soothes me. He rolls my top up a little further and tucks it under itself to stop it getting in his way. His movement is gentle yet business-like. The way his hands move with purpose over my skin causes my cheeks to burn rosier than before. I close my eyes. This is so unlike me. I curse myself for being unprofessional and a bad friend. I've known Zac for years. I try and focus on the beautiful design Zac has drawn being permanently etched on my skin for me to take everywhere with me. But my brain has other ideas and is in a bit of a fog. I'm not sure whether to laugh or cry over how Zac's touch is affecting me. I want to laugh because I'm being ridiculous, he's my good friend and this is not the time nor the place to be turned on. And I want to cry because I didn't think I could feel like this again. In the months after I learnt about Scott's affair the idea of another man touching me made me feel nauseous and guilty. This evening I feel nothing but welcome tingles.

'Are you ready, hon? After three.' Zac lets me know before the gun connects with my skin. I draw a sharp intake of breath with the first scratch and then drop my shoulders, releasing my pent-up nerves. I concentrate on being in the moment, inhaling, exhaling, and following Zac's strokes, picturing the mountains and scenic views of Colorado. Minutes pass, my side is throbbing with a dull ache. My skin is sore by the time Zac wipes me down. Once I'm wrapped up and ready to go, I thank Zac and pay, feeling proud of my small accomplishment. Madi grabs my cheeks and kisses my forehead; I think she's proud of me too.

On the walk back to Madi's, I feel as though with each new step I am shedding my old skin. I can't believe I just did that. On the spur of the moment, one hundred per cent spontaneously, I got a new tattoo. Between snowboarding, hot tub nights under the stars, having my first original script made into a movie, standing up to Scott, meeting Dean and Sophie and living with Madi these last few months, I feel like a new woman.

'So, you know I'd never rush you and I'll always follow your lead and respect your time of healing, but I was sensing a little sizzle when Zac touched you. How are you feeling, Harp? Did it feel good?' Madi asks. The way her voice is filled with both concern and a hint of mischief makes me giggle.

The evening breeze soothes my heated skin. My tattoo stings under its wrap as I glance at Madi, then up at the sky.

'It felt good,' I say, my mind wandering to Zac's touch. It's a relief to feel a shiver down my spine and know that my body isn't numb. 'But I don't know, Mads, I've come to find that I am enjoying being on my own, being with you, learning something new about myself every day. It's wonderful to know that I don't need anyone. It's quite liberating and a lesson I hadn't realized I would ever need to learn or even want to learn.' I pause, hesitating on my next thought. Madi intertwines her fingers through mine.

'I can one thousand per cent respect that, babe. I have loved spending so much time together again and just so you know, Harp, your beauty shines like no other. You had Zac in a tizzy back there, not least because you looked sexy as sin but because you wear your heart on your skin and it's like magic getting to see that. I'm proud of you that you didn't let Scott take that away,' Madi notes, squeezing my hand a little tighter. 'And . . .?' she adds, giving me a side-smirk.

I laugh. Her words mean everything to me. Madi has always been my role model, my inspiration in life. If I know anything about staying true to who you are no matter the obstacles you face, then I've learnt it from Madi. She's had to be a warrior since the day she was born, and she's never let the way her parents treat her affect the way she treats people or her self-worth.

'And, I'm not really looking for just a thrill or a moment of pleasure. I think I have a better understanding of what I'm looking for now and when it happens it happens.' I'm not exactly keeping secrets when I don't bring up Dean. I've told Madi all about him and Sophie, but as far as my mind drifting to Dean at Zac's touch, I keep that to myself. I don't want to get ahead of myself. I have no intention of rushing the universe's plans, which brings so much peace to my mind, and besides, with Madi's words there are other things I want to discuss.

'Have you told your parents about Em?' I ask. Madi lets out a soft chuckle at my swift change of subject. It's been years since I spoke to Madi's parents. Madi's resilience and persistence with them is commendable. Though I'm not a hateful person, I've never been quite as forgiving of them in their treatment of my best friend.

'I'm working my way up to that. There's no point in freaking them out just yet. It's still early days,' she says, swinging our hands back and forth. The road is quiet and we're coming up to Madi's house.

'Are you doing OK?' I ask.

'Of course, Harp. I'd tell you otherwise. You know I love them, they're my parents, but loving people and missing people doesn't have to mean you need them in your life. It's better this way. Keeping my distance right now is what I need to focus on my happiness,' she explains. I understand. 'Now!' she starts, stepping up to her front door and putting her hands on her hips like she's about to make a big announcement.

'All this talk of moving to Colorado that has been flitting about over the past few months has me thinking we need to sit down and have a good chat. What do you think?' She leans forward wiggling her eyebrows. My heart skips a beat.

Chapter 20

'I'm officially Harper Hayes again,' I say brightly to Bella, whose beautiful face is staring at me from my laptop screen. 'It feels good.' Though I've been using my maiden name regularly since Christmas, seeing it change on legal documents has been liberating.

'It has a nice ring to it. I like it.' Bella nods enthusiastically. She's holding up her phone and walking around her house in a unicorn onesie that matches Poppy's. I can see her stepping over bits of Lego and crayons as she steps out of the playroom and into her gorgeous yellow kitchen. There are sunflowers, real and fake, decorating the wooden kitchen table and window ledge and in between the log-cabin-style beams is a pale yellow paint that makes me smile. It's just a happy colour and suits Bella perfectly. It's exactly how I would picture Bella's house to be. 'I saw the movie trailer yesterday. I love it, Harp, and oh if it didn't make me want to come and visit you there in England. The scenery was breath-taking.'

I laugh thinking about the views Bella gets to witness daily outside her kitchen window – the wintry wonderland of pine trees, magnificent mountains, peaks and valleys of adventurous paths, not to mention magical hidden springs – but I guess it's different when you live in a place and see it every day. It can do you good to step away from it so you can then appreciate it on a whole other level when you get back. There is no doubting our countryside's green beauty, but I long to witness the snow-covered mountains again soon. It's actually the purpose of today's phone call with Bella.

'Thank you,' I say referring to her comment about the movie teaser. It officially aired on the Pegasus channel over the summer during Pegasus's Christmas in July – just a short clip as the movie is still in the editing stages. The movie will be released 25th December; yes, I got the Christmas Day premiere slot. I'm still pinching myself. I'm pleased that Bella liked the teaser. Madi can't stop raving about it to anyone and everyone. I've had messages from all the girls back in Colorado. Mum and Dad rang to tell me how thrilled they were for me and how they have already set it to record. I even got a message from Dean congratulating me.

'So, I've been attending "The Skills to Foster" course here and I wondered if that would help me should I come to Colorado for a bit?' I ask Bella, doing my best to sound nonchalant. I bite my lip waiting for her reaction. She scrunches up her nose and looks at me through squinting eyes. Her words come out slow and suspicious, not like her usual fast-paced, enthusiastic tone.

'Erm, I will have to look into it for you.' She pauses, then continues. 'I will speak with my social worker later if you'd like and get some information. You do know that you need a house though, Harp, or an apartment – your parents' house is awesome, but the kids need a structure. Wait, of course you know that, you're not stupid, so why are you asking about fostering here?' As the question leaves her lips, I watch Bella's eyes go wide and her hand flies over her mouth. No doubt she doesn't want Poppy and Evan to overhear. Every time we have Skyped, they have asked about my return. It's incredibly heart-warming and all the more reason why I want to do this. My eyes crease with a smile.

'You know I've been telling you Madi and I have been looking to visit again soon, just for a holiday; well, that's not entirely true.

We've sort of been house-hunting and contemplating moving.' I pause as Bella full-on squeals. 'Don't tell anyone yet. It's not confirmed but I was looking at houses today, just for fun, and I kind of fell in love with one. Madi's out at the offices today so I was going to show her tonight. With the money I got for the sale of mine and Scott's house, it feels like it's meant to be.' Bella is now jumping up and down in her kitchen. I'm nervously twisting my hair around my fingers, knowing I'll regret it later when I come to brush it. It is well past my butt now and a nightmare to untangle, but I love it.

'Oh, Harper, this is amazing news. Poppy and Evan are going to be stoked and does Em know? Oh, Em is going to freak out,' Bella sings with glee. The thought of spending more time with Poppy and Evan lets lose a flurry of butterflies in my stomach and the idea that Em and Madi can be together makes my heart skip a beat.

'I think Madi might have mentioned it, but it's super early days. But gosh, they are so loved up it's beautiful. You should hear Madi on the phone every night, and sometimes you don't want to hear Madi on the phone at night. My best friend is head over heels and has one hell of a dirty mind.' I chuckle and Bella rolls her eyes and laughs.

'They are truly the perfect match then.' She guffaws.

I nod and walk past the kettle, flicking it on to make a mug of tea.

'Bella. Bella,' I hear Poppy shouting and then come into view on the screen. She's tugging on Bella's arm and when she spots me on the camera her doe eyes widen, and she gives me a sweet, toothless grin. 'Harper, are you coming back soon?' she asks innocently.

'Soon, sweetheart,' I say before Poppy turns her attention back to Bella.

'Can we go outside, Bella? It's sunny,' the little girl whispers politely.

'Of course, we can, Pop. Why don't you and Evan go and get

175

your jackets and I'll meet you at the door to get our boots on,' Bella replies, her voice kind.

'Bye, Harper. See you tomorrow,' Poppy says, pulling the camera right up to her face so all I can see are a few eyelashes and her pupils. She pulls at my heartstrings.

'I like her idea of soon.' Bella smiles at me. 'OK, Harp, I've got to go, but keep me posted won't you and I'll message later with what I find out about fostering.' Bella blows a kiss through the screen.

'Me too. I will, Bell, have fun.' I blow a kiss in return and hang up.

*

We're tucking into a veggie burger of halloumi and portobello mushrooms, which is all I have wanted to eat lately thanks to my mother's recipe sheets and her spoiling me when we were in Colorado. Just thinking about being around the corner from her again and being able to eat her cooking has me feeling like this is the right decision more and more. I was going to wait until we had finished dinner and my hands weren't greasy to show Madi but I'm too excited. I take a sip of tea to calm my nerves, praying that she falls in love with the house I'm about to show her. I haven't planned for what happens if she doesn't get the same vibes from it as I do.

'OK, Mads, I have something to show you. Put your burger down and pay attention.'

Madi eyes me curiously over her burger, which she is holding with both hands. She pauses, her lips parted, then quickly takes a giant bite before putting it down and wiping her hands on her napkin. I smirk as I watch her trying to chew the enormous bite without choking. I should probably give her time to swallow it but instead I thrust my laptop in her face holding it aloft with the picture of the house enlarged on the screen.

I sense Madi is gobsmacked but doing her best not to drop her jaw and spray cheese all over my laptop. Her eyes are bulging, and she is flapping her hands in the air. I quickly move the laptop away and click 'next' to bring up another picture of the inside of the house. Madi takes a glug of tea and swallows down hard before gasping for air.

'I love it,' she yells. 'Oh my God, I love it. That's our house. Harper, that's our house.'

'You think?' I ask, feeling the floodgates about to open but I rein them in as I place the laptop on the coffee table and wipe off my sweaty palms on my own napkin.

'We're really doing this, Madi. I was speaking to Bella today, just putting feelers out there for how the foster care would work and I should be able to transfer over my training, but of course they would need to interview me again once we have the house set up, do further background checks, and there will be more courses and I'll need to sort a visa through Mum and Dad or work. I'm still going to write. Did you speak to Lara and find out more about their Colorado office?'

'We're really doing it, Harp. And yes, yes. Lara said the office out there is a much smaller scale, a tiny one in fact that simply oversees talent and the network there. She can transfer us quite easily, which would sort out our visas. They have been looking into building up the brand out there for some time. She thinks now might be the right time to do that with us on board. They're looking for a creative director,' Madi explains. It's my turn for my jaw to hit the floor. I move to the edge of the couch; I don't know what to do with my hands. Madi helps me with that by handing me my mug of tea.

'That's unbelievable,' I manage feeling a touch overwhelmed by all this information. It feels like our casual planning and pipe dream to move to Colorado just went from zero to real in nought point one seconds. 'So, I'm going to get to look after kids, write and spend time with my parents and you're going to have Em and possibly run an office?' I'm still gawping in between words. I've forgotten how to close my mouth.

'It seems that way.' Madi shrugs with a sly smile curving up at the corner of her mouth. She clinks her mug against mine. 'Cheers.' I cheer back and take a refreshing and welcome sip of lemon tea. 'Here's to working hard, making it happen and facing our fears,' Madi announces to the room, holding her mug in the air like she's royalty. 'Now show me more of our new home. Actually, let's send it to Em and she can go and check it out for us and get the ball rolling with an offer. Eek, fingers crossed.'

Madi sits down and starts tapping away at the keyboard, bringing up her email account, more pictures of the house and the estate agents we need to contact. She's super-efficient and organized, which is just one of the many things I love about her. As I sit back and watch her, I wonder for a moment what her parents will make of all this; what will they think of their only child moving across the world? Will they miss her? It's hard for me to comprehend someone not missing Madi. I can't go an hour without her, but it saddens me knowing that her parents have never felt the same way about her that I do.

Madi speaks to them to check in maybe a few times a year. Her enthusiastic conversation is always met with loveless tones and uninterested tuts from her parents, who have never approved of Madi's lifestyle choices and have never held back on letting their disappointment in their only daughter be known. I don't believe they ever truly wanted kids and if they did it's clear that they had their heart set on a prim and proper young lady, but even at four years old it was clear Madi was eccentric, colourful and meant to stand out. She often turned up to nursery with frayed dresses and knots in her hair, after trying to spruce up her ordinary outfits and putting plaits in her hair, much to the frustration and annoyance of her mother and father, whose faces permanently resembled someone who had smelt something awful. Looking at the incredible woman before me, I'm in awe of how fabulous she turned out and count my lucky stars that it was my nursery class she waltzed into in her cut-up pinafores and felt-tip-dyed hair.

I catch a glimpse of our (fingers crossed) soon to be home on the laptop as Madi flicks through the pictures to send Em. I feel like I'm dreaming. The past six months feel like they have blown by in a mad whirlwind. My first original script has been made into a movie, I'm divorced from Scott, have sold my home and instead of fearing about the future and not having kids I've made the decision to go into fostering. It's been a mixture, an obscure concoction of good and bad. I'm no longer a ball of anxiety but a content and happy woman.

I'm ready to get back to Colorado; to the fresh mountain air. I want to snowboard and do yoga under the stars and have snowball fights with Poppy and Evan and enjoy crazy outdoor log chopping with my parents. I want this fresh start; this change.

'Right, I sent the estate agent an email and Em is going to check it out tomorrow. This is so exciting. I'm proud of us,' Madi proclaims. 'And I'm so bloody proud of you, Harp. What Scott did to you was despicable, all this time after he just continues to show his true colours. I can't say I miss him, but I know that's much more difficult for you, having been his wife, but you have handled this with such grace and love, and I admire you for that. Em was ready to get on a plane and start a bonfire with his belongings and put up posters around town warning every one of the cheat he is. But you've stayed true to your kind heart and that's commendable. It really is, Harp. I hope you know that.'

I shrug, uncomfortable with the praise. I cringe at the thought of blasting what Scott did to the world and burning his stuff. I didn't abstain from doing it to be kind, it came out of my weakness in not wanting to hurt the man I'd loved. I don't exactly feel like a role model for women, but I don't want to dwell on those moments of weakness. Tonight, I feel strong. I've moved past those thoughts now.

'Thank you, Madi, but let's move on now. I appreciate Em having my back but I'm not a saint. I've been angry, I just couldn't bear doing anything to him that would hurt him the way he hurt me. I wasn't exactly being graceful and empowered.' I pause as Madi's words and the words I am speaking spark a light bulb above my head. 'You know what? No, I wasn't being weak and actually it did feel empowering to react without malice or spite. Still, I'm not a saint, Madi; bad thoughts crossed my mind, but I'm going to stop looking at myself as weak now. Loving others *is* an empowering feeling,' I finish with a confident nod of my head and a glug of tea. Emotions do not make you weak. They mean you care, that you leave pieces of you in each moment and that is a powerful thing. When I glance at Madi, who's swilling the tea in her mug like it's wine around with small wrist movements as she gazes at me, she has a loving expression on her beautifully contoured face.

'I love you, Harper Hayes,' she says sweetly. Between the tea and her words, I feel warm and fuzzy inside. 'Now, we're going to need some new outfits to brave the Colorado weather, I wonder if they do a leopard-print snowsuit.'

I burst out laughing picturing Madi on the mountains resembling a wild cat and lean back into the red and white polka dot cushions to enjoy this moment with my best friend. I'm not thinking about the past. I'm not worried about the unknown. I'm living in this moment, a moment that I have been gifted with one of the truest and complete loves of my life, Madi. I feel like the luckiest girl in the world.

Chapter 21

It's the middle of August, my top lip is sweating with the heat from the blazing sun burning my bare back. I should have worn flat shoes because my high heels are making me walk painfully slowly and with a slight limp in fear hitting the ground running and I mean that literally not figuratively. I'm late to the annual company summer party, for very good reason, but still I'm nervous about making a scene. That and my movie's teaser trailer has had more than a million views, with its release being highly anticipated. Lara gave me a list of people to introduce myself to. I try and shake off my anxiety and simultaneously trip up over the golden trim where the stone steps meet the carpeted entrance of the London building.

I'm almost to the white double doors when Madi bursts through them looking as pale as a sheet.

'Madi, Madi, what's wrong?' I say hurriedly, sick rising at the back of my throat. I'm a million miles away from the fragile person I have been in recent months. I know Scott will be in there but I'm not afraid of seeing him. Madi doesn't have to protect me this evening. But the look on her face does nothing to ease my rising sickness. What's going on?

She's grabbing my arms and pulling me to a secluded spot

181

where it's just the two of us before I can demand she speak.

'I'm sorry, I'm sorry. I promise it's OK, please don't panic. I'm sorry. Your dad is in hospital,' Madi says softly. It's a good job she still has hold of my arms as my knees give way. 'Sorry, Harp. I'm supposed to be calm. Your Mum said she couldn't get hold of you. I only just got off the phone with her. He's OK. He's stable, but they are at the hospital.' The words are not computing in my brain: my dad, hospital, stable? My dad is tough. He's the strongest man I know. Why is he in hospital?

The blood has drained from my face. I can feel it as it tingles all the way down to my toes, ignoring the vital organs on its way down, making me feel weak. 'What's going on, Madi? Why?' I manage calmly, trying to understand the situation.

'Your Mum said just a silly accident with the axe this morning and slipping on some ice.' My stomach lurches. I don't want to know more right now for fear of being sick.

'OK, let's go. Are you OK to come with me?' I ask, already knowing the answer but at the same time not wanting to pull Madi away from such a prestigious evening for our company.

'I'm right behind you,' she replies without missing a beat. We hadn't planned on being in Colorado to start the next chapter of our lives until late October. However, my dad being stable isn't registering in my brain; he's in hospital and I need to get to him. I'm reminding myself to breathe and remember all that I have learnt this past year and a half about going with the flow and keeping a level head when facing challenges.

We're sitting in silence in the back of a black cab on the way to Madi's house. Madi is holding my hand until I retrieve my phone from my over-the-shoulder crocheted purse and return Mum's call.

'Hey, Mum, hey,' I manage before tears start trickling down my face. 'Mum, what's going on? Are you OK?' I stutter. Madi puts her hand on my knee and scoots up next to me to wipe my face with a tissue. I rest my head against hers so she can hear my mum too, and for comfort.

'He's doing fine, sweetheart. Goodness me, he just wanted to give us all a fright,' Mum says. I know she is trying to keep me calm, but her voice is shaky, and a nervous flutter of a laugh escapes her when she speaks. I know this has shaken her up. My strong mum sounds broken. 'We're going to be fine, girls. Look after each other for me, please. I do worry, but I know how much light you both have in you.'

'We're coming to see you, Mum, OK? We will be there soon. We love you. You look after yourself and Dad for us too. Please tell him we're coming.' She doesn't even fight me on cancelling our plans and heading to Colorado sooner. I try not to dwell on it, but my heart is pounding in my throat. This means she needs me.

'OK, girls. We will see you soon. We love you both,' she says, her voice a humble whisper. I place my mobile back into my bag just as we arrive outside Madi's. We ask the taxi driver to wait and rush inside. We both make a dash to the bedroom and strip off our evening dresses, trading them for sweatpants and matching hoodies. The house is neat, but there's no time to worry about that now. I throw a few more clothing items into my backpack and check we have our work bags ready to go. Madi had planned to keep a room locked for bits and pieces that we're keeping here in London when we move, but there's not enough time to organize that now; moving is happening now. I do a quick scan of the downstairs while Madi sees to the upstairs and less than twenty minutes later we're back in the taxi on our way to the airport.

*

I don't think I've ever felt turbulence like it before. I'm not sure if it was the rattle already in my brain or my heart, not having gotten off the roller-coaster ride it jumped on the moment I saw Madi fly through the doors at the party, or if the plane truly was encountering every bumpy cloud in the sky, but by the time we reach Eagle County Regional Airport I'm ready to kiss the ground and I'm certain my skin looks green.

I'm too far gone in a state of shock – on autopilot hailing a cab with only my dad on my mind – to think about the temperature drop from London to Colorado. I don't care about the weather or if I'm wearing the right shoes. I just need to see my dad.

It's pitch black outside. Fortunately, there are plenty of taxis lined up in arrivals and it doesn't take long before we're winding down the paths towards the hospital. Surprisingly the weather is cool and there is no snow to be seen, not that I can see much – it's gone 10 p.m. Madi informs me that she has texted my Mum to let her know we are on our way. I count to ten slowly, appreciating the taxi driver can only go so fast in keeping with the rules of the road and traffic lights and all.

'He's going to be OK,' Madi offers, squeezing my hand. Her nose is bright red from being rubbed raw through sniffles and trying to keep it together, and her cheeks are flushed. Her eyeliner is a little smudged from tears and sleeping on the plane and her hair that fifteen hours ago was up in a sleek pin-up-style bun, now resembles a beehive. Somehow, she still rocks it. I've rubbed my eyes so many times I don't believe there is a touch of concealer left on my face, but it's not important. The dark trees whizz by in a blur. I can barely focus on the twilight beauty that surrounds me or the fact that coming back here was supposed to be a celebratory occasion. I will celebrate once I've seen my dad and when I know he is going to be OK.

I can see streetlamps ahead and a large rectangle building with more giant buildings around it. It looks out of place in the picturesque landscape of gingerbread houses. When we pull up, I thank the driver while Madi springs to action collecting our things and paying the man. My hair whips around me when the driver spins the car away and the trees begin to pick up speed with the night-time breeze. I help Madi with the bags and quick-march inside in search of the reception desk. It doesn't take long to find it as when I turn the corner I bump straight into my mother.

I drop my bags and immediately hug her tight. She's shaking slightly. Though she does have colour in her cheeks, her eyes are droopy with grey bags underneath. Both Madi and I managed a few short restless naps on the plane, but if I know my mum, she's not slept a wink, instead choosing to stay awake with the moon and heal my dad.

'Oh, Harper. You're my star,' my mum says, stepping back and running her hands through my matted hair. 'Thank you, honey, thank you for coming. Madi, darling come here,' she whispers looking past me and reaching out to Madi for a cuddle. My body feels drained, like I haven't slept for a week. I can't imagine what my mum feels like; she must be exhausted. We follow my mum as she nods at the nurses and doctors and guides us to where my dad is being looked after.

I suddenly feel the cold creep into my bones when I catch sight of my dad lying in the hospital bed with wires sticking out every which way. In this moment I will myself not to cry. I want to be strong for my dad like he's always been strong for me. I walk over to him and at the sight of me, his hazel-grey eyes light up, and a faint chuckle escapes his lips.

I want to joke about him missing me so much he had to put on this fine display to get me here, but the words get lodged in my throat. I want to make light of the situation, tell him to pull himself together and come home, but he looks to be in a lot of pain. I need to talk to someone and find out what happened so I can help.

'I love you, Dad. I'm here now; you're going to be just fine,' I say confidently and kiss his forehead. I see bandages on his shoulder furthest from me and padding peeking out from under his head. I bite my lip as they start to tremble. 'I love you,' I whisper again before stepping back and allowing Madi to say hello. I turn to hold Mum, unaccustomed to seeing her look so fragile. I gesture for her to sit in the chair before stepping out of the small room and going in search of tea. As I walk the neon lit corridors, I'm reminded of something Mum used to tell me when I was younger about courage. She used to say that courage isn't about being fearless, it's about facing obstacles, taking leaps and trying new things even when you are afraid. She used to tell me to become friends with my fear, to treat it as a sidekick; to look it in the face, smile and jump.

Another thing she would say is that there will be times in life where you don't get a choice of whether you wish to be courageous or not; sometimes life will present you with a moment or moments where courage is thrust in your lap because others need the courage you hold inside of you. The older I get, the more I understand her words of wisdom. I don't feel so courageous right now, but I can see that my mother needs my courage.

I find a vending machine and acquire two cups of peppermint tea to take back to Mum and Madi. I'm walking back to the room, the warm paper cups heating my hands and bringing some colour back to my cheeks. I hadn't realized how frozen I was until they start to thaw my fingertips and it's not even icy out.

'Harper Hayes?' I hear my name and pause. Quickly I look around, my brows furrowed. I'm disorientated in a new hospital and I'm getting anxious that I have been gone too long from my dad's side. I think I might be hearing things, so I take another step forward, flustered that my mind is playing tricks on me out of tiredness. 'Harper, is that you?' I recognize the voice but can't place it in my current delirium. It's coming from behind me. I look over my shoulder and see Dean standing tall with a clipboard, blue doctor's attire and a dashing smile on his face. I blink wanting to be certain that he is not a mirage and I take a step closer to him. His smile is contagious. My lips curl up into a small side-grin at seeing his familiar, friendly face.

'Hi,' I croak. 'It's me,' I manage before without warning I feel my face crease and within seconds water leaks from my eyes. I have no way to stop it flowing with both my hands being out of service due to the steaming hot cups of tea I'm holding.

Dean closes the gap between us, lifts the teacups out of my hands, places them on an empty chair in the corridor, then gently steps into me putting an arm around my shoulders and an arm around my head. The tears and emotions I have been holding in since Madi informed me of my dad's accident some sixteen hours ago come barrelling out. My shoulders are bouncing up and down as Dean strokes my hair.

'Thank you,' I whisper when my tears become less like a river. I pat my face with my palms and step back. Dean tucks my loose waves behind my ears and offers a warm smile that creates that dimple in his right cheek. I don't feel the need to apologize for my emotional outburst to him and from the way he looks at me, I sense that he isn't waiting for me to say sorry either.

'Anytime, Harper. Now, how can I help?' he asks, his grey eyes crinkling with a mixture of concern and confidence. I pick up the tea as he picks up his clipboard and I start walking in the direction of my dad's room. 'Wait, Jerry Hayes?' With the inflection at the end of my surname I nod to answer his question as he registers why I am at the hospital. 'He's going to be OK, Harper. I promise you,' he adds as we reach the door. I go inside first and pop the tea on Dad's table. Madi is holding his hand still, chatting away to him. Dad looks more awake, his lips rosy and grinning at whatever Madi is telling him. They've always had a strong bond. My dad loves her as if she was his own daughter. He would most likely claim she is too, if anyone were to ask. My mum is dozing on the chair, which tugs at my heartstrings. She needs her rest. I'm quiet as I tiptoe over to my dad.

'Hi,' I whisper. Madi squeezes his hand and wanders over to the table to take a sip of tea.

'I love you, kid,' my dad says gruffly. I somehow manage to control my waterworks this time as I bend down and kiss him once more on his cheek. When I stand up Dad's eyes land on

Dean standing by the door. 'To what do I owe the pleasure this time, Doc?' I can feel my pulse slowly returning to normal with every word my dad utters in his usual laidback tone. I ignore Madi looking from me to Dean with curious eyes.

'Checking in, Jerry. No more prodding and probing today, I can assure you. We just need you to rest,' Dean says with a wave of his clipboard. With his words, relief floods me.

'See, will you tell your mother to get some rest. I'm fine.' My dad winks at Dean making me chuckle. He'll forever downplay his pain if it means my mum doesn't worry about him. I look over to her still snoozing in the chair. My dad can't see her with being unable to move his head.

'I will do,' I reply softly.

I get up and walk to the door to thank Dean for popping in. If he has time, I hope to possibly learn what happened to my dad. I don't want my mum to have to relive it.

'Is he really going to be OK?' I ask, standing just outside the door so our voices don't wake up my mum.

'He really is,' Dean answers, giving me his full attention. 'Your mum didn't see what happened but couldn't wake him when she saw him lying in the yard. When the paramedics arrived, it appeared he had slipped on the ice while chopping wood yesterday morning. He was concussed when they found him but coming to; but he has a nasty wound and severe bruising on his left shoulder. The cut will need monitoring – it's deep and we don't want it to get infected. And of course, we're keeping an eye on him to make sure there's no damage or fluid around his brain due to knock against the ice, but so far so good.'

I let out a shaky sigh, taking in this information but not wanting to picture my beast of a Dad lying in the cold bleeding and unconscious. Dean touches my shoulder. I snap out of my drifting thoughts knowing that even if I lived in Colorado at the time, I still might not have been there to stop the accident from occurring. I meet Dean's gaze.

'It says on your dad's notes that he lives here? You live in London?' he asks, his eyebrows quirking upwards. He looks puzzled but hopeful, of what I'm not quite sure.

'He does yes, him and my mum have lived here seven years this year. And I do kind of live in London, but we had plans, Madi and I, to move out here. We were all set for October, but that process got sped up a little last night and here we are,' I say softly, raising my hands at my sides and dropping them back down while blowing out air. Dean squeezes my shoulder. 'I actually live here now. Anything I needed to sort out over the next few months, I think I'll just do from here now so I can be with my dad. I couldn't bear to leave him again.' I thought it might sound strange the first time I said I live in Colorado, but it doesn't. I'm in Colorado right now and it's home; I don't have any desire to leave.

Dean's smile broadens. 'I'm sure that makes your parents very happy. I take it you jumped on a plane the minute you heard about your dad?'

'I haven't actually told them yet; they knew we were planning another trip and wanted to visit again for the holidays, but they don't know anything yet.' I shrug casually as a mischievous smile creeps on to my face. A giddiness takes over me. I want it to be a surprise; to take my parents to Madi's and my new house and see the looks on their faces when I reveal it's ours. I will have to make sure my dad rests and get him better so my little surprise can go ahead. 'And yes, we did. It's going to be nice living so close to them now.'

'You're full of surprises, Harper. You didn't mention your parents or that you were planning a move,' Dean says with a twinkle in his eye.

I look down at the floor, contemplating why I hadn't told Dean that I was planning on moving out here. I think it over for a minute before a smile tugs at my lips.

'I wanted to make certain I was doing it for me, and I've been

189

working on putting my faith in the universe a little more,' I say confidently, unable able to hide my grin. There's something about Dean that stays with me every time we speak. It nestles in the corner of my heart and doesn't budge. I can't explain it, but it doesn't feel like it needs to be rushed; instead it simply gives me a feeling of contentment.

Dean pushes his black-rimmed glasses up his nose and nods with a crooked smile. 'Ah, the universe. It knows the way.'

A moment passes as I let Dean's words sink in and then take in his doctor's uniform. 'You couldn't play a dairy farmer but a doctor – I think you've got that down no problem,' I say with a chuckle. But then my nose wrinkles and I tilt my head to one side. 'Can I confirm that you did say you are not an actor? So, I am safe to assume that my dad's in good hands and you're not prepping for a role on *Casualty*?'

His head quirks at 'Casualty'; I wave it off forgetting that it's a very British TV show and I'm not talking to a Brit.

'Born into a family of doctors and still not very good at acting.' He winks, but then glances subtly at his clipboard. I need to let him get back to work.

'I best let you go then. I can't thank you enough for taking care of my dad,' I say bringing my hands together in prayer position and truly hoping my words right now are enough to show him my sincere gratitude as I don't have a box of chocolates or a tin of McVitie's biscuits on me.

'Don't mention it.' He pauses and I take a step back towards my dad's room, wanting to head back in and check on everyone and make sure they're doing well, even though I've only been outside the door for five minutes. I wave and nod, Dean does the same, and I duck back into the room, feeling content in the knowledge that my dad is on the right path to a full recovery and he has the best doctor looking after him.

My mum is now awake sipping on what must be cold tea by now, but she's not complaining. My dad is grinning and the complete definition of bearing it. I want to tell him that he doesn't have to put on a brave face for me, but Madi is practically beaming too, so I don't wish to spoil his fun.

'What's made you so happy?' I ask, leaning against the edge of his bed and taking his hand carefully in mine. Mum pulls the chair up next to the bed, while Madi is sitting on the bed next to my dad.

'You tell her,' Madi whispers to my dad, nudging his right shoulder encouragingly. There's no mistaking he loves her as he flinches but doesn't say a word.

'You only went and got shortlisted for "romance screenwriter of the year", kid,' he informs me slowly, his gravelly voice thick with pride. His eyes are glistening and there's no holding back the tears on my end now. Before I know it, my face is wet and there are arms all around me as I'm in the middle of a Mum and Madi bear hug with Dad squeezing my hand. Despite Dad's condition, getting to share this moment with the people who matter most to me in this world is a dream come true. It makes our decision to move to Colorado feel all the more right. My understanding of the universe moving you and shaking you up to get you somewhere, like Dean had said, resonates within my core.

Chapter 22

It's been two months since Madi and I jumped on a plane in a mad dash to get to my dad's bedside. It was another example of how in life things don't always go to plan and you sometimes must rewrite your script as you go.

There had been no time to inform the fostering agency that I wouldn't be able to make my appointment. It had been scheduled for the day after we ended up flying. And there was no time to pile all of our belongings into storage or give Lara enough time to inform the office here of our arrival. The plan had gone up in smoke and we had to adjust here and there and learn to be OK with that. All things considered, our plot twist is shaping up nicely and I very much feel at home here in Breckenridge. Madi has gone on a short trip back to the UK with Em to get her house in order. She had planned on renting it out for a couple of months after our initial move so she's clearing away personal belongings and bringing what she can here; basically, tying up all the loose ends that were lost on us when my dad was in hospital.

I've welcomed the clean slate and besides a few notebooks, the odd framed photo of my family and some lace staples in my wardrobe, my suitcase marked Colorado was light. I'm in no rush to go back to London and be away from my dad, even though his recovery has been going well, and so I left Madi and Em to it. When I'm not with Dad or helping Mum, I've been meeting everyone at the Pegasus office here – taking the lead a little with Madi being out of town, working on my new script and, with Bella's help, going through each stage in the fostering process.

My biggest obstacle to contend with so far has been Madi's and my new house. We had planned on surprising my parents over the holidays and with my dad's accident, decided to stick to that plan. There was too much going on and it worked out better this way, as I've been able to stay at my parents' and help him in his recovery. I knew Mum would be busy running the shop and so I was happy to lend a helping hand. I love their house and seeing my dad looking more like my dad each day is incredibly reassuring.

Keeping our secret under wraps hasn't been too difficult, now I think about it. Between Madi having sleepovers at Em's and my sleeping over at Bella's, we've managed to nip to our house to decorate, tidy and get it up and running. The house is more magnificent than the pictures conveyed. We have our own ginger-bread log cabin with a wraparound deck, sliding glass kitchen doors, like at my parents' place, that let in the sunrise and sunset, an open-plan kitchen and dining area and a stunning square living room. With four bedrooms, it's perfect for visitors and wonderful for fostering. I can't wait to surprise my parents. They are both none the wiser, just thrilled and overjoyed that I refused to go back to the UK. I told them that I would be writing from here until Dad was one hundred per cent again.

Dad's face lights up every time I tell him I'm off out on the slopes to meet Hayley and they couldn't beam brighter seeing Em and Madi together. Mum has expressed that she sees the spark back behind my eyes again and therefore hasn't asked too many questions, instead just allowing me to go with the flow of whatever my instincts are telling me.

Since last Christmas, I had made sure to phone my mum more

often; in fact my phone calls with my mum became everyday occurrences when back in London and I was loving life because of it. I can't quite believe I had ever shut her out. Her words and affirmations keep me grounded and lift my spirits each day. I think of one of the last phone calls we had, before Dad's injury, when I was explaining to her in a roundabout way about fearing something big coming up, and she said, 'Feel that fear, baby; it's OK because we're here to listen to it. You must look it in the eye and decipher what it's trying to tell you. When you do that, the fear weakens. You realize it's not something to be feared, it's simply calling to challenge you and give you a door to new adventures. Opportunities will come if you deal with these things head on. You're allowing the door to open and giving yourself access to the magic that's behind it.'

I am currently heeding my mum's words as I'm pacing the ski lodge café with fear rumbling in my stomach. I completed my additional skills to foster care course over a period of three days at the end of August and have since completed my application, interviews, both medical and background checks and my visa was rushed through thanks to my job at Pegasus Entertainment. I'm now waiting to meet a little girl who needs looking after two weekends a month to give her foster carers some respite. I'm so excited to meet Erin but riddled with fear that she's not going to like me. The thought that mine and Erin's lives were meant to cross paths and that the universe is holding open this door for me is making me look fear in the eye, challenge it and see it as a friend.

Suddenly I spot my social worker, Jess, walking hand in hand with the cutest, daintiest thing with a short blonde bob, anxious smile and wearing a yellow polka dot snow jacket, towards the café.

'Breathe, Harper, don't scare her,' I whisper to myself.

Jess greets me with a cheery hello, I nod and smile brightly back with one of my own.

'Erin, this is Harper, who we talked about,' Jess tells Erin. Erin looks up at me through her long lashes, her vivid grey eyes wide. I bend down to introduce myself, offering my hand. She hesitates for a second before looking at me curiously. Slowly she reaches out to touch my hair. I styled it in lose waves this morning with a flower headband – it's my safety blanket today.

'Like *Tangled*,' she squeaks.

I smile – this little pixie has captured my heart in two words. Erin's parents were drug addicts, so she was put into foster care just shy of eighteen months old and has since bounced around from carer to carer. Her current carers requested two weekends a month respite and that's where I come in.

'*Tangled* is my favourite,' I say and receive a giggle in return. I'm sensing the magic that my mum was talking about.

'Ooh, what's Harper got planned for today?' Jess says with an enthusiastic tone, her hands gesturing over to the nearby booth, her eyebrows wiggling at Erin. Jake has set up the table for us to decorate cookies, as I've been told that Erin has a creative streak and loves to bake; she also has a sweet tooth, which makes me smile and think of Dean for a second. Jake has set out bowls with every kind of sprinkle that would rival my mother's Christmas stash. Erin's grey eyes sparkle when they wander over the display, then she takes Jess's and my hands and scurries into the booth.

We spend the next hour chatting about Disney movies and her friends at playgroup while Erin carefully places each sprinkle on to specifically placed splodges of pink, purple, blue and rainbow icing. She's done a stunning job. I felt compelled to use lots of colour on mine too. My biscuit has become a yellow and pink tie-dye mix, which I notice Erin has tried to replicate on one of her biscuits – oh this girl is precious. We eat one each of our creations while Jake preps the others for us to take home. Jake did a delicious job of the vanilla cookies. Both Erin and I eye up another one as they disappear into a box, but Jess is already getting her ski jacket on. Next on the agenda is going for a walk around my neighbourhood to show Erin where I live to get her better acquainted to where she will be staying over the weekend.

By the time our few hours are up, my cheeks ache from smiling so much. Erin is a delight to be around; so whimsical and heart-warming. I immediately race to my parents' house to tell them all about my afternoon, though I must tweak the details in order to not ruin our Christmas surprise. Therefore, they think I've been hanging out with Bella, Poppy and Evan at the Grand Colorado Peak meeting Santa. I find them both sitting on the deck, my dad reading the newspaper, my mum with her head in a book. Their faces light up when they see me and I take a moment to appreciate that I was just able to dash over to their house around the corner; after six and a half years of them being a plane ride away it's something I do not take for granted. Phone calls were lovely, but this is everything.

'How did it go, kid?' my dad asks, lifting his head slowly from the paper. With his physiotherapy sessions, his neck and shoulder are healing nicely, but it's still a slow process. I go to sit on the small bench in front of them, so he doesn't have to strain his neck to look at me.

'The kids are beautiful,' I gush. I know it's not going to be smooth sailing. I understand it will be different when Erin comes to stay with me, but I just know I want to do my best for her. I'm thinking over the afternoon in my head and how happy Erin was to take her cookies with her, while trying to keep my lips sealed and not divulge all this information to my parents just yet.

'Children are special,' Mum says, brushing a strand of hair out of my eyes. 'They change you in ways you never thought possible. I think being a mum is the closest I've ever felt to being a superhero,' She notes with a laugh.

'You're the best superhero there is, Mum,' I reply, kissing her cheek. 'Can I get you both anything?' I enjoy a cup of tea with my parents before I disappear off to mine and Madi's house.

I spend the evening pottering around at the house, feeling

inspired by Erin to get her bedroom ready. I told my parents that I was just heading into the office to get a head start on tomorrow's scripts before dinner at Bella's. Heading into the office would probably be a smart thing to do with the amount of work that needs doing there, but I'm enjoying painting sunflowers on Erin's wall and soon it's time to put my head down and get some rest before my alarm clock sounds and I really do have to be at work.

Chapter 23

Madi may have outshone me on that first day we strapped our feet into our snowboards, but I can't say the same when it comes to her ice-skating skills. I'm actually quite pleased with myself; I've not fallen once and have taken to it like a pro (not really) compared to snowboarding. I hide a snigger as I try and prise Madi's hands off the barricade.

'Whose idea was this?' she exclaims dramatically, mock glaring at me. Her pink polka dot scarf has shifted from its perfectly positioned style on her bright blonde mane, leaving Madi with wispy baby hairs representing her frazzled state.

'I think it was Em's,' I say innocently flashing Madi a cheeky smirk.

Em is currently somewhere amongst the throngs of people with Erin, Bella, Poppy, Evan, Jake and Colt. Ariana and Hayley are both busy with clients; it's been tricky getting the whole group of us together lately with work schedules, but Erin has met them all on different occasions over the last two months and she's been a gem – not showing favouritism, though Madi will claim otherwise. I've overheard her arguing with Em: 'I'm her favourite.' 'Yes, hon, whatever you say, but did you see the way she hugged me earlier?'

It wasn't Em's idea to ice-skate today; it was in fact mine. It feels lovely to be out this Sunday afternoon and doing something together. Poppy and Evan are growing fast. They are five now and have taken Erin under their wings; they treat her like she's their triplet. Evan has even given her a nickname: 'E'.

E's weekends with me have been wonderful so far, minus one weekend back in November. She'd had contact with her birth mom and from her withdrawn attitude and her need to be alone, I gathered it hadn't gone well. I don't know too much about what happened, her social worker could only pass on that Erin's mom liked to make promises she couldn't keep and was clearly still not entirely clean. The situation breaks my heart and I often pray for Erin's mom. Erin spent the weekend disorientated and snappy, not wanting to do any of her favourite things. It was a learning curve for me, which in all honesty I had been preparing for since Erin's arrival; after all she's only two and a half and is growing, learning and expressing herself, which I want her to feel comfortable doing in my presence.

Considering her pinball life thus far, she's such a happy child with a heart of gold. She loves keeping up with Poppy and Evan and being outdoors and if we're ever indoors we're baking. When she's not with me I'm thinking about her and what I can plan for her next visit.

Today, with all her friends on board we decided on an adventure at the ice rink, the snow is coming down heaver now, now December is here, the blizzards making outdoor activities difficult, but Bella suggested the indoor one recently so I thought we'd try it. 'E' is a pro. She demonstrated a no-fear approach and threw herself onto the ice; I had to dive on to keep up with her, but it turns out ice-skating is something I am more natural at, though my skills on my board are getting a thousand times better.

'Madi, I help you,' Erin says as she and Em lap us for the fifth time. I feel steady on my feet but my insides jiggle as I try to suppress a laugh as I take in Madi willing herself to look cool and uphold her favourite friend status in Erin's books, but precariously taking a step forward, her knees bow inwards.

'Go around one more time, sweetheart, and then I'll be ready,' Madi replies with a forced 'I'm OK' smile.

Erin and Em zip off to find the rest of our group; filling their gap a tall shadow looms and I look up to catch Jake wiggling his eyebrows at me as though he's gearing up to play a trick on Madi. Madi doesn't even have to look up, she can sense him.

'Jake, go away and don't even think about it,' Madi says to the floor. She has a spidey sense for Jake's teasing. With Em being his best friend, the four of them, including Ariana, have spent a bunch of time together since we moved. Jake and I have become close too as a result of being Em and Madi's respective best friends; Em is at our house most nights so Jake pops over a lot. I treasure his friendship and find that I can go to him for advice. He reminds me a lot of my dad: a giant of a man's man with a liquid heart and wisdom to impart.

Jake winks at me and chuckles. 'I was merely going to suggest you take my hand and maybe leave auditions for *Dancing on Ice* until next year.' Jake receives a thump to his bicep before Madi grabs his hand. I take her other hand.

Slowly but surely, we start to manoeuvre around the track, keeping Madi upright.

'You're doing it, Mads,' I hear Evan shout with delight.

'Yay!' Poppy claps and squeals.

'That's my girl,' Em hollers, which Erin repeats in the cutest sing-song voice that sends butterflies of joy whizzing around my stomach.

*

Outside the window it's nothing but a swirl of grey and white as snowflakes zoom around the sky; the clouds low, the blizzard dense. I can faintly hear Elton John's 'Step into Christmas' in the background but the howling winds are making stiff competition for even Elton's powerful voice. I'm miles away from the fun of yesterday's outing at the ice rink and the relaxation of stringing popcorn at our house for the afternoon. It's Monday morning and the office is manic.

Madi and I had been lucky when discussing our wanting to move to Colorado with Lara. Though slightly hesitant at first over us being so far away, she worked with us to come up with a plan and see if it was feasible. Being able to write from anywhere wasn't the problem, but little things like the time difference had to be taken into consideration when thinking about deadlines and meetings; meetings which I had been more involved in since the production of my first original script back in April.

Working massively in our favour was that Pegasus Entertainment had a small office in Colorado that the group had been looking to build up. Our films had been picking up ratings on our international station and management wanted to look into growing the platform. Not to mention one of Pegasus's more sought-after actresses in recent months had come from the very office I am in now; Sophie Turner was adored by the Pegasus faithful, her movies ranking top of our board. Not only that but she had texted the other day to tell me she had landed a role in a pilot for an upcoming prime time TV show. There was certainly room to grow out here, which had been wonderful news before we actually saw the state of the office.

Writing over the years has been a solitary job for me, unless you count mine and Madi's two-woman workshops, which I don't really because Madi more often than not adds to the calm and inspired aura of the room whenever I am scribbling away, but since we took on this new role there's a lot more teamwork involved.

Madi stepped into the role of creative director, as Lara believed that what she may lack in experience in that specific department she more than has the skill set to learn as she goes along, and they really needed someone for the job after the last director jumped ship to a competing channel with a total and unprofessional lack of notice.

I've slipped into the more casual title of 'head of the writing team'. They're a fun-loving bunch of writers, all with doe eyes and that whimsical look about them that suggests they are mentally somewhere in a fairy-tale land of meet-cutes, heroes and heroines and not in a dim office. I know we've only been here a little over three months, but I plan on coming in over the holidays and sprucing the place up a bit. I'm sure no one would mind. It could do with a pop of colour and some ambience to get the creative juices flowing. I can't see management having a problem with it, should it motivate this group of individuals to actually complete a script. It's no surprise to me now why Sophie auditioned for a role in the UK. This office is behind and the scripts have dried up. I need to bring my team out of fantasy land and, I can't believe I'm saying this, get them to put down their Pegasus novels for just enough time to complete a new, fresh and entertaining script.

'Arrrgh, Harp, can you come here for a minute?' Madi shouts over the booming wind and the sound of 'Fairy Tale of New York' playing from her corner booth three desks across from me. I jump up narrowly missing the stack of scripts I must read through at some point to see if any can be salvaged and bounce over to her; with her sounding desperate.

'How can I help, Mads?' I say crouching over her shoulder to see her computer screen. The Pegasus logo shadows the play arrow.

'Can you watch this and tell me what you think? It needs to be sent across to our channel in . . .' Madi pauses and looks at her watch '. . . in approximately six minutes,' she finishes with a sigh. The trailer is three minutes and even though I think my best friend is a genius I don't believe three minutes is enough time to change anything I don't like now. I cross my fingers that it's going to be fantastic.

'Sure, Mads.' I click the arrow as Madi leans back in her swivel chair, squinting her eyes under her long wispy fringe.

In addition to my original, we've had a total of seven original movies for the Pegasus faithful this Christmas. With only three days to go before Christmas, Madi and her team have been working around the clock to get the last few sizzle reels and trailers pumping across our channel to keep up with the demand and the excitement. Viewers have been loving this year's 'Countdown to Christmas' and I have to say Madi has been doing a brilliant job with the advertisements and her suggestions for videos. Though I can tell by her slightly smudged eyeliner, and an inch of roots showing on her gorgeous head, that she is exhausted.

'It's great, Madi. I love it,' I say enthusiastically and truthfully. I know how much input Madi had with this one and how difficult it had been getting it finished when everyone was already in holiday mode. While Madi herself doesn't man the editing software, she's the brains behind the clips, cuts and tying it all together. The advert was captivating, colourful and the teasing of specific scenes worked perfectly to make it a must watch for the viewer.

'I was hoping you'd say that.' She breathes with relief.

We're the only two left in the office by the time eight-thirty in the evening rolls around. I'm determined to try and dwindle down these scripts, have a go at editing some myself while making a pile for the writing team with notes to look over and see if they can rework some and bring them to life – maybe insert some holiday magic into them, but that holiday magic is seeping into my bones right now and the lure of a cosy fireplace and catching up with tonight's premiere on Pegasus sounds way more appealing. I also have a stack of both Pegasus novels and my general TBR pile to see to and I'm trying to remain hopeful that I will be able to accomplish such a task this Christmas.

A knock on the door draws my attention away from chewing my pen and tapping the gleaming white sheets of paper. I notice Madi tapping away on her keyboard and so jump up to unlock the office door; though she's closer, she hasn't heard it.

Em is stood in the doorway, bundled up in her leopard-print

ski jacket carrying two big brown paper bags and wearing a beaming smile. The smell and heat emitting from the bags makes my stomach rumble to attention. I step aside to let her in.

'What's up, Harp? I thought you ladies might be hungry,' she says brightly, placing the bags on the empty table by the window before bounding over to Madi, wrapping her arms around her shoulders and whispering something into her ear. Madi doesn't take her eyes off the screen, but her cheeks glow pink as a grin creeps on to her face. I hear the familiar clicks of her saving her work and leave them to their greeting as Em swivels the chair around with a creek so Madi is facing her.

Unloading the bags, I'm drooling as the sweet scent of cinnamon wafts up to my nostrils and the smell of warmed peaches teases my taste buds. I lay the dishes out on the table but before tucking in, nip back to my desk to retrieve my phone and send a thank you text to Colt for our scrumptious dinner; no one makes waffles and peaches like Colt.

We don't leave the office until eleven, by which point both Madi and Em have helped me whizz through two scripts, giving me suggestions for the endings. The writers on my new team clearly have talent, but the endings seem to be where they struggle if the couple of scripts I have read through are anything to go by. The dim office space has been made much more festive with the addition of the sugary perfume filling the air, but my eyelids are getting heavy and not even the agave syrup swimming around my system can keep me awake much longer.

Mum and Dad think I'm having a sleepover at Hayley's tonight as her place isn't far from work and by now, they are accustomed to Madi spending most nights at Em's, so we head back to our place with no need to disturb anyone. I kiss Madi and Em goodnight and thank Em for being so thoughtful and bringing us dinner before rinsing off the day and climbing into bed.

Chapter 24

This time last year I was doing my best to hold it all together as Mariah Carey crooned 'All I want for Christmas is you' over the speakers. The year before that my marriage had come to a messy end and I was struggling to find the star on the top of the Christmas tree. My mind was a battlefield of self-doubt, insecurity and loss even while my family and new friends tried to breathe love, happiness and warmth into my soul. It was an internal battle I had to see to, but they gave me hope that my mind and heart would soon work together again and be at peace; now here we are.

I'm currently putting the final touches on my homemade Christmas cake. The house smells of roasted vegetables, hot sourdough and citrus when the doorbell rings. Bella rushes enthusiastically through the kitchen to the front door to let my parents in. This year with Dad having to take it easy with his shoulder and being on the slow road to recovery, I suggested we do Christmas at 'Bella's house'. Having never been to Bella's house before Mum and Dad are none the wiser about Madi's and my plan; a plan that has been in the making for over four months.

Madi is making sure the table settings are in place, with Em overseeing this difficult task, while Jake adds more logs to the fire in the living room, under instruction from Ariana and Hayley.

The house is part open-plan. I can see into all the rooms from the kitchen, but there are sliding doors should I want privacy, or should I want to keep the entire house from smelling of garlic.

Bella bounds back into the kitchen as I'm placing the cake on the window ledge out of the way until later.

'False alarm, it was just this one,' she says with a giggle. She hasn't even had a mimosa yet.

'Hi, Colt. It's great to see you,' I say, giving him a quick kiss on the cheek. 'Now, no chefs in my kitchen please. I can't cook under scrutinizing eyes.' I shove him playfully on the chest towards the living room and then watch as Bella ushers him out with her hands around his waist. My heart does a somersault seeing Bella so loved up. It took her a minute to get there. Colt has liked Bella for years, but Bella wanted to take it slow. He asked her out last Christmas and she only answered him back over the summer regarding the date. They talked and hung out around friends, but I remember her messaging after the first date where it was just the two of them and she couldn't stop laughing at how long it had taken her to agree to a date. Needless to say, she'd had a fantastic time and Colt has fitted in to our group seamlessly, getting on with each of us, kids included. Watching the two of them now I adore how Colt looks at Bella, a look of sheer pride and wonder in his eyes. It's beautiful.

Speaking of beautiful, Hayley walks into the kitchen, her bright blue eyes wearing a hint of glitter, her sandy blonde hair out of its usual ponytail. She's wearing black jeans and a slouchy white tee. She's a knockout in her snowsuit but now she just takes the cake.

'Can I help with anything, Harp?' she asks, putting her hands suspiciously close to the bread bowl.

I laugh. Hayley is always hungry. 'You can take the bread to the table,' I tease, giving her a mock serious glare.

'You know that's not going to happen without me devouring half of it,' she mock threatens back.

'Help yourself – my parents should be here soon. When is

your dad getting here?' I ask, pulling a veggie lasagne from the oven to check on it.

'He said he'd be around this evening. He'll finish up lunch at his girlfriend's first, if that's OK?' Hayley says, heeding my offer of helping herself and nibbling on a bread roll. Hayley hasn't divulged much more about her family life; I only know that her mom and sister live out in LA and it's just her and her dad here. I don't want to pry and am here when and if she wants to open up.

'Of course, there's no rush and there'll be plenty of leftovers and I've got food for tonight too,' I say, feeling so at home and excited to cook for my friends and family.

'They're here,' I hear Madi shout from the living room. I pop the lasagne back in the oven. It should be ready once we've indulged in the starters.

I make my way to the front door where everyone is gathered making a fuss over my parents, well except Hayley, who claps my dad on the back of his good shoulder and says, 'I need you back on the slopes soon, Jer, the competition is only two days away.' My dad responds with a hearty laugh. I don't want to interrupt their snowboarding talk and so move to say hello to my mum, who is fawning over how marvellous Bella's house is and how it has such a positive aura about it.

I nod in agreement and wonder how I'm supposed to get through lunch without busting at the seams from holding in mine and Madi's secret for so long. Maybe we can tell them once everyone is seated at the table? That way I can relax and enjoy the wine and the food without any pressure. I mosey into the living room to ask Madi and walk in on her and Em making out under the mistletoe.

'You do realize what you've got yourself into living with these two?' Jake says, swigging a beer. I do, I think, smiling from ear to ear. We've had plenty of secret sleepovers over the past four months while decorating the house, though Madi has stayed at Em's a lot too, and no amount of steamy make-out sessions would make me regret living with Madi and Em.

I adore them both, though I can't help but tease, 'I'm hoping Madi will be so busy running the creative team at the Pegasus office and Em will be so swamped with yoga classes that they'll rarely be here, to be honest. That or I'll just scare them away with a bunch of kids running around,' I joke loud enough that I know Madi will hear me. Jake lets out a laugh.

'I heard that,' Madi says coming up for air and pouncing on me, wrapping her arms around my neck in an affectionate, love-drunk hug. 'Let's go tell Joan and Jerry now. I can't wait until after,' she adds skipping off hand in hand with Em and reading my mind.

My heart feels fit to burst when I see everyone sat around the table. It's been a year since we all met, but when Madi and I got back in August, it was like everything fell into place, almost like we had never left – only we had, and a lot of things had changed. I no longer have a husband or a house in London. I have a new tattoo. I've had my first original screenplay brought to life. I took the leap into fostering, about which I am thrilled. Bella and Colt are an item. Madi and Em are officially together and I feel as though I've been given this brand-new opportunity to seize each moment and go after my wildest dreams.

Madi jingles her knife against her glass, pulling me away from my reflection. She gives me a short nod, her red plump lips curve into a huge smile, she looks at my mum and dad and then back to me. I clear my throat.

'Mum, Dad?' I say brightly. They both turn to me. My dad's jaw is relaxed but a few wrinkles pop up on his forehead, indicating he's slightly anxious about what I'm going to say. Last time I was here I wasn't exactly one hundred per cent myself, the light inside me not shining so bright, and I knew it bothered him that he hadn't been able to protect me where Scott was concerned. Mum's sweet face on the other hand is crinkled with adoration. The wrinkles around her mouth are there because she is smiling at me with a sparkle in her eyes. No matter what I say she believes in me, believes that I am strong enough to get through it and that

I'm capable of figuring out what the universe is trying to tell me. 'Madi and I bought a house together.' My dad visibly lets out a huge breath and pats me on the elbow. Mum reaches across to both Madi and I and touches our hands.

'That's wonderful news, sweethearts,' Mum says. Reading the wrinkles around her eyes I can see she's torn between letting me go and wanting to hold tight.

'That's great, my love,' Dad says, his smile not reaching his eyes. His hand gives a slight gesture to the food as though he's not ready for me to start talking about heading back to London yet. Madi and I have been here for the past four and a half months aiding him in his recuperation while nipping back and forth to this house to work on it. It has required many a white lie about sleepovers with the gang to get us through. We wanted everything to be a little more set in stone and for Dad to be in good health before we told them the news. I hope my parents will forgive the secrecy and lies once they know why.

'It's this one. You're in it right now,' Madi blurts out, which causes me to burst out laughing and break the silence in the room. All our friends have been sitting so patiently with kind smiles on their faces watching the exchange. My mum bursts into tears. My dad remains solid, but his eyes are wet. Madi leaps up to hug them both and I simply sit back and observe for a moment. My best friend looks delightfully content in giving my mum and dad such happy news. I know it means a lot to Madi too; to feel like people care about her; that they are ecstatic to have her around the corner, when her own birth parents didn't bat a single eyelid about her moving across the world and being so far away from home. It hadn't been the most joyful conversation to overhear; Madi on the phone to her mother and father thrilled about finding love and taking a leap into the unknown and travelling across the world, to receive no 'we're proud of you' or 'congratulations honey'. No, there had been none of that, just an airy silence as if they couldn't be bothered to even pretend to invest in their only daughter's dreams.

Madi always put on a brave face after these calls. When she put the phone down, she put it down on her parents' world, shut them out until the next time she attempted to connect with them, putting herself through the rigmarole all over again. Of course, I could see past the bravado. Her eyes would dim, and her aura would shy in on itself for a few hours, sometimes even a day, before she moved on and was back to being her vibrant self. It wasn't that she was burying her emotions. We talk about her parents, it is never off limits and she doesn't get mad at me if it's me who brings them up in conversation; however, she much prefers to focus on the happier things in life and the people who actually love her.

This brings me to the scene before me; my parents squeezing Madi tight, hugging Em too. My dad is playfully wagging his broad fingers at Em telling her to look after Madi because she is a daddy's girl and he won't stand to see her hurt. Em is smiling, taking it all in her stride. She's a feisty one but she shows my dad great respect; listening to his every word not the least bit offended by being put on the spot. No one can predict the future or say for certain if a relationship will last but hurt can be avoided somewhat if we communicate and treat our partner with respect, kindness and truth; I've learnt that much.

Em leans down and puts her arms around my dad's shoulders gently. 'I promise to look after her,' she whispers in his ear. I see tears start to pool in my dad's eyes. He's never been afraid of his emotions, one of the many reasons my mum loves him, but he can be private with them, saving all of himself for my mum and me. But the tears start to roll when Madi kisses him on the cheek and he catches my eye.

I wave my hands over the table and gesture to the food. 'Everyone, please dig in,' I say before it's my turn to lavish my parents with kisses and cuddles on this jubilant Christmas Day. A clatter erupts from the table as everyone starts passing plates to each other, serving up the dishes and chatting away. It's music to my ears.

I squat in between my parents' seats and they each put a hand on my shoulder. 'I love this,' I say. 'I love being here with you.' Then I kiss each of their cheeks.

'Harper bee, this is the most precious Christmas present I could ever have wished for,' Mum says, cupping my face and kissing my nose.

'Well, besides that time you made us your own perfume from the pond water and pigeon feathers you had found in the garden.' My dad chuckles, kissing my forehead before I move around the table and take my seat once more. Madi squawks out a laugh as she piles my plate high with bread rolls and prawn cocktail.

'We did that,' Madi cries, passing the bread rolls to my mum, tears of laughter in her eyes. 'I still don't know why you didn't let us make our own range of perfume for the shop.'

My dad winks in our direction and helps himself to a seeded bun.

The food is wonderful; the company even more so. Right here, right now, I feel fit to burst with the love that surrounds me.

*

'Scoot over!' Madi cries. I can't say for certain if it's merely Em she is buzzed on or the wine that has been flowing, but her energy is contagious as she drops herself practically in my lap. We've moved from the dining room to the living room where everyone has made themselves comfy sprawled out across our chunky cream sofa and armchairs. My movie is due to premiere in two minutes. Strangely enough I don't feel nervous. This movie looks at the love between friends, family and yourself and to appreciate and nurture that love with the same time and energy we put into our romantic bonds. It feels humbling to be surrounded by the people who helped me see that.

'Before it starts, I just wanted to say how insanely proud I am of my very best friend in the world. You are my heart and soul, Harper, *and* "romance writer of the year" for Pegasus Entertainment.' Madi lets out a holler. 'Have I mentioned that before?' she adds with a shrug and a knowing giggle. She told the postman yesterday and I'm pretty certain everyone at the ski resort – staff and tourists alike – has heard about my recent accolade in the week since we found out. I kiss her shoulder as she's half sat on my thigh squashed up on the couch with Em next to her and Hayley at the end.

'I couldn't have done it without you.' I say softly.

'We're so proud of you too, honey,' Mum says echoing Madi's sentiment, raising the glass of elderflower she has been nursing. My dad clinks his beer bottle to the glass.

'Congratulations, kid,' my dad says to a round of applause and more clinking bottles.

'Thank you,' I respond as the credits start to roll and the room descends in silence. It's not a bad way to celebrate Christmas.

Chapter 25

This afternoon the mountains are enchanting. There is a light drizzle of snow falling refilling the trodden footsteps along the slopes. The wind carries laughter and joy, whipping around my eardrums, squeezing my heart tight.

'Harper, Harper, it's your turn.' I stare down into the piercing grey eyes that are staring up at me from the tiny person tugging at my snowsuit. Erin's nose is bright red, her cheeks flushed pink and the smile brimming on her face lights up my world.

'She's not as fast as us,' Evan shouts, running past us quickly then slowing down as the slope becomes steep. I take Erin's hand and we run, laughing as we too get stuck inching our way up the mountain of snow to get to the top. I'm dragging our sled behind me.

'She is too fast,' Erin quips at Evan, standing up for me. Everything this child says melts my heart.

'But I'm the fastest.' Poppy gives her two pence as she catches up with us, Bella in tow.

'This is the last one, guys. Hayley will be here soon for your lesson,' Bella informs our group and receives a unanimous vote of excited cheers. Hayley has been taking the kids for snowboarding lessons and they are loving it; like ducks to water, or polar bears to ice, the three of them. Erin has been with me two weekends a month for the past three months and I adore her. We're rarely indoors when I have her and it suits me just fine.

The Pegasus office has been demanding to say the least. Madi is doing a wonderful job elevating the workload and making this office a more dominant fixture within our company. Our script intake has risen drastically, and four upcoming movies are set to be filmed out here in Colorado in the coming months. It's been incredible to oversee, but very much all go in the office. We have lots of changes to make in the New Year, my in-tray is never empty and I still need to get in and give the place an overhaul. So, weekends on the slopes are a welcome respite.

However, I'm never without my laptop or notebook and pen, despite the stress of the office and some of the more unenthused members of my team, my own ideas and inspiration have skyrocketed since moving to Colorado. Furthermore, after the success of my movie I have been assigned to create two new original movies for Pegasus this coming year, including one that is currently doing its rounds back at the UK office. I'm anxiously awaiting the team's verdict.

I never could have scripted two years ago what has happened for my career or Erin coming into my life and keeping me busy. I've never met anyone with a purer heart and a sweeter nature. My mum and dad fuss over her, and Poppy and Evan want to keep her around all the time, but her foster family are lovely and it's still early days. I don't want to interrupt our routine, even though dropping her off at her foster family's house is becoming increasingly difficult every Monday morning.

We're all panting by the time we reach the top of the slope. Evan is eyeing me mischievously. Poppy is already clambering onto her sled while Erin waits patiently for me to sit down first. She's trying to keep up with the others and show no fear, but her grey eyes shine with a touch of nervous anticipation. I tuck my knees to my chest allowing room for her to sit between my legs. Her little frame jumps in and she wraps her arms around my knees, holding on for safety.

Evan gives us the countdown and after three we are all hollering and whooping down the snowy hill. By the time we reach the bottom, there is no fear in Erin's eyes but glistening sparkles of happiness, as she screams, 'We do it again.'

'Hayley's here now, sweetheart. We can have another race after your lesson, OK,' I tell her. When she spots Hayley, she squeals and runs right up to her, hugging her leg. Poppy and Evan gather around her too, eager to get started. Hayley shoots us a wave and gets the troop to follow her to retrieve their boards and gear. As they reach the gate, Erin turns around and trots back over to me. I bend down to greet her, worry creasing my brow. She loves snowboarding and she loves Hayley. Bella and I are usually content to leave them to it, so this is a first.

'Be back soon,' Erin says in her sing-song tone, putting her tiny arms around my neck and giving me a squeeze. I choke back tears not wanting her to think I'm sad.

'I will be here,' I say as she releases me and dazzles me with her pretty smile, before running back to join the others. Bella is grinning at me when I stand up. I look away watching the kids until they disappear inside with Hayley. Then we start walking to the café, which has become our Saturday treat, catching up over hot chocolate for an hour while the kids have their lesson.

'I know it's early days so I'm not trying to rush things, but you've taken to fostering really well. That kid is happy in your care and, well, I think she adores you. You're doing a wonderful job, Harper,' Bella tells me as we take our seats. We've barely been sitting for two minutes before Jake appears with two hot chocolates and a thick slice of vegan beet chocolate cake, which he lets me know he's trying to perfect for my mum after he was blown away by hers at Christmas. Then he leaves Bella and I to natter.

'Thank you,' I start, truly grateful for the compliment. I'd been nervous about doing or saying the wrong things and scaring Erin.

She has already bounced around from house to house, foster home to foster home all before the ripe old age of three. 'It's Erin though, she's so full of love and light.'

'Because she soaks up and projects what you give her. It's not always like that, Harp. Love is what they need but it's not always what they get. They meet you and they can feel it, that warmth and heart. I've met Erin before, seen her at the social meetups, and this is the happiest I have ever had the pleasure of seeing her.' Bella's words send a wave of goose bumps up my thermal-covered arms. Talking about Erin often gets me emotional. I wipe at my eyes trying to stem the tears before they leak.

'She's an honest to goodness doll,' I say, picking up my fork and helping myself to the first bite of cake. It's heaven on my tongue. How there's no sugar in it is beyond my logic; it's delicious. Between my mum and Jake's fascination with all things vegan, since the gang have stopped by for Sunday lunches at my parents' a lot over the past couple of months, my diet has become much more plant-based. I can't lie, I feel like I have all the energy of my twelve-year-old self back again and I certainly need it to keep up with the kids, the office and when racing down the mountains with Hayley.

'Like I said, I don't want to get ahead of myself but I just want to put it out there, even if it's just to keep you in the loop or get you up to speed with the process, but you know adoption is an option should it be an avenue you ever want to venture down?' Bella states, picking up the fork and breaking off a chunky piece of cake. I watch her chew the piece carefully, eager to see her reaction while also biding my time unsure of what to say next. It's not really a question, more like a hint at what she believes is a great idea for me.

'And he wants to convince me that this has beets in it?' Bella laughs, mock incredulous. She's pointing at the cake with her fork. I chuckle and nod. I take another bite of cake and look over the mountains. I can just make out the kids on the far side of the mountain, on the small beginners' slope with Hayley. For two and a half years old, Erin shows signs of taking after Hayley. I'd be entering her into competitions in a matter of months, should she wish to partake; she's a little natural on the board like she's a natural on the ice. Watching her, my heart squeezes.

'I want to be good enough for her,' I confess, my voice low, a whisper. It's been twenty-four months since I found out Scott was having an affair. I've moved across the world and have an amazing job and an incredible group of supportive people around me. I am in love with my life. Erin gives me purpose, a reason more powerful than anything I could ever describe before, to be better, to bring my best self to every day. But I want to be good enough for her. Scott was able to leave. Erin's a baby. She wouldn't get that choice and she must be happy. I want to know that she is happy every day and that I am doing right by her. My throat catches. I let out a small cough, choking a little on a chocolate crumb. I've not thought about what happened with Scott in a long time.

Bella reaches out and takes my hand. 'Harper, are you good enough for you?' she asks me gently, the weight of her words hitting my chest instantly. It's a question I asked myself countless times after Scott left. And my answer was always that I wasn't good enough for him, for me, for anyone. Yet as each day passed, my strength grew, and I made it through. I stood tall and made decisions. I embraced life, opened myself up to new friends like Bella, buried myself in work, moving up in a job I love and though I may not be in the position to have kids of my own right now I leapt outside my box, opening my eyes to the kids out there who needed love; who didn't get it the normal way. I'm happy with who I have become, how I have evolved since Scott left, since our divorce, but it's been a while since I asked myself this question. It surprises me that today I have a different answer.

'Yes.' The word tumbles out. I smile, acknowledging that yes, yes, I do believe I am good enough. I gasp, a little shocked at myself.

'Then you will be more than good enough for Erin,' Bella replies. Her words resonate to my very core; my hands tremble. I can do this on my own. I can support this little girl. I can make it so she knows that she is capable of anything; that she must always dream big. And I can give her all the love in my heart. I want to give her all the love in my heart. I want to give her the sun, the moon, the stars.

I let out a nervous chuckle. My mum was right all along; I thank the universe.

Chapter 26

There is a feel of magic in the air that only the aftermath of Christmas Day can produce. It's that limbo between Christmas and New Year where no one is quite ready to get back to work yet, there are tubs of Quality Streets lying open on every surface and the odd twinkle of glitter sparkles from the rug that the wrapping paper left behind.

My new daisy-print slippers and the roaring fire are keeping my feet nice and toasty, and the tiny being curled up next to me is making certain I'm full of warmth. *Frozen* is playing on the TV as Erin and I are finishing up our last dregs of hot chocolate. I'm wondering if she's going to make it to midnight when there's a knock on the door. Erin's drooping eyes spring open as she sits up straight, allowing me to get up and see who it is. She sits on her heels, peeking over the couch; shy until she gets to know a person. I open the door, speculating as to who it could be at this hour.

Madi, Em and the girls are out, and my parents like to ring in the New Year from the comfort of their bed these days. I was content in having a quiet night in – just Erin and I – and was not expecting visitors. I feel the icy chill the minute I open the door, but it's quickly replaced by a hot flush when Dean fills the

219

doorframe in his fleece-trimmed denim jacket and black-rimmed glasses.

I've only seen Dean a handful of times in the last few months when taking my dad to his physiotherapy sessions. He's wonderful to talk to, as always, and I have been able to learn a few more titbits about him such as he has been a doctor for six years, loves his job, dislikes avocados (how could I possibly take him home to my mother?), is not a fan of spiders (would make a terrible roommate, who would get rid of them then?) and adores camping, which he'd love to make more time for. We've chatted about fostering and my list of Colorado desserts I must try now has a notebook unto itself.

I'm about to ask him what he's doing here when I hear a squeal behind me and a little pitter-patter of feet.

Erin runs past me to Dean. 'Hey, peanut,' he says, ever so affectionately. Erin gives another giggle.

'How do you two know each other?' I ask, a little perplexed and a little taken aback that my ovaries were just attacked without warning at the current scene of Erin doing her best impression of a koala, her arms wrapped around Dean's leg. She just about reaches his kneecap.

'He reads me books,' Erin pipes up finding her voice amongst her excited giggles, before squeezing him tight with sound effects and bouncing back over to her spot on the couch.

Dean scrunches up his nose, his lips curve into a small side-smile and he offers a shy shrug then lowers his voice. 'Erin had a few trips to the hospital before she was put into care,' he says, clearing his throat. My own immediately restricts with a fierce need to protect Erin. I look away from his features; he's staring at Erin with warmth and concern in his grey eyes. I follow his gaze. She looks adorable curled up in her Pascal blanket.

'When I finish my shifts early, I like to pop down to the kids' ward and read to them,' Dean says. When I turn back to look at him, his eyes are already watching me closely.

'Of course you do,' I say with a playful wink, teasing. I take my hand off the front door to pull my jumper down over my lace pyjama shorts, suddenly realizing how cold it is and Dean is still stood outside. I was just trying to process him being here, him knowing the little light of my life and reading to children after long and exhausting shifts as a doctor, that I had yet to invite him in.

'Would you like to come inside?' I say shaking my head apologetically and gesturing for him to come in.

'You can sit next to me,' Erin shouts, looking over at us both and patting the couch next to her. Her crystal grey eyes are wide with happiness as Olaf bursts into song.

'You don't have to stay long if you have places to be tonight,' I assure him, closing the door behind him as he steps inside.

'Erm, yes, no, of course. I didn't mean to disturb your evening,' Dean replies and I notice a slight blush rise in his cheeks. Did he think I was kicking him out already?

'Sorry, no you're welcome to stay and celebrate with us but if you have friends to meet or parties to attend that's OK too.' I try to reassure him as I make my way back over to the couch. Dean follows me tentatively. 'Please, make yourself at home,' I add as Erin lifts her blanket to indicate where she would like us to sit.

I tuck my feet underneath myself to Erin's right, while Dean makes himself comfortable on her left. I feel a smidge of jealousy when Erin scoots a little closer to Dean and leans into him. As if sensing my insecurity, she reaches out and takes my hand, keeping hold of it while she gets cosy once more.

Watching the sisterly love being portrayed on the screen makes my eyes glisten, not least because of the love I have for Madi but because I'm getting to experience it through Erin's eyes. I'm witnessing the way her delicate features crease with concern, her eyes grow huge and a rosy hue creeps into her cheeks. Her innocence and sweet and pure heart are admirable considering she has been to hell and back at such a young age. She still shows empathy for Anna and Elsa despite it all.

I swipe my eyes with my fingertips as subtly as I can and twirl a strand of hair around my finger, not wanting to disturb the moment Elsa's warm hug saves her sister. I catch Dean looking at me. He offers me a cute smile, his grey eyes twinkling under the Christmas lights reflecting in his glasses. I return his smile before he looks away, absent-mindedly brushing Erin's hair out of her eyes as she lies curled in a ball, her head on his lap.

The room feels so full of love and togetherness. Dean has a tenderness to him and when he looks at me, it's all-embracing and makes me feel fuzzy inside. I no longer feel the need to shy away from my emotions or feel embarrassed about my tears. When Dean is around, I feel like myself; like my old self, my new self, the person I was and learnt from and the person I want to be, all at the same time. I sense he sees and accepts it all and I appreciate that about him.

As the credits roll, I get a surge of empowerment while I prepare to scoop Erin up and carry her off to bed. I make to stand when her eyes suddenly spring open and she shoots off the couch, grabbing Dean's hand. 'Dean didn't have any hot chocolate.' She gasps like it's the worst thing in the world; which I suppose it is considering how delicious it is.

I let out a chuckle as Dean copies her gasp and plays along naturally. The three of us dash into the kitchen and I set about turning on the crockpot to warm up our hot chocolate. We had made extra for Madi and Em. Erin climbs on to a chair by the breakfast bar and sends a puppy dog glance my way. 'Harper, can Dean have a cookie too?' she asks politely, her fingers edging closer to the plate of multi-coloured sprinkled cookies we had made earlier with my parents. Dean hovers beside her making sure she's steady and not going to fall off the high stool.

'If he would like one, of course he can. Would you like to ask him?' I say dropping a kiss on her head as I retrieve a wooden spoon from the drawer to stir the simmering cocoa. Dean takes the seat next to her, scooting up his stool a little closer to hers and Erin turns to face him.

'Would you like a cookie? I licked the bowl; Harper said I can do that,' she says leaning in and whispering to Dean like it's a secret, her face etched with glee.

'It's not really baking if you don't get to lick the bowl now, is it?' Dean replies in a matched hushed tone. 'They smell amazing,' he adds as Erin pushes the tray towards him. I can see her attentive eyes surveying the plate and even though we used natural sugars and there are no E numbers in our bakes I have some trepidation about ruining her sleep pattern; but it is a night for celebrating after all, with ten minutes to go before the New Year.

I ladle some hot chocolate in a mug for Dean and half a ladle for Erin in her Rapunzel mug and place them on a tray.

'How about we go and sit on the deck and watch the fireworks and we can have one more cookie to celebrate,' I say and wiggle my eyebrows. Erin giggles and claps. Dean helps her off the chair as I add the plate of cookies to my tray and lead the way on to the deck under the heater.

Once again, I find myself under the illuminated Breckenridge sky to bring in the New Year. Whereas last year I was both a bundle of nerves and excitement to face the year ahead, this evening I feel accomplished and contented. I don't think I could ever tire of the mountainous view or the fact that my garden now boasts enormous pine trees and vast snowflakes littering the grounds. There's a party in the sky as fireworks of every colour explode around us. It's a stunning scene, though not quite as stunning as taking in Erin and Dean munching on vanilla cookies and sipping on their hot chocolates as the sprinkles sparkle in their eyes from the light bouncing off the night sky.

We remain quiet for a little while, just the crunching of our cookies can be heard against the pops and whizzes of the fireworks and the cheers and howls from the houses down the valleys and those that surround us a fair few metres away. Erin clambers onto my knee and is careful not to sit on my hair, gently moving it with her tiny caring hands, as I ease the rocking the swing makes with her movement as the countdown can be heard all around us.

Five, four, three, two, one . . .

'Happy New Year, sweet girl,' I whisper as Erin turns around and kneels up on my thighs and gives me a kiss on my cheek. She then pulls Dean towards her so she can kiss his cheek too and my cheeks sting with the smile brimming to my ears.

'Happy New Year, ladies,' Dean says, and it warms my heart. Erin wears a bewildered expression for a moment looking from me to Dean. I'm aware she hasn't quite grasped the concept of New Year yet and is probably a little confused by all the commotion and by the fact I have let her stay up when it's dark out, but then her face moves to an inch away from Dean's and there is a cheeky glint in her eye.

'You didn't kiss her,' she says, matter-of-fact.

'I didn't, did I?' Dean replies after a pause. Both now look like they are in a meeting I have not been invited to. I stroke Erin's hair and lean back, not wanting her to see me laugh at her innocent comment. I feel strangely relaxed, though even in the dim light of the deck I can see Dean's cheeks are flushed, but he's doing his best to remain confident for Erin's sake. He leans over from next to me on the swing and I chuckle, putting him out of his misery, meeting him halfway so he can kiss me on the cheek.

By the look on Erin's face you'd have thought Santa had just appeared for round two.

'Right, munchkin, it's time for bed,' I say, scooping her up and onto my hip. She leans across to Dean and gives him a squeeze around his neck.

'Night night, thank you for the best night ever,' she says softly, causing me to choke back tears.

'Night, peanut,' he says, hugging her back a little gentler.

I nod at Dean to indicate I won't be long. He stands as I head into the house waving at Erin who has her arms wrapped around my neck, her head already lolling off to sleep.

It doesn't take long to brush Erin's teeth and get her tucked up in bed. She makes no complaints and the minute her head touches her pillow she's fast asleep.

I pass the kitchen on my way to the decking and stop in to pick up a bar of Rocky Mountain birthday cake truffle chocolate as I have no doubt that Dean and I could polish off Erin's cookies and I couldn't do that to her – though I know she'd be more than fine with it as long as I was happy and enjoyed them. She's got that kind of beautiful and considerate soul.

When I step out onto the deck, Dean is sitting on the edge of the swing, his hands intertwined, looking across the peach horizon. The world has gained some peace now that the barrage of fireworks has stopped. The odd sizzle and crackle can be heard in the distance.

'Hi,' I say as I rejoin him on the swing, tucking my legs up underneath me though I'm not feeling the cold with Dean around. The night is gorgeous and fresh with thankfully no blizzard or chilly breeze whipping around us.

'Hi,' he croaks before clearing his throat, rubbing his hands on his trousers and leaning back so his shoulder rests against mine.

I snap the bar and hold it out to Dean who takes a piece and pops it in his mouth. I do the same. The chocolate satisfies my sweet tooth and my desire to celebrate this evening in my own way. Dean places his arm over my shoulders on the back of the swing and I find myself leaning into him a little. I offer up the bar and Dean cracks off another piece.

'Birthday cake truffle,' he starts before mulling over the packet with a grin on his face.

'It's my favourite,' we say in unison. I can't help but close my eyes, breathing in the woodsy lingering scent of the fireworks, the burning logs from neighbouring bonfires and Dean, who smells like the outdoors on that first day of summer: fresh, clean and yummy. The corners of my lips are curving upwards and as Dean casually kisses the top of my head, I breathe out, knowing that here right now, on this porch with Dean, is where I'm meant to be.

And do you know what? This scene isn't going to weave its way into one of my scripts. This one I'm keeping just for me.

Acknowledgements

Thank you to the amazing and wonderful Cara Chimirri for all your guidance, support, kindness and encouragement. I have loved sharing Harper with you and getting to work together on her story. It has truly meant the world to me and I'm grateful to have had the opportunity to work with you. Thank you to all the incredible team at HQ Digital UK and HarperCollins for all the work that goes into bringing my books to life. To Helena Newton for going through the copy edits, the awesome design team for designing such a gorgeous cover that I adore, Dushi Horti for proofreading and catching my oversights, and everyone at PR who organized my blog tour; you are all fantastic and I appreciate you all very much.

I don't even know how to put into words how grateful I am for every blogger, reviewer and lovely persons of social media for your continued love and support with my books. Every tweet, mention, share and picture fills my heart with so much love and gratitude; I thank you all and am sending you all massive hugs. Shelby, Amanda, Kate and Matt, sending extra super big hugs to you all for your inspiration and for always making me smile.

Maxine Morrey and Katie Ginger, I adore you both so much. Thank you for always being a message away and for inspiring me every day. To all the amazing authors I have met (and those who I haven't yet), thank you for being such an awesome group of people who support, encourage and lift each other up daily. I'm truly honoured to know you all, be it in person or through social media.

To my family, thank you with every piece of me. This book is very close to my heart and through all the plot twists and re-writes in my life, you all make me feel the magic and power of love each and every day. You truly are my world and I can't thank you enough for everything. Also, to my family up above, there's not a day that goes by that I don't think about you all. Grandad, I am grateful every day for the strength and guidance you give me. I miss you so much, but you continue to inspire me in all that I do. Thank you!!

Turn the page for an extract from *How to Bake a New Beginning* by Lucy Knott . . .

Turn the page for an extract from *How to Make a New Beginning* by Lucy Knott

Chapter 1

Beans on Toast

Ingredients:
Bread

Butter

Heinz baked beans (Always stock up when you go to Target)

What to do:
Toast bread and heat up beans in a saucepan or microwave.
(Never tell Amanda you use the microwave.)

Butter toast and drizzle beans over the top. (Doesn't taste quite like home, but it will do, I suppose. Don't get sad, you're living your dream and don't be ungrateful, the boys are awesome, and you've worked so hard to get to this point. Mmm beans, I wonder what Levi is up to? Why does England have to be six hours ahead when you're spending another night alone and could do with a sister chat? Just eat your beans.)

Sabrina realized that she had been mindlessly shuffling paper for the past fifteen minutes. It was gone five in the afternoon and she needed to go home and pack. Yet, she was sitting at her desk, eyes wide, staring at the mini chandelier that hung from the ceiling. The crystals bounced light off the walls and led to the dreamy state Sabrina found herself in as she daydreamed about the day that Levi first burst into her office.

Why did she always do this to herself? Every Christmas for the past two years she couldn't get him out of her head. Was she really that lonely? Couldn't she fantasize about men who weren't off limits? Better yet, couldn't she stop fantasizing altogether and venture into the real world and meet a non-rock-star man who wasn't way out of her league? She huffed to herself as her phone rang, startling her. Seeing that it was her baby sister, Louisa, she put on an enthusiastic smile and answered with the cheeriest hello she could muster.

'Are you all packed? Do you have everything ready for tomorrow?' her not-quite-as-cheerful-sounding sister asked abruptly.

Sabrina blinked away the dancing crystals of the chandelier that were starting to give her a headache and went back to shuffling papers as she answered her sister's questions. 'Yes, yes, of course, Lou. I have everything organized – you know me, what am I if not organized?' She felt a twinge of guilt for her white lie, but she didn't want her sister to worry. Normally, she was the queen of packing, but with the band's new release approaching and her brain often getting distracted by a certain drummer, she hadn't quite been herself lately.

'OK, so you *will* be on that flight tomorrow?' Louisa asked, her voice a little imperious.

All Sabrina's attempts at bubbliness evaporated. She snatched the band's schedule from the desk and made her way to the door to head to the photocopier room. She was too tired to deal with Louisa's sceptical, patronizing tone.

'Lou, please. It's Grandpa's ninety-sixth birthday; of course I will be on that flight tomorrow. I *am* going to be there,' she said with force. Her heels echoed along the deserted corridor. The cool office interior, bland cream walls and stark white furniture personified elegance and a modern flair in Lydia's eyes, but at this time in the evening when most of the staff had gone home, it screamed cold to Sabrina. It lacked vibrancy in her mind and could do with some fresh flowers and a pop of colour.

'Well, I'm just checking. It's not going to be some glam, flashy party,' Louisa added, a hardness to her voice that stung Sabrina and caused anger to bubble in her stomach.

'I know it's not going to be a bloody glamorous affair and I don't bloody care. You know how much Nanna and Grandpa mean to me. I wouldn't miss this for the world. I miss them, and I miss you all and I will be on that plane tomorrow, so please, give it a rest.' She practically punched the copier to life and let out a frustrated sigh. She was growing tired of her sister's guilt trips over missing family affairs, especially when Louisa knew how hard she worked, and especially as Louisa knew she was busting her butt for their big sister Amanda's best friend and not just some random pop act.

Sabrina made a mental note to start adding pictures of the piles of paperwork and late-night sessions to her Instagram, to break up the once in a blue moon flashy press events – maybe this would appease Louisa.

'We all miss you too and can't wait to see you,' Louisa whispered after a minute or two.

Sabrina collected the photocopies and decided to call it a day. She picked up her pace, wanting to get back to her office and get home to pack. It had been months since she had been home and though she felt nervous about leaving her boys, she could do with the break.

'Look, I'm sorry for getting snappy with you but I'll be there, and it would be nice if you believed me, for once,' she said, softer now. As she walked past Lydia's office she noticed the light was on. It hadn't been on earlier. She had thought Lydia had gone home for the day. Squinting her eyes and sending a quizzical look through the glass, she noticed Lydia was not alone and her breath caught.

'Is everything OK, Brina? I'm going to head to bed now – it's pretty late here,' Louisa said.

Sabrina tiptoed into her office as quickly and quietly as she could and gently closed the door behind her. She steadied her breath to answer Louisa: 'Erm, sorry, yes, Lou. I'm fine and gosh, yes, please get some sleep. It's already morning there. I love you and I'll text you tomorrow.'

'OK, love you, Brina,' Louisa said before putting the phone down.

Sabrina placed her phone in her bag and shook her head. She needed to pull herself together; she was being ridiculous. Tears pricked her eyes as she gathered her belongings and dashed out of her office. Without glancing back at Lydia's window, she took the lift to the ground floor. When the doors opened she marched to the huge glass doors and swung them open with force, letting the cool LA breeze graze her warm cheeks.

She felt ashamed for her dramatic performance and scolded herself for allowing Lydia to get to her so much, but this had been the final straw. Lydia could boss her around, criticize every move she made and talk down to her all she wanted – it was business; it was work – but to mess with her heart in this way was beyond ruthless.

How could she work for such a horrible woman? It was Lydia who had warned Sabrina to stay clear of dating clients. The company didn't tolerate it and Sabrina was asked to promise that she would not date any member of San Francisco Beat. This rule, however, had only come into play after Lydia had heard that Levi and Sabrina had got rather close at the band's album launch party two years ago. Sabrina had never heard of it prior to the event. And Sabrina hadn't intended to be unprofessional, but it just sort of happened.

Naturally, she had pulled away from Levi, worried about being taken seriously, scared that she would get in trouble, that she was breaking rules. How silly had she been to throw away what she and Levi had – and for what? There hadn't been any rules then, but now Lydia had gone and created and enforced those stupid rules. And she'd made it abundantly clear that when one of the boys dated it should be with a fellow star – a model, an actress, someone who could raise their profile, someone who was definitely not Sabrina.

She dragged her feet along the sidewalk towards her apartment. How could she have been so naive? Of course, Lydia had only been jealous – she had wanted Levi for herself. Sabrina realized this, but it was too late. The image from moments ago now burned in her brain: Lydia with her arms wrapped around Levi's neck, falling with him onto the couch in her office.

Sabrina shuddered. She didn't know what hurt more: the fact that this woman hated her so much or that she had thought Levi had felt the same way she had that night they kissed. Who was she kidding? What guy waited two years for someone? She didn't live in a fairy tale; this was real life and in real life she had chosen work. She had stomped on the book of love without turning another page, and in doing so had well and truly placed Levi in the friend zone.

She didn't have a right to be sad. It had worked out well for everyone. The band were doing fantastic and she had progressed tenfold with her job in spite of Lydia. Yet here she was, with another Christmas upon her, daydreaming of Levi. Whether she had the right to or not, she did indeed feel sad. She needed her grandpa's pizza and she needed it now.

Chapter 2

Grandpa's Pizza

Ingredients (I'm sure this makes a lot of mini pizzas; need to check on pizza for one?):

10oz yeast

1lb flour

Olive oil

1oz butter

Mug of water

Cheese and sauce

What to do:

Once yeast dough is formed (thank you, Grandpa), roll it out to fit the trays/baking sheets.

Place trays in clear bags (not Tesco bags like Grandpa did once; they will melt) and leave in warm oven until risen.

Once the base has risen, take the trays out of the bags.

Turn the oven on and when ready, cook one side of the base until golden brown.

Flip over and add sauce and cheese like Grandpa does.

Place back in the oven and allow cheese to melt and edges to turn golden.

With a tear in his eye Grandpa reached out and touched Amanda's arm. He pulled her towards him and gave her a kiss on the cheek.

'Thank you,' he said with so much sincerity that Amanda couldn't stop her eyes from welling up too. She paused for a moment to take in his features. His bright blue eyes glistened, the wrinkles on his round face crinkled up and a small smile developed at the corners of his mouth as he looked at her. If hearts could leap from one's chest, smile and do happy dances, Amanda was certain that's what hers would be doing right now. Her chest felt fit to burst, she loved this man so much.

'Grandpa, *grazie*. I'm so excited. I think I finally have it all up here now,' she said, knocking her knuckles against her forehead. She then wrapped her arms around his waist and squeezed him tight. 'Come on, let's go and sit in the living room and have a break.'

Before they could leave the kitchen, Grandpa did his usual check. Deep down, Amanda knew he didn't doubt her knowledge in the kitchen, but at the same time she was aware that Grandpa liked being thorough. He loved teaching her and repeating the steps to every recipe numerous times and she loved learning from him and could listen to those steps every time he repeated them.

'It will take about . . .' Grandpa started.

'. . . an hour,' Amanda finished. Both were looking at the oven door.

'Ah, you know.' Grandpa's face lit up as he said this. He nodded and walked in the direction of the front room to join the others. He had his arms outstretched, touching the walls as he walked. They were his guide now; he didn't quite trust his failing eyesight. His shoulders were hunched from years bent over the kitchen counters and his legs wobbled delicately with each step he took.

Amanda puffed out her chest. She loved the feeling of making her grandpa proud. Then she subtly walked behind him, his shaking legs making her anxious that he would fall. They had been in the kitchen for the better part of an hour, making pizza dough. At ninety-five years old that was no mean feat. You still couldn't get him out of the kitchen when he had his heart set on cooking. These days, however, he knew when to stop and rest, when his legs couldn't take his weight much longer and no amount of his determination and strong will could hold off the aches and pains.

Grandpa went to sit down beside his youngest granddaughter – Amanda's baby sister, Louisa – on the soft grey couch. Louisa placed a hand on the small of Grandpa's back, guiding him down, aiding him with his balance as his old knees did their best to bend. Then she scooted up to give him some space and make sure he was comfy.

Amanda made for the little blue chair in front of the fireplace. This had been the girls' favourite spot to perch when they were kids. In the cold months, they would run in from school, drop their schoolbags at the foot of the stairs and race to the living room, ready to fight for the chair. With their arms outstretched over the flames they would try to capture the heat, as Grandpa shouted, 'Careful not to roast,' with a chuckle. They would tell their *nonni* about their day and what they had been up to while taking it in turns to sit on the chair, indulging in soft, buttery Bauli cakes as crumbs sprinkled the carpet.

Things hadn't changed much, except these days Amanda had to position herself more carefully in the chair. When she looked up she caught sight of Louisa who was grinning, her brown eyes looking from the chair to Amanda. They weren't kids any more. The precise movement – a twist of the hips and a gentle shuffle to avoid getting stuck between the armrests – was certainly a sight to behold. She couldn't help but reciprocate Louisa's grin. She would not get stuck today; she'd mastered this by now.

'Grandpa, would you like a biscuit?' Louisa asked, picking up the tin and offering it to him.

'Just one?' he questioned, making both girls laugh. Amanda watched him tuck into his chocolate biscotti. Tears threatened her eyes again as she replayed his 'thank you' in her mind. Though Grandpa could be impatient at the best of times, his passion for cooking knew no bounds and it was getting harder for Nanna to help him in the kitchen.

The girls' mum would often tell him that he couldn't start whipping up things left and right and then leaving it for Nanna to finish and clean up. Mum would have to explain to him that Nanna was getting old too. This frustrated Grandpa. He would get bossy and occasionally snap when the girls tried to help him.

Today, hearing him say 'thank you' after Amanda had helped him mix up the pizza dough and prep it to rise in the oven had melted her heart. Not only because in that moment he seemed to acknowledge his sometimes-bad moods and apologize for them, but also because she couldn't imagine not being able to cook whenever she wanted. She understood his need to be in the kitchen; after all, he had passed on that same passion to her. She knew how important cooking was to him. His 'thank you' had been filled with gratitude – all because of the simple act of being there for him, allowing him to do what he loved.

'One for Amanda too,' Nanna said to Louisa, pointing at the gold tin of biscuits on the coffee table. Tins of biscuits were a permanent fixture in the living room. '*Mangia, mangia,*' Nanna continued, as she turned to look at Amanda.

'I am, Nanna, I am, look,' Amanda replied, her nanna's voice snapping her out of her thoughts. She stood up out of the chair, with a ninja-like swivel of her hips, so they wouldn't get caught under the tiny armrests, and took a biscuit from the tin. She smiled at her nanna and stuffed the whole thing in her mouth.

'You're a cheeky girl,' Nanna said, with a tut and a shake of her head.

Amanda took another biscuit and bent down to kiss her nanna on the forehead. 'I love you,' she said, with a mouthful of amaretti.

'God bless you,' Nanna replied, her voice wobbling slightly. '*Grazie, grazie* for helping Grandpa.'

Amanda leant down and kissed the top of her forehead once more, her nanna's rose scent filling her heart with contentment.

'What time is it?' Grandpa asked, squinting through his round glasses, to see the clock above the fireplace better.

'Nearly time, Grandpa,' Louisa answered. Both sisters knew all too well why he was asking. Amanda and Louisa's sister, Sabrina, was due any minute and Grandpa had spent the better part of the morning looking at the clock. It had been a while since he'd had all three of his granddaughters together. His excitement was clear from the sparkle in his eyes.

'Ahh, I ask you too many times,' Grandpa said, shrugging his shoulders and placing his hand on top of Louisa's biscuit-free hand.

'No, no, it's OK, Grandpa – we're excited too. We understand,' Louisa replied, chewing a crunchy Pirouette thoughtfully.

'But what more is there for me to think about?' he continued, turning to face Louisa.

Amanda smiled, knowing this action meant Grandpa was about to impart some wisdom.

'At my age, what is more important than family? What do I have to think about? To make sure they are fed, me and Nanna have food for them. I must think about you girls being safe. Your mamma, yes, she looks after you and well, yes, your daddy can provide for you, but me and Nanna, we can only do so much. We can help too. We are always thinking like you are our own daughters.'

Her grandpa's broken English made Amanda's heart soar. The girls were fluent in Italian, but they often alternated between the two languages when speaking with their *nonni*. It helped them all: the girls to keep their Italian fresh and their *nonni* to understand English better for when they needed to speak with English family and friends.

At that moment, the doorbell rang. Both girls looked at each other with Cheshire-cat-like grins. Louisa sprang up from her seat. Amanda stood up, less frantic. Both Nanna and Grandpa sat upright, their eyes shining like they had just won the lottery.

'She's here,' squealed Louisa, gently shoving Amanda out of the way and racing to the door. 'I'll get it.'

Amanda merely chuckled and walked behind, allowing her little sister to take the lead. Louisa often got angry with Sabrina for moving away to LA and leaving everyone behind, but it never changed how excited she got when Sabrina came home. Amanda, on the other hand, was a little more reserved. She was pleased her sister had followed her dreams and over the moon that Dan and his band were in good hands, but there remained a part of her that stubbornly missed Sabrina and was mad with her for being so far away too.

'The eagle has landed,' Mum reported as she came through the front door first, arms loaded with birthday balloons and cards, having just picked up 'the eagle' from the airport. 'Safe and sound – she's home,' Mum said. Her eyes shone as she kissed Amanda and Louisa, as they passed each other in the corridor. Mum continued to the living room to say hello to her parents, as Amanda walked leisurely outside, and Louisa practically flew.

Like a local celebrity, Sabrina, the middle child, was standing in the middle of the path, between the cherry trees and the fence. Her sandy blonde hair was blowing in the breeze and she had clearly picked up an LA tan. Amanda noticed her bronzed skin glowing under the soft British sun, as Sabrina waved and said hi to the neighbours.

'All right, Jennifer Lawrence, it's only been an entire year – we all haven't missed you that much,' Amanda shouted into the street, from her position leaning casually against the doorframe.

Sabrina turned to face them at the same time Louisa leapt outside and nearly bowled her sister over with a hug.

'I've missed you, Brina,' Louisa said, sweetly, as Sabrina gasped for air, Louisa's hug choking her. Amanda looked on in amusement.

241

'I've missed you too, Lou. It's good to see you. It feels good to breathe in this British air.' Sabrina took a big breath in, as Louisa let her go, and then she let out a deep sigh. Amanda knew she loved parts of her life in LA, but it comforted her to know that it hadn't stolen her sister just yet. Watching her hazel eyes soften as she took in the surroundings, she could tell Sabrina was happy to be back and that nothing compared to home.

'You look exhausted. So, what presents did you bring back?' Amanda asked, leaving her position by the front door and wandering over to join the party.

'Always so kind with the compliments, aren't we? I might have gifts for you, but I'll be needing a hug first,' Sabrina said, and waved her arms in the air, dramatically motioning for a hug, while giving her big sister her best puppy dog impression.

'That we are, and it better be an awesome gift. I can't just be giving away free hugs,' Amanda said, rolling her eyes and stepping forward to hug her sister.

'Come on, Brina, Nanna and Grandpa are so excited to see you. You know what Grandpa's like – he hasn't stopped asking about you all day. Plus, we've held off with the birthday celebrations till you got here,' Louisa said, grabbing her sister by the arm and pulling her towards the house. Amanda strolled calmly behind them. Though she didn't quite display her emotions on her sleeve like Louisa did, there was no hiding the bright smile that was now etched on Amanda's face.

*

The dining room was full of colour. Red, green and white balloons were bunched up – dangling from the doorframes and curtains – and wrapping paper had been strewn across the table, as had bags of pasta and vibrant Italian cake boxes.

Sabrina's eyes drifted round the table. She took in everyone's features, everyone's movements: her mother's chocolate eyes sparkled with pure delight; Dad had his hands resting on his stomach as he leant back in his chair, stuffed and happy from all the food; Grandpa's eyes twinkled; Nanna's smile reached all the way to her ears, making her look twenty-one and carefree again; Amanda's green eyes focused intently on the food in front of her and Louisa simply watched her grandpa, making sure he had everything he needed.

Everyone talked over one another, laughing uncontrollably in between devouring each piece of pizza quicker than the speed of light. In that moment, she felt content, like there truly was no place on earth she would rather be. All the stress and drama of work melted away like the mouth-watering mozzarella she was chewing; it was heaven on earth.

'Grandpa, I sure have missed this,' she said, holding her piece of pizza in the air, like it was a trophy.

'You can get pizza in America, no?' Grandpa replied with a cheeky grin.

'Ha, you know as well as I do, Grandpa, that no pizza on the planet tastes as good as this. No one will ever be able to make it taste as amazing as you do,' Amanda said.

Sabrina loved the passion her sister had for their grandpa's food. It made her laugh hearing Amanda's voice rise with pride when talking about his pizza.

'It's crisp, yet chewy, with the perfect amount of crunch, and it's as light as air,' her big sister continued.

Sabrina watched as Grandpa's gaze met Amanda's and he gave her a small wink. They were like two peas in a pod.

'Hear, hear,' Sabrina chanted, raising her wineglass now that her pizza had been demolished. She felt dizzy on love and Lambrusco, but her eyes threatened to roll back in her head. Amanda had been right: she not only looked exhausted, she absolutely felt it too. Her bones were heavy, her neck tight. She rolled her head from side to side, hoping it would loosen up.

'It's good to have you home, sweetheart,' Dad said, raising his glass and clinking it against hers.

'It feels great to be home, Dad.' Sabrina smiled softly. It really did feel wonderful to be home. Her shoulders relaxed at the thought of not having to deal with her wouldn't go amiss in a Disney villain line-up, Cruella de Vil of a boss, Lydia, for the next few days.

The warmth of the room and the bubbles from the Lambrusco made her feel a world away from LA. Tonight she was surrounded by the people she loved more than she could say, and who genuinely loved and cared for her. '*Buon compleanno*, Grandpa,' she shouted, raising her glass to the room once more. Seeing her grandpa's face light up would keep jet lag at bay for a while longer.

'*Mamma mia, grazie, grazie*. How many girls have I got here now?' Grandpa said. His voice filled the small dining room, his happiness radiating to each of them.

'*Buon compleanno*,' Nanna shouted, clapping her hands together. 'Louisa, get the *pandoro*. Come on, come on.' Nanna too was thrilled to have all her girls round the table together. Any time this happened was cause for cake and celebrations, but when it came to birthdays and special times like Christmas, Nanna looked like a child, her face etched with glee. She looked to her husband and whispered, '*Buon compleanno*, my dear,' before cutting a huge slice of *pandoro* and placing it in front of him. She then went back to cutting more big chunks of cake and passed everyone a piece. 'Be happy, happy,' Nanna continued. 'Ahh *grazie*, God.'

Sabrina wasn't sure her stomach could handle the mountain of *pandoro* in front of her, after eating so much pizza and drinking a fair bit of wine, in addition to jet lag that had now kicked in, but it smelt so buttery and delicious and Nanna was staring at her expectantly. Not eating it was not an option – it was never an option. Plus, she was only in town for a week. She had to eat all her favourites while she could get them, and it was Grandpa's ninety-sixth birthday after all.

With these thoughts sloshing round her brain, she laughed to herself and took a huge bite. No sooner had the vanilla flavour hit her taste buds than her slice had gone. So much for not having any room left.

'*Grazie*, Nanna,' she whispered, with a chuckle.

Dear Reader,

I'm having a pinch me moment wondering how I got here; here to my third book. It's still incredibly surreal to me, a dream come true. Did you see that I have an 'Also by Lucy Knott' section now? Eeek, I can't stop grinning while shaking my head in disbelief.

I absolutely adore writing and can't thank you enough for picking up my book and giving it a read. I sincerely hope you enjoyed Harper's story. If any of you, like Harper, have been going through a rough time – maybe struggling with your own plot twist – please know that you have the strength within you to re-write your own destiny. Please reach out to family or friends or anyone that you feel you can talk to, (there are places like @PennineCareNHS and @healthymindsPC on twitter that can also be a great help) to help you make sense of it or get through it. May I also suggest you pick up a pen and write? Writing can be a wonderful helper and healer.

Thank you again for giving me and my book a chance.

All my love,

Lucy xx

Dear Reader,

We hope you enjoyed reading this book. If you did, we'd be so appreciative if you left a review. It really helps us and the author to bring more books like this to you.

Here at HQ Digital we are dedicated to publishing fiction that will keep you turning the pages into the early hours. Don't want to miss a thing? To find out more about our books, promotions, discover exclusive content and enter competitions you can keep in touch in the following ways:

JOIN OUR COMMUNITY:
Sign up to our new email newsletter: po.st/HQSignUp
Read our new blog www.hqstories.co.uk
: https://twitter.com/HQDigitalUK
: www.facebook.com/HQStories

BUDDING WRITER?
We're also looking for authors to join the HQ Digital family!
Please submit your manuscript to:
HQDigital@harpercollins.co.uk
Thanks for reading, from the HQ Digital team

If you enjoyed _Wishes Under a Starlit Sky_, then why not try another delightfully uplifting romance from HQ Digital?